More praise for
SOMEONE TO LOVE

"SOMEONE TO LOVE is a funny, poignant, absolutely charming romance that is guaranteed to make you smile. This book has it all—humor, heartfelt emotions, adventure, and a ghost you can't forget. SOMEONE TO LOVE is hauntingly good fun. A delight from start to finish."
    —KRISTIN HANNAH
    Author of *When Lightning Strikes*

Also by Lori Copeland
Published by Fawcett Books:

PROMISE ME TODAY
PROMISE ME TOMORROW
PROMISE ME FOREVER

SOMEONE TO LOVE

Lori Copeland

FAWCETT GOLD MEDAL • NEW YORK

A Fawcett Gold Medal Book
Published by Ballantine Books
Copyright © 1995 by Lori Copeland

Library of Congress Catalog Card Number: 94-90869

ISBN 0-449-14884-X

Manufactured in the United States of America

First Edition: May 1995

10 9 8 7 6 5 4 3 2 1

To Nan Ryan and Heather Posserere

HAKUNA MATATA!

Prologue

Hoodee Doo Mining Camp
Colorado, 1857

"Butte Fesperman! Get your worthless hide out here. I'm going to blow your no-good, claim-jumpin' head clean off your rotten shoulders."

Now, in order to understand the story and Butte Fesperman's role in it, we'd better pause and examine Butte's intelligence, or lack thereof.

Who in their right mind would respond to a threat like: "Get out here, I'm going to blow your no-good, claim-jumpin' head clean off your rotten shoulders"?

I wouldn't; would you?

But, Butte, now Butte was stubborn and ornery and full of himself. He talked two hundred miles a minute (with gusts up to four) and in his opinion—which was widely acclaimed to be worthless as teats on a boar hog—he had as much right to stake a land claim as the next man.

So, Butte claimed and staked a piece of land in Colorado that Ardis Johnson insisted was his.

Butte said it wasn't. Ardis could say whatever he liked, but when Butte had come across the mine it was deserted.

Ardis said he hadn't deserted it. He'd left it long enough to go into town for supplies, and a little female association.

Well, the mine sure for the world looked deserted to Butte, so he'd claimed it.

Butte's voice came back from the mine's entrance. "Blow it out your ear, Ardis!"

Ardis Johnson, flanked by the sheriff and his three deputies, moved in closer. "You're on my land, Fesperman. You got five minutes to get off, or I'll pump your worthless hide full of lead!"

Butte didn't care. Ardis could threaten all he wanted; he wasn't budging. And he didn't scare easy, neither. He'd been a loner most his life, so he didn't have a thing to lose, even if Ardis carried out his threat.

"You know the rules, Johnson! It's my mine now, and you're the one who's trespassing!"

A vein throbbed in Ardis's neck. "I know *all* the rules I need to know. Show your ugly face, Fesperman. I'm gonna make a lead sinker out of it!"

Butte's voice came back loud and clear, excited now. "You want to know the rules, Ardis? Here's the *rules*, Ardis!

"Number one. Each person can hold one claim by virtue of occupation, but it cain't be no more than a hunnert square feet." He paused to make sure Ardis heard him. "You claim you own five hunnert and forty feet. Let's just say that I done you a favor and took that spare forty feet off your hands—the forty feet the mine's sittin' on. *Heh, heh, heh.*"

The sheriff restrained Ardis.

"That make you mad, Ardis? I didn' write the rules, I jest learned 'em by heart!"

"Show your thievin' face so's I can blow it off!"

Butte continued, only faster. "Number two. A claim or claims, if held by purchase, must be under a bill of sale, and certified by two distinguished persons as to the genuineness of signature and of the consideration given!"

"I *told* you, Fesperman, I've got that bill of sale someplace!"

"Lemme *see* it." Anybody who knew Ardis knew he wasn't worth a hoot when it came to organization.

"I told you, I can't find the blasted thing, but I've got it!"

Butte went on with his carefully memorized recitation. Oh, he'd boned up on this—he'd boned up real good! "Number three: A jury of five persons shall decide any question arising under the previous article."

Ardis took a menacing step in his direction. "I've got all the jury I need right here with me."

The sheriff and his deputies tightened their hands around their rifles.

"There's no use trying to reason with him," the sheriff said under his breath. "He's crazier than a bedbug."

Butte's maniacal laughter resonated through the hollow. "Number four. Notices of claims must be renewed every ten days until water to work said claim is to be had."

"Quit stalling, Fesperman. Discussion over! I ain't gonna argue no more! Git out here!"

"If there's any shootin' to be done, I'll be doing it," the sheriff warned.

"He ain't gettin' my mine, Jonas."

"All right, all right. Keep your britches on."

"And last but not least—now listen close, Ardis. Number five. As soon as there is enough water for working a claim, *five* days' absence from said claim, except in case of sickness, accident, or reasonable excuse shall forfeit the property."

"I *had* an excuse. I was in town!"

"Doing what?"

"None of your dadburn business!" He'd already told him what he was doin' and he wasn't tellin' him again.

"You were gone *over* five days. I been here *six* afore you came back!"

"I was unavoidably detained," Ardis returned sullenly. Gold Pan Molly had been more woman than he'd anticipated.

"Drinking and fornicating. That don't seem to

fall under the column of 'reasonable excuses,'
Ardis. You lose," Butte cackled.

Ardis glanced at the sheriff. "What's unreason-
able about drinkin' and fornicatin'?"

The sheriff shook his head. "I told you, you're
wastin' your breath arguing with him. You might
as well talk to a fence post. Let's get it over with."

"You've stalled long enough, Butte. You're on
my land, and you've got," Ardis consulted his
watch, "precisely three minutes left to get off."

"Not gonna give it back, not gonna give it
back!" Butte jumped up and down, his temper getting the best of him. "Cain't make me, Ardis,
cain't make me! It's my claim; ain't you or no
girly-talkin' sheriff gonna make me give it back!"

Deputy Waters edged closer to the sheriff. "Let
me shoot the old coot."

Sheriff Wickler's eyes steeled with resolve. "Get
out here, Butte, or we're coming in after you!"

Butte Fesperman suddenly loomed in the doorway, his wiry five-foot frame braced for battle.
Eyes as blue as the Colorado sky contrasted
sharply with a flowing white beard as he shouted,
"Here I am! Come an' git me!"

Strapped around his chest were ten sticks of dynamite, fuses smoldering.

The sheriff and his men took several hasty steps
backward.

"Butte, you idiot." Ardis's voice cracked as he
continued backing up, eyes riveted to the burning
fuses. "Put those things out!"

"Cain't make me, Ardis. Cain't make me!" Butte

jumped up and down, up and down, savoring the moment. He'd never liked Ardis, ever!

"You're not only going to kill your fool self, you're going to blow the shaft! Won't no one get the gold!" Ardis shot back, still retreating.

Butte's bizarre antics suddenly ceased.

Casually strolling toward the men, he grinned. "Why, Ardis, that's kinda how I got it figured."

Fuses hissed and sputtered. Five men turned and bolted for safety. Sliding rocks and spinning gravel spilled down the mountainside as they scrambled for cover.

As their backsides disappeared, Butte, still grinning, calmly wet his fingertips to extinguish the sparks.

Dern bunch of lily-livered cowards, he thought, watching their backs disappear.

As if he would be *stupid* enough to blow himself to smithereens.

Glancing down, his eyes bulged when he saw the ends of the fuses still glowing bright red.

Whipping his fingertips back to his mouth, he frantically pooled spit and licked, trying to accumulate enough wetness to extinguish the time bomb.

But, alas, even man's best-laid plans occasionally go astray.

Ho boy.

Butte Fesperman shot up like a rocket, shattering the Rockies' majestic serenity, and putting an end to the squabble once and for all.

Or, so they thought.

Chapter 1

1893
Wokingham, an itty-bitty town in England

"A what?"

"A gold mine, mum."

"A *gold* mine?"

"Yes, mum. A gold mine."

Maggie sank back on her heels, staring at Kingsley Dermot as if he'd lost his mind.

"I know the news comes as a bit of a shock," the aged retainer granted. "Madam's death ... was most unfortunate."

A woman with Eldora Snidelyshire's heart condition admittedly should not have been frolicking with a stable boy a mere fraction of her age, but then no one who knew Madam found the incident surprising. To be sure, Madam was a bit of a stinker at times.

Removing a large envelope from his leather carrier, Dermot handed it to Maggie. "I fear Madam enjoyed life to the fullest. Once the estate was settled there was little left—with the exception of the mine, and a few hundred pounds, which you will find in the envelope."

Maggie stared at the envelope at a complete loss for words.

"Oh, yes ... your mine is located in Colorado, mum."

Maggie glanced up. "Colorado? America, Colorado?"

"Yes, mum, Colorado. It seems the mine was a carryover from," he cleared his throat, "Madam's sixth husband's estate." Whipping a timepiece from his vest pocket, he consulted it, wagging his head apprehensively. "Dear, dear, dear, I must be on my way if I am to make the four o'clock train."

Reaching for his hat and cane, he sidestepped Maggie and the pail of soapy water, and promptly took his leave.

As the door closed behind him, Maggie sat in stunned silence. *A gold mine?* Aunt Sissy died and left Wilson and her a *gold* mine?

Her mind raced to recall her father's flamboyant younger sister. Though Maggie had met Eldora Snidelyshire only once, she remembered Aunt Sissy well.

Eccentric, affluent, Aunt Sissy was the proverbial black sheep of the family. She drank, married, and traveled extensively. The order in which she conducted her bohemian lifestyle depended entirely upon the mood to which she had succumbed at the moment.

At sixty and three years, still having failed to

achieve any semblance of order in her life, Aunt Sissy had died, leaving her estate to her deceased brother's children, Maggie and Wilson Jr.

Numbly dropping the scrub brush back into the pail, Maggie grappled with the stunning news. Why had Aunt Sissy left all of her earthly possessions to Wilson and her?

Why hadn't she included her own sister, Fionnula, and Fionnula's two daughters, Mildred and Gwendolyn, in the estate?

"Mary Margaret?"

Upon hearing her aunt's voice, Maggie hastily stuffed the brown envelope into her skirt pocket. "Here, Aunt Fionnula!"

"Was that someone at the door?" Fionnula Wellesford descended the long staircase with her usual stately elegance. Her tall, noble bearing could intimidate the most casual observer.

Maggie bent her head to her chores, vigorously scrubbing the stones in the entryway. "Yes, ma'am."

For the time being she didn't want anyone to know about the inheritance—especially Aunt Fionnula—until she'd had time to consider her windfall. She wasn't given to deceit, but she'd barely had time to savor the news, much less assess its value.

Pausing on the bottom step, Fionnula peered down her nose. "Well? Who was it?"

Maggie scrubbed harder. "No one important— just a solicitor."

The dowager's features hardened. "You informed him that peddlers are received at the back entrance?"

"Yes, ma'am."

"Riffraff," Fionnula observed. "Will they never learn their place?" Proceeding down the hallway, she called over her shoulder, "See that Mildred's pot of chocolate is served on time today, dear."

"Yes, ma'am."

"And make certain that it's the proper temperature this morning. Mildred has a delicate stomach, you know."

"Yes, ma'am, I know. I'll be careful."

"Has the butcher delivered the chops?"

"Yes, ma'am, here with the cock, he was."

"Try not to overcook them again. You know how upset Gwendolyn gets if the lamb is overcooked."

"Yes, ma'am." *She'd be mad as a hornet.*

Fionnula disappeared into the parlor, drawing heavy French doors closed behind her.

Dropping the brush into the pail, Maggie wiped her hands on her dress, then extracted the envelope from her pocket again. Her eyes, bright with excitement, scanned the legal document.

A gold mine.

It wasn't a dream. She and Wilson owned a gold mine! Sighing, she cradled the paper tightly against her breast. Why, this could mean a whole new world for them!

"Mildred's waiting," Fionnula reminded from behind the French doors.

"Going right now, ma'am."

Carefully refolding the document, Maggie slipped the envelope back into her pocket and quickly got to her feet.

Picking up the pail of soapy water, she set off for the kitchen, whistling.

A gold mine!

It was turning out to be a bit of a smashing day!

"A gold mine?"

"Yes! What do you think of that?"

Honestly, Wilson didn't know.

As Maggie and Wilson shared their evening meal at the kitchen table, Fionnula, Mildred, and Gwendolyn ate in the formal dining room.

Skillfully maneuvering another forkful of peas beneath his mound of potatoes, Wilson tried to share his sister's excitement while Maggie filled Wilson in on the day's unexpected turn of events.

"Exactly what are we going to do with a gold mine?"

The inheritance was a nice thought, but not very practical. But then, from what he knew, Aunt Sissy had been anything but practical. What they really could've used was hard cash. A big wad of good, hard cash.

"Shhh." Maggie leaned over to recover the buried peas. "I haven't told anyone yet."

"I don't like peas," Wilson reminded her as she carefully arranged them back in a neat pile on his plate.

"They're good for you."

Sighing, he quietly went to work hiding his carrots.

Buttering a steaming wedge of cornbread, Maggie let her mind drift, pleasantly contemplating all the things they could do now that they were rich. Wilson needed shoes, and she needed a new dress—maybe even two or three!

"You haven't told Aunt Fionnula about the inheritance?" Wilson asked.

"Not yet."

"She won't like it," he predicted.

"Maybe not," Maggie allowed. She wasn't sure how Fionnula would take the news but she'd already made up her mind to claim the inheritance. She'd do whatever it took to make a better life for Wilson and her. The mine would mean that Wilson could attend college and have all the things Maggie wanted for him.

Fionnula supplied life's necessities, but she'd made it clear that once Maggie reached eighteen, she was expected to provide for herself. Wilson would be free to stay on until he reached like age; then other provisions were to be made. Maggie was worried sick about what would happen if she were unable to support them when that time came.

Wilson reached for his glass of milk. "Is the mine nearby?"

"No, it's in Colorado."

Choking, Wilson peered back at her through bottle-thick spectacles. "Isn't Colorado a long way from here?" Geography was his absolute worst subject.

Nodding, Maggie recalled the map she'd consulted earlier. Colorado was so far away she couldn't even calculate the miles! "But it doesn't matter." Sitting up straighter, Maggie made a decision commendable for her seventeen years, eight months, and three days. "We're going to Colorado, no matter how far it is."

Wilson sighed. Talk about impractical. "But Aunt Fionnula—"

"I know we have to consider Aunt Fionnula. She did take us in when no one else would."

"But not without considerable gain for herself," Wilson reminded.

Every cent of their parents' estate had gone into Fionnula's coffers. True, it wasn't cheap to rear two additional children, but everybody knew Uncle Frank had left Fionnula well-off.

In Wilson's opinion, their parents' estate should have been placed into trust for his and Maggie's future. Instead, Fionnula had commandeered the funds and presided over them with an ironclad fist.

"Still, she took us in when no one else would," Maggie reasoned.

"Yes, the train wreck was calamitous to all," Wilson concurred, thinking of the dark days following his parents' death. Had it not been for Fionnula, they would have been orphaned.

Maggie sent him a reprimanding glance. "Wilson, where *do* you learn those big words?" He was eight going on forty.

She didn't know where he got his wisdom, but at times he seemed the adult instead of her.

Wilson shrugged. "I have a flair for English."

Grinning, she reached over and tousled his flamboyant thatch of carrot orange hair. "With all that money, we'll be able to buy those new glasses now."

"That's nice." He picked up his piece of cornbread and coated it with peach preserves. "Does this mean I can have a pet now?" Aunt Fionnula strictly forbade pets. They were too messy.

"Sure, you can have as many as you want."

Taking a bite of bread and preserves, he frowned. "I wouldn't be counting my coins yet if I were you."

Her brows lifted curiously. "And why not?"

"I doubt we'll ever see our gold mine."

"Nonsense. It's ours. See?" She pulled the envelope out of her pocket and waved it at him.

"Aunt Fionnula, though basically a decent woman, won't allow us to go to Colorado," he concluded, taking another bite of bread.

"Baloney," Maggie reiterated. "How can she stop us?"

"Well, that I don't know," he contended patiently. "I'm only eight, but I sense she will find a way to keep us here."

"No, she'll be disappointed that Mildred and Gwendolyn were not included in the will, but she can't blame us for that. Aunt Sissy most likely felt bad because she wasn't able to care for us when Father died, and since Aunt Fionnula doesn't need the money, she left us her entire estate—which amounted to nothing, really, but the mine and a few hundred pounds." Maggie chewed a bite of meat thoughtfully. "Aunt Fionnula won't prevent us from claiming our inheritance. If anything, I think she'll be relieved that she's no longer responsible for us."

"I think not," Wilson maintained.

"Poppycock, Wilson!" Sometimes he could be so darn logical.

"Who will do the work? You do everything," he pointed out.

Well, that much was true, but Maggie didn't mind. She was happy to earn her and Wilson's keep.

"She has Mildred and Gwendolyn."

He gazed back at her assiduously.

"But I still say she'll be glad to see us go."

Wilson's eyes returned to his plate. "You can be so naive, dear sister."

They ate for awhile, mulling over the situation.

Finally, Maggie looked up again. "Are you suggesting that we don't tell her?" She thought about what such an act would imply. To slip away without telling anyone would smack of ingratitude. Yet to remain and reveal the inheritance did present a certain element of risk. If Fionnula were to seize possession of the mine while Maggie was still underage, it could, as Wilson hinted, be lost to them.

"Let's think about it."

They did, thinking long and hard.

"Well . . . perhaps it would be best if we just run away. Once we arrive in Colorado I can write Aunt

Fionnula and tell her where we are—although that does seem callous," Maggie conceded.

"But profitable for us." He gazed at her with wisdom far beyond his years.

Her confidence continued to spiral upward. "We could . . . yes, we could do it! I believe in us, Wilson!"

"You believe in everyone." That was her flaw. She believed in *everybody*. "How old are you?"

"You know how old I am. Seventeen."

"Seventeen—but even more important, three months and twenty-seven days away from your eighteenth birthday, if my addition serves me right. At the tender age of eighteen you get booted out of the house. Correct?"

"Correct."

"What funds have you set aside for our welfare?"

"Well, there's what's left of Father's and Mother's estate . . ." Her words wavered when she saw him shaking his head.

"I doubt those funds even exist now." When she was about to argue, he continued. "Have we seen any—even one pound of those funds in the three years that we've been with Aunt Fionnula?"

"No, but it takes a lot—"

"Aunt Fionnula has a *lot*, none of which she plans to squander on our well-being. If this mine is profitable—" He paused, his eyes hopeful.

"I don't know," she admitted. "Mr. Dermot didn't say anything about that. The deed only indicates that the mine is located within a day's travel of Denver. But it has to be profitable, doesn't it? Weren't most gold mines profitable?"

"Well, silver would be better, but a good gold vein is capable of producing a handsome profit," Wilson mused. He seemed to recall Colorado had more silver than gold. He'd have to read up on that.

Maggie leaned closer. "You think we should do it? Just slip off without telling anyone and go to Colorado?"

"Most assuredly." He slid a piece a lamb into his mouth. "There is only one problem."

"What?"

"We're penniless."

Smiling, Maggie waved the brown envelope in front of his face. "There's enough in here to get us to Colorado, and, if we're thrifty, enough to see us through a few lean months."

"Then it's settled. We'll go," Wilson said. "Must I eat the carrots?"

"Yes."

Taking a drink of milk, Maggie weighed the wisdom of embarking upon such an adventure. There would be perils to consider. She knew nothing about mining, or Colorado. It would be daring of her to leave the security of family to start life anew in a land that might prove to be harsh and uncompromising.

If they were to venture off without Aunt Fionnula's blessing, they might not be welcomed back. Yet, if they told her about the inheritance, she would surely scheme to control the money.

In less than four months, Maggie would be eighteen and able to do what she wanted. But in less than four months, she could have the mine producing enough gold so that she and Wilson would have endless financial freedom.

Go, or stay?

Sneak away like a thief in the night, or tell Aunt Fionnula about the mine and risk losing the only asset they had left.

To be certain, it would be a tremendous undertaking—an eight-year-old and a seventeen-year-old—Maggie glanced at Wilson. But then, Wilson wasn't like most eight-year-olds; she intuitively trusted his wisdom and insight.

Maggie pushed back from the table as the bell from the dining room sounded. "Mildred wants more lamb."

"Mildred needs more lamb like I need thicker glasses."

"Wilson, be nice," Maggie scolded as she dished up the remainder of the chops from the iron skillet.

"Mildred isn't nice." Wilson took a bite of carrot, wincing. "And Gwendolyn is downright mean." Why, only yesterday she'd made him read to her from a novel by Beatrice Harraden called *Ships That Pass in the Night* while she sprawled on the settee, drinking tea and stuffing her face with raspberry scones. The tragic love story had her blubbering like a whale.

Balancing the heavy platter on her slender hip, Maggie hurried to the door. Lowering her voice, she whispered, "Eat your carrots and peas. You're going to need your strength."

Wilson glanced up. "To make our escape?"

"No, silly." She winked. "To mine *gold*."

Chapter 2

A steam locomotive, hauling a combination baggage coach, regular coach, and an open, flat-roofed observation car, slowly wound its way up the steep incline.

Black smoke rolled from the engine's stacks as it huffed, straining to pull its heavy load up the narrow gauge railway.

Surrounded by magnificent beauty, Maggie clasped her hands in awe as she viewed Colorado's snow-covered peaks silhouetted against a flawless blue sky.

Searching for the proper term to describe such breathtaking beauty, she found none. Yellow pines, Douglas firs, and blue spruces covered the mountainsides. Just below the timberline, hardy bristlecone pines, gnarled by the constant winds, dotted the land. And the aspens! Their magnificent broad leaves shimmered and danced in resplendent gold beneath the warm September sun.

On the lower slopes, mule deer browsed on grasses and lichens. Elk and bighorn sheep leapt among the crags at higher elevations.

How could she recapitulate such splendor—such grandeur—when she wrote to tell Aunt Fionnula about their adventure? How could she describe the wonderful landscape?

How could she explain why she and Wilson had sneaked away like two thieves in the night?

Sighing, she dismissed her nagging conscience, breathing deeply of the pine-scented air.

As far as the eye could see, there was nothing but rugged valleys and towering peaks. Surely, God had a special place in his heart for Colorado. When he finished his wondrous masterpiece, he must have sat back and simply stared at his miraculous handiwork.

"Maggie, look!" Wilson's nose had been mashed against the coach window for the past hour. The train was crossing a deep gorge in its continued ascent up the mountainside.

Switching to the seat across the aisle, Maggie peered down on the yawning chasm spread below them.

"How'd you like to fall down there?" Wilson marveled.

"Wouldn't," Maggie decided. Even looking at such depths gave her the willies.

The elderly couple sitting across the aisle listened to the lively exchange with growing amusement. The old man chuckled at the boy's appreciation of Mother Earth. Leaning over, he observed quietly, "This your first glimpse of Colorado, son?"

Wilson glanced expectantly at Maggie, remembering her earlier warnings about strangers. He wasn't supposed to talk to any.

Maggie smiled, granting him permission to speak.

Turning back to the stranger, Wilson nodded. "Yes, sir—is everything in Colorado this deep?"

"Some parts even deeper," the old man allowed.

The man's eyes shifted to Maggie. "Are you and the boy traveling far?"

"To Hoodee Doo."

"Hoodee Doo, eh?" The man nodded, familiar with the mining camp. "Got relatives up there, have you?" He thought he detected a bit of an English accent in their voices.

"No, no relatives," she said.

His wife gently reached over to silence him. Franklin never met a stranger. He'd talk the quills off a porcupine if she didn't stop him. "Now, Franklin, perhaps the young lady doesn't want to state her business in Hoodee Doo."

"Oh, I don't mind," Maggie said. Slipping to the seat opposite them, her face fairly glowed as she explained. "My Aunt Sissy passed away and left us a gold mine."

A frown crimped the corners of the old man's eyes as he drew thoughtfully on the stem of his pipe. "Gold, eh?"

Maggie smiled. "Actually, Wilson and I have never been anywhere near Hoodee Doo. We've lived in England the past few years, but we're looking forward to the new experience."

Edie and Frank traded hesitant looks.

Aware of the exchange, Maggie leaned toward them hopefully. "Are you familiar with the area?"

"Yes," the old man said. "We know the area."

"I had a cousin who lived in Hoodee Doo for a time," Edie supplied.

Maggie could barely contain her excitement. "Tell me all you know about it." She was eager for any tidbit, however small, concerning their soon-to-be new home. "Do they have a school?"

At first she'd thought about home-schooling Wilson, but after considerable thought, decided otherwise. Wilson needed to be with children his own age. Primarily, he'd been with adults all his life, and she thought he needed youthful, carefree days. The good Lord knew he'd seen little of those.

Besides, she would be too busy running the mine to school him at home. She had to set up a household, hire a crew—oh! There were so many things to be done!

"Hoodee Doo's like most mining towns around these parts," the old man said. "Good school, I understand. Most of the bigger mining companies have taken over. In order to have their families with them, most men settle for an hourly wage now. Understand they mine a good deal of silver up there in Hoodee Doo."

Maggie's brows lifted. "Silver?"

Franklin and Edie exchanged that look again.

"Yes . . . silver is quite the thing now, you know," Edie ventured.

"See, that's what I told you!" Wilson said. "Gold in Colorado—not much of it, I hear tell."

Maggie turned to stare at him. "What?"

"Gold," he articulated. "The books I've read say there's more *silver* than gold in Colorado. That's what I've been trying to tell you, Maggie!"

Maggie was dumbfounded. "*When* have you tried to tell me that?"

"When you weren't *listening*." She never listened. Since she'd inherited that old mine, her head was *always* up in the clouds.

According to history, gold had been found in Colorado, but not in great quantities. Men, in their quest for riches, bypassed the heart of the Rockies and headed for California. But in 1860, the cry of "Silver!" was raised, and for more than two decades now, the mountains of central Colorado had ridden the crest of the silver boom. Everywhere, mining magnates had built impressive homes, and miners had plenty of work to support their families.

When the Sherman Silver Purchase Act was enacted in 1890, the pot grew even sweeter. The legislation obligated the U.S. Treasury to buy the equivalent of the entire U.S. silver production. The silver was to be paid for with treasury notes redeemable for gold or silver. The measure sought to increase the amount of currency in circulation and blunt the movement of free silver.

"I'm sorry, Wilson. I guess I wasn't listening," Maggie apologized. Was it possible they had come all this way, given up a stable home, to claim a worthless inheritance? Her heart sank when her dreams for their future suddenly dimmed.

"Well now, dear, I wouldn't fret. There's gold in

Colorado, plenty of it around these parts," Franklin assured her kindly. "They find it every day. It's just that silver is more profitable now because of the Sherman Act."

Her face fell. "I didn't know that."

"Well, there's talk of repealing the law . . . you never know."

"Well, I wouldn't worry," Edie said brightly. "Hoodee Doo can't keep cooks at the local cafés," she encouraged. "A body can always find work!"

"Yes, ma'am," Maggie said lamely. All this way for a worthless mine.

"Yes, a body can always find work in Hoodee Doo," Franklin agreed.

Resting her head, Maggie stared at the roof of the train, feeling slightly ill.

Now what? They could hardly return to England —not after the way they'd left. Aunt Fionnula would never understand.

Franklin sat up straighter, pointing to an animal grazing on the hillside. "Say! Will you look at that!" Leaning toward the window, he pointed to a splendid elk. "Have you ever seen an elk up close, son?"

Wilson, round-eyed again, gaped out the window at the magnificent creature. He'd never even seen elk from a distance! "No, never," he breathed, absolutely enthralled.

The old man's and young boy's voices faded as Maggie closed her eyes, listening to the wheels rhythmically clicking along the rails.

Wheels that were taking her to a worthless *gold* mine.

* * *

Cutthroat, Randy Doddler, Fiddle Creek, Jackass Hill, Shirttail Diggins, Bloody Run, Bladdersville, Gouge Eye, Humbug Creek, Red Dog, Tenderfoot Gulch, Lost Horse Gulch, Whiskey Gulch, Gulch of Gold, Mad Mule Gulch—there were a hundred and one gulches where her mine could have been.

Unfortunately, hers was in Hoodee Doo.

Nearly every man in Hoodee Doo wore a beard. That's what struck Maggie as she jerked Wilson out of the path of a careening wagon.

Wading through ankle-deep mud to cross the street, she stared at the large assemblage of masculinity. Not one man in a hundred had a cleanly shaven face. Some looked to have cut a swatch of hair from around their mouths so they could feed themselves more easily, but in general they all looked alike: flannel shirts, heavy boots, trousers saturated with muck, and long, matted hair.

The town itself was an eye-opener. Tucked at the base of a mountain, a day's ride west of Denver, the camp appeared on the surface to have no civilized refinements.

A vast sea of tents sprawled at the foothill of a mountain, interspersed with crudely assembled buildings that looked to have been thrown up with rampageous zeal. Wagons were lined up, people living out of the back of them.

Traffic had no right of way, many vehicles traveling right down the middle, Maggie decided, as she jerked Wilson from the path of another oncoming wagon.

The stench emitted from the livery stable was crippling. Manure from thousands of mules, horses, and oxen that freighted up and down the main street every day was piled high.

A round of six shots erupted from one of the nearby saloons, sending patrons scrambling out of windows and doors in search of cover.

Holding tight to Wilson's hand, Maggie forged her way down the crowded sidewalk in search of the land office. Her eyes watered from the blend of odors of livery stable, chicken feathers, grimy cats and dogs, and unwashed humanity.

Wilson, wearing his Sunday best, made a face as his shoes, oozing with mud, make a sucking sound with each step.

"I'm not going to like it here," he predicted. Pinching his nose between his thumb and forefinger, he hurried to keep up with his sister. "It smells as bad as Gwendolyn's socks in late August!"

"It'll be fine," Maggie soothed, more concerned over how she was going to find the recorder's office than the odors around her.

Coming down the middle of the street was a small funeral procession. The bereaved walked hand in hand, grim-faced. Some wept openly. Stepping aside to allow the mourners to pass, Maggie restrained Wilson, waiting as the small cortege stopped in front of a modest looking house with an open grave beside it.

A couple of sturdy looking chaps gently lowered the casket into the ground as the minister, a tall, sparingly built man with ruddy cheeks and a receding hairline, opened his worn Bible and began to read.

"Brethren, it is a sorrowful occasion that unites us this day. In this most solemn of hours we gather to pay our final respects to Sister Oates—let us pray!"

The minister's powerful voice washed over Maggie as she nudged Wilson, and they bowed their heads with the mourners.

"Heavenly Father, we ask that you look down on Sister Oates's family and her precious loved ones. Grant them the peace that passeth all understanding . . ."

Out of habit, one of the mourners began to examine the dirt he was kneeling on as the preacher droned on.

"Sister Oates was a *kind* and *obedient* servant, Lord. Those who are left behind take comfort in knowing that at this very *hour* she walks hand in hand with loved ones who have gone before her."

Finding the gravel thick with traces of color, the mourner began to edge his way to the mound of fresh dirt piled high beside the grave, passing the word to the fellow next to him. *Gold!*

The preacher shot him a disapproving look, but continued. "Ashes to ashes, dust to dust . . ."

Whispers of "gold" gained momentum throughout the crowd as first one man and then the other started to paw the ground. The preacher, moving his Bible aside, gazed thunderstruck at the ground, then shouted, "Gold! You're all dismissed!"

Dropping to his knees, the man of the cloth

clawed the dirt, the solemnity of the moment shattered.

Shaking his head, Wilson watched the spectacle taking place. "It bears repeating: I'm not going to like it here."

Grasping him firmly by the hand, Maggie crossed the street, glancing over her shoulder to watch the greedy frenzy. The casket was dragged out of the grave and moved to a different spot to allow for more digging.

"Oh dear," she murmured when she finally spotted the land office and saw the line was backed up clear to the street.

"It's going to take forever, isn't it?" Wilson said nasally, still holding his nose from the stench.

"A while, I'm afraid."

Taking their place at the back of the line, Maggie looked around her, dismayed to see the recorder's office was every bit as chaotic as the streets. Yet she had no other choice but to wait. She hadn't the slightest inkling where her mine was located. Someone familiar with the area would have to take her there.

Taking the deed out of her purse, she studied it again. The mine didn't appear to be far, but it would be foolish for Wilson and her to set out alone when they knew nothing about the area.

For more than two hours they stood in line, wedged between smelly old men who shouted, and pushed, and shoved, and said awful things to each other as they waited to stake new claims.

Recalling the earlier conversation with the man on

the train, who said that most men in Hoodee Doo worked for the larger mining companies, she leaned forward, having to shout above the din to the man standing in front of her, "What's going on?"

"New strike—big one, over near Poverty Flats!"

"Gold?" she asked hopefully.

"Silver!"

As Maggie edged nearer to the building's entrance, she noticed the noise coming from inside was deafening. Around two o'clock her head began to pound. She glanced down when she felt Wilson yanking on the hem of her jacket.

"I'm hungry."

"It won't be much longer." She patted his head consolingly. It had been hours since they'd eaten, but if she stepped out of line she'd lose her place and have to start over again.

"I'm tired, and my shoes are too tight," he complained. He sagged against her, weary from the long journey and the extended wait. They had traveled for weeks to claim their inheritance. Over land and sea they had come in search of a bright, new tomorrow. Maggie was starting to wonder if she'd done the right thing. What if the mine *was* worthless? What if it yielded so little gold she would be forced to return to England? What if Aunt Fionnula refused to take them back?

Here, in a strange town, with even stranger-looking men flanking her on all sides, doubts assailed her. She and her brother had sneaked off like bad eggs, and now, if anything were to happen to them, there would be nowhere to turn for help.

For more than an hour she had been aware of a ragamuffinish-looking individual two places in line ahead of her. He was, without exception, the most tattered and torn man she had ever seen. He was a caricature of an old miner, unkempt hair, beard falling to the center of his chest, the rim of his old brown hat ready to drop down on his shoulders at a moment's notice. The battered sides had severed all connections to the crown. To keep the fabric from coming completely apart, he had tied a string around the top to fashion a hatband.

His hair hung in fiery red locks around his shoulders. What had once been a flannel shirt now hung in ragged tatters down to his soiled trousers.

Her eyes meandered to his boots and found that they were more holes than leather.

"Look, Wilson," she whispered. "There's a man with hair like yours."

Wilson looked, appalled.

"Except yours is cleaner," she added.

"Maggie!"

"Much much much cleaner."

The man suddenly turned, his eyes nailing Maggie.

For a moment, she couldn't breathe, his arresting blue gaze holding hers. Caught off-guard, color flooded her face as she realized he knew she had been staring at him.

He suddenly smiled, about to doff his hat when he thought better of it. It was entirely possible he might lose it altogether. Instead, he graciously bowed from his waist. "The boy is weary. Would you like to trade places?" His hand indicated their chaotic surroundings. "It won't help much, but some."

Moving Wilson protectively closer, Maggie summoned her best Christian smile. "No, thank you. We'll wait our turn."

Conceding with a gracious nod, the man turned back to continue the wait.

The hands on the clock crept from three to four. Wilson reeled with fatigue, clinging to Maggie's skirt like a wet blanket.

"Are we *any* closer?" he asked, so hungry his stomach rumbled conspicuously.

The line moved at a snail's pace. Men's voices rose and fell with anticipation and anger. The room was so hot Maggie could hardly breathe. Loosening the top button on her collar, she took deep breaths, giving the evil eye to the man who kept stoking buckets of coal into the stove in the corner. It was hot enough to cure meat in the room, but the man didn't seem to notice. Every half hour he stepped to the stove to feed it another bucket of coal.

Maggie had worked her way to within five places of the desk when she suddenly became light-headed. Fighting the weakness that threatened to consume her, she squeezed Wilson's hand tighter.

Wilson's glasses tilted askew as he sagged against her, catnapping now.

The minutes ticked by. Sweat trickled down the small of Maggie's back. Bringing her handkerchief to her forehead, she blotted perspiration, willing her eyes to focus. *Only four more*, she told herself. Then she could seek a breath of clean, blessedly cool air.

She was third in line when her knees buckled. With a whimper of despair, blackness consumed her and she wilted to the floor.

Wilson fell on top of her with a loud thump.

Startled from a sound sleep, he sat up, wide-eyed, trying to orient himself.

The noise in the room swelled to a frenzied pitch as someone dragged the tangle of bodies out of the way so the line would keep moving.

Wilson scrambled to his knees, frantically groping for his glasses. Locating them, he quickly fastened the wire hooks around his ears, then crawled to his sister's side, trying to fan her awake.

"Maggie—Maggie! Wake up!"

A shadow suddenly fell across the floor. Wilson looked up, his mouth going slack when he recognized the dirty, red-headed giant who had offered them his place in line earlier.

Shrinking backward, Wilson stared up at the man, terrified. Fire shot from the stranger's eyes, and white smoke belched from his enormous nose.

Wilson's ears started to ring. Run! something told him, but he couldn't leave Maggie!

Over the roar in his ears, Wilson saw the giant open his mouth to speak, his powerful voice reverberating across the room like a mighty storm, rattling the boards of the wooden floor.

"Do you need help, son?"

The giant's words came to Wilson slow and lumbering. He was going to faint. No, throw up—no, faint. *Throw up, faint, throw up, faint.*

Backing away, Wilson shook his head as the giant leaned over to touch Maggie's forehead.

"No!" Squeezing his eyes tightly shut, Wilson struck out at the giant, willing to defend Maggie at any cost. "Don't touch her!" His eyes flew open, frantically searching the room for help. But the men in the room pretended they didn't see the giant. They kept on laughing and talking, acting as if nothing unusual was happening.

"Need to get her outside," the giant rumbled. "Needs fresh air."

"No! No! You can't have her!"

Kicking and screaming, Wilson battled the giant, but a giant was a giant, and giants were seldom affected by eight-year-olds.

Scooping Maggie's limp body up in his enormous arms, the giant strode across the room, his huge boots thundering against the wooden floor. Before Wilson could stop him, he disappeared out the front door.

Struggling to his feet, Wilson's eyes were awash with tears. The dirty, red-haired giant carried Maggie off and not a single person tried to stop him.

Blinking back tears, Wilson fought the urge to howl; he was too old to howl. He was too young to defend Maggie, and too old to cry. It wasn't fair!

Sitting back on his heels, he started to swipe

away tears of frustration. The room was powerfully hot, and he was starving hungry.

And now a stupid, dirty, red-haired giant had stolen Maggie.

A shadow fell over the floor again. Lifting his eyes slowly, Wilson's despair reached bottom when he saw the giant glaring down at him.

Shrinking aside, Wilson clambered behind a random leg, but the giant collared him and dragged him back out.

"Gotta come with me, kid," the giant ordered.

"No! I don't want to come with you! Stop! Help—someone help me!" Wilson cried.

The men waiting in line watched the altercation with mild amusement.

Ignoring his pleas, the giant picked Wilson up by the scruff of the neck and hauled him out the front door.

A blast of cold air hit Wilson in the face, stiffening his resolve. Doubling up his fists, he tore into the giant, trying to break his ferocious hold.

Setting him down on the sidewalk, his captor calmly held the boy at arm's length and let him swing away.

Wilson fought until the last ounce of strength deserted him. Sagging hopelessly to his knees, he panted, glaring up at his foe with brimming eyes.

The giant, hand on his hip, stared back at him. "Are you through?" he asked.

Wilson, screwing his face into a determined scowl, confronted him. "What have you done with my sister?"

The giant's eyes moved to the wooden bench in front of the building where Maggie was just sitting up, holding the back of her head.

With a cry of relief, Wilson ran to her, clasping her tightly around the neck. "Maggie, oh Maggie! Are you all right?" He took her hand, his bespectacled eyes inspecting her for damage.

"I'm sorry ... I must have been overcome by the vapors." Maggie straightened her hat, feeling both annoyed and embarrassed to be so delicate.

"Are you sure? He didn't hurt you?"

"Yes, I'm fine, really." She smiled back at her brother wearily. "I'm sorry if I frightened you."

Scooting closer, he lowered his voice. "Never mind that, we've got a problem."

"A problem?" she whispered, her fingers gingerly testing the back of her scalp for tenderness.

Nodding his head, his eyes gestured toward the man who was standing not six feet away watching the hushed exchange.

"The giant," he urged. She must've taken a good whack on her head if she hadn't noticed him!

Woozy, Maggie looked around. "The giant?"

"Over there," Wilson whispered crossly, feeling the giant's molten gaze spearing him. "Right there! ... Don't you *see* him?"

Maggie didn't see him. All she saw was the kindhearted miner who had carried her out of the land office a moment earlier.

"See him?" Wilson insisted, his voice bordering on impatience now.

Since Wilson wasn't given to flights of fantasy,

Maggie was puzzled by his insistence. "No . . . exactly where is he, Wilson?"

Wilson's eyes nonchalantly returned to the miner, willing hers to follow.

For a long moment they stared.

"Him?"

"Yes." Were there two?

"Wilson," she scolded, hoping the miner hadn't heard him. "He isn't a *giant*."

The man was tall, his raggedy appearance fierce looking, but why Wilson imagined him to be a giant escaped her.

The giant stepped forward, and Wilson's head dived for safety in Maggie's skirt folds.

Pausing in front of them, her rescuer asked quietly, "Are you feeling better now?"

"Yes, thank you," Maggie said gratefully. "It was so hot in there . . ." She suddenly realized what happened. "I'm sorry you lost your place in line."

He shrugged. "It doesn't matter. I'll come again tomorrow." He studied her flushed features intensely. "What about you?"

Sighing, Maggie retied her bonnet strings. "I can't come back tomorrow. I have to find my mine tonight." Her funds were rapidly melting, and she couldn't afford another night's lodging.

The man's eyes moved to her skirt, where only Wilson's glasses protruded from the folds. "It's getting late," he said gently. "And the boy is hungry. Can't you wait until morning? The lines are usually not so long."

"I can't." Maggie took Wilson's hand, trying to comfort him. He was bone weary and neither one of them could go much longer without eating. "I have to wait."

Although he was aware that it was none of his business, the man still tried to talk her out of it. "It will be dark soon."

For a moment Maggie was tempted to tell him, but knew it was foolish to encourage conversation with one so disreputable-looking. Yet he had been kind enough to help her when no one else had.

"You're new in town," he observed when her silence stretched.

"We arrived this morning. From England."

"England?"

"Yes, England." She smiled, and he was drawn by its surprising warmth. "When our parents died we were sent from New York to England to live with our Aunt in Wokingham." Sighing, Maggie noticed that it was getting dark. "I'm afraid I have to get back into line. We have to locate our mine tonight."

Prominent blue eyes assessed her. She was no bigger than a gnat. When he'd picked her up she'd been as light as goose down. Around here the women were as sturdy as oxen. They had to be if they hoped to survive the elements.

Her hair was different from the other women's, too. It looked clean and he imagined it smelled that way. She wore it loose, the unfettered locks reaching to her waist. She was also very young. Maybe seventeen or eighteen, the boy eight or nine.

"You don't know where your mine is located?"

"No." Loosening the string of her purse, she searched for the deed. "Have you been here long?"

"Long enough." At times it seemed he'd been here all his life.

"Then perhaps *you* might know where the mine is." If he did, she wouldn't have to stand in line again. It would be the only thing that had gone right all day.

Rummaging through her purse, she absently handed him a handkerchief, a small leather pouch, a comb, various disheveled papers, a skeleton key, a needle stuck in a spool of black thread, and a faded blue button.

"It's here somewhere," she promised.

When his hands were piled high, she finally located it. "Here it is." Smiling, she handed him the deed, watching hopefully as he shifted the contents of the purse back to her.

She frowned. "You do know how to read?"

"No pictures?" he asked dryly.

"No, only words," she apologized.

Unfolding the deed, he held it up to the fading light, squinting to make out the boundary lines.

Getting a closer look at his hands, Maggie was surprised to see they were strong and tanned. Why, he wasn't nearly as old as she'd first thought. No one to take care of him properly and hard living, she suspected when she detected a faint whiff of whiskey, had wizened his features beneath the scrubby beard.

"Well?"

Refolding the deed, he handed it back to her. "I know where it is."

Relief flooded her. "Can you take us there?"

"No, ma'am." He turned to leave, and she called after him, "I'll pay you . . . a little." A paltry little, she added silently. Her money wouldn't hold out long at this rate.

He was about to call back that it didn't matter, he wouldn't take her there for any amount. He knew about the Hellhole. There wasn't a man, woman, or child around who didn't.

He had himself geared up to tell her so when he turned around and saw her looking at him. Hope was written all over her face.

Annoyance flared. She had no call to expect anything of him; none at all. He'd carried her out of a hot room when she fainted. Any man in the room would have done the same. That didn't obligate him to her, or her to him, and he'd have no trouble telling her so.

"Ma'am . . ." His words suddenly stuck in his throat.

She stood shivering in the mountain air, holding tightly to the kid's hand. They looked at him as if they'd just gotten off the oprhan train and he was their new father.

"I know it would be an imposition," she said softly. "I'm genuinely sorry to impose upon you, but we have no one." A stiff breeze ruffled the

feather on her bonnet, a frivolous little thing made
of pink silk, rimmed with black ribbon and a black
feather, with black lace around the front. Totally
inadequate mountain wear. "It will be dark soon,
and we're weary. If you could only lead us part of
the way, we could travel the last distance alone."

"You'd be better off waiting until morning," he
said shortly.

"Is the mine a good distance away?"

"No, not far, but as you said, it will be dark
soon and the mountains are treacherous if you
don't know them."

A smile filled her eyes. "But you do know them,
don't you?" She wasn't sure why, but she trusted
him. She wasn't foolish. For all she knew he could
be dangerous; yet she sensed he wasn't. His out-
ward appearance did nothing to disclaim the notion, yet his eyes gave him away. Maggie saw a
sense of nobility in them.

Hard times might have stripped him of dignity,
but they were powerless to take his pride.

"You do know the mountains?" she asked softly.

A muscle flexed on his bearded cheek. "I know
them."

"Then I'm sure we could not ask for more capable assistance." Her pleas formed a soft vapor in
the air.

Glancing at the boy, the man realized he was
outnumbered. Up until now, he hadn't realized he
was such a soft touch for a pretty face. "We'll need
lanterns."

"I have enough money to purchase one," she

said. "And a few basic necessities to tide us over until I can get the mine operating."

Which will be comparable to a cold day in hell, he thought, but he said instead, "Bundle up tightly. It will be cold."

As they descended the wooden steps, Wilson hurried to match strides with the giant.

Peering down at the top of the boy's head, the giant asked, "Hadn't you better stick close to your mother?" One thing he *didn't* intend to do, and that was mollycoddle either one of them. Deliver them to the Hellhole and be on his way. That was all.

"She's not my mother, she's my sister."

The giant glanced over his shoulder. "Your sister?"

"Yes, sir. Maggie Fletcher—that's her name."

Sidestepping a barrage of buckboards, the three grimly waded across the street. When they reached the other side, Wilson continued to stick close to the giant. It looked as though he didn't intend to eat them, and he would be a definite asset if they ran into trouble.

"What's your name, son?"

Wilson swallowed, panting to keep up with the man's long strides. "Wil . . . son."

"Wilson?"

Wilson nodded, wishing giants didn't have such long legs.

"You good with your fists, Wilson?"

"Not very . . . but with a name like Wilson I should be, huh?"

A hint of a smile appeared on the giant's lips.

"Well, I wouldn't worry, Wilson. They call me Gordie."

Wilson glanced up, almost losing his balance. His breath was coming in gasps now. *"Gordie?"* That was a rather inappropriate name for a *giant*. "Why do they call you *that*?"

"I don't know," Gordie admitted. He had acquired the name in childhood and had failed to rid himself of the embarrassing stigma.

"Gordie," Wilson mused. Hmmm. The name was every bit as humiliating as Wilson. Suddenly, Wilson felt a developing camaraderie with the giant.

"We got the same color hair, you notice that, Gordie?"

"I noticed that, kid."

Gordie hoped the boy didn't plan to get cozy. He didn't take much to kids.

Looking up, Wilson beamed at the giant, deciding that since they had so much in common, like red hair and unmanly names, he just might change his mind and like him.

In fact, he decided as he reached for the giant's hand as they approached another busy intersection, he might just decide to like him a lot.

Chapter 3

"The what?"

He held the lantern higher as Maggie got down on her hands and knees, trying to make out the lettering burned into the weathered board staked to the ground. "He—Helhail—Hello—Hel—"

"Hellhole."

She looked up. "What?"

"Hellhole," he repeated.

"Hellhole?"

"That's the name of your mine. Well, The Hellhole, if you want to get technical." Pulling his collar closer to his neck, he realized he needed a drink. A good stiff one. By the time they'd climbed the narrow, twisting path leading to the mine, darkness had overtaken them. Cold was seeping into his bones, and his joints felt like raw meat.

"Boy oh boy." Wilson's eyes grimly surveyed the desolate setting. He didn't know what a gold mine was supposed to look like, but this one sure didn't look like what he thought it would.

A ray of moonlight splayed across the weather-beaten boards arbitrarily nailed over the entrance to the big hole. That looked to be the extent of their inheritance, just a nailed-up hole in the side of a freezing cold mountain.

Wilson wished he was back in Wokingham, in a nice warm feather bed, eating Maggie's strawberry scones.

Getting to her feet, Maggie dusted dirt off her gloves. "Well, it isn't exactly what I'd hoped for, but the name isn't important." A name could always be changed. It didn't matter what the mine was called as long as it produced.

"Isn't *exactly* what she'd hoped for," the man chortled under his breath, wondering if she were making a joke or if she was just plain simple.

Glancing around, Maggie sought to bolster her careening spirits. As she said, the mine wasn't what she'd hoped for, but it was good enough. "Where are the living quarters?"

Right now the only thing she cared about was getting Wilson in out of the cold. She was no stranger to problems. Granted, by the looks of things, the mine would present its fair share, but anything worth having seldom came easy.

"*Living* quarters?" Gordie snickered. He'd heard tales about the Hellhole's living quarters—or lack thereof.

Maggie's strength was quickly ebbing. Her day had been long and trying. Her head was pounding and her stomach ached with hunger. She desperately needed a bite to eat and a bed.

Rummaging through her purse for the deed, she did some disconcerted mumbling of her own. Someone had made a mistake. Surely he recognized that!

"The deed clearly states there is some sort of dwelling on the land," she declared.

"The deed," he granted, "says a lot of things."

Maggie's heart took a nosedive. There *had* to be a dwelling. Where would she and Wilson live?

"Are you telling me there are *no* living quarters?"

"Well, now, ma'am, I suppose that's a matter of who you're asking."

Her eyes revealed a good deal more than fortitude now. "I'm asking you."

"Well, then." He motioned for her to follow him.

The wind howled through the mountain pass as they picked their way across the frozen ground.

The moon stretched higher in the September sky. Wilson stayed on Gordie's heels, his eyes anxiously searching beyond the lantern light. There were bears out there; big ones—along with a herd of gigantic elk with those big old horns he'd seen out of the train window earlier.

Some hundred feet from the main shaft someone had tunneled into a steep hill face and then drifted right and left three or four feet, fashioning a dark earth chamber about eight by ten feet. A six-by-four, crudely built wooden door sagged on the frame at a comical angle.

Holding the lantern higher, the man motioned for Maggie to come closer.

She did so with a sense of trepidation. "What is it?"

"Your 'dwelling.' "

"Maggie," Wilson groaned. *Good grief!* Now they had to live in a *cave*? Dreams of grandeur were quickly dissipating.

"Shhh," Maggie consoled. She refused to accept the absurdity of the situation. First she was told that her mine might be worthless, and now the visual evidence!

It was a mistake; it had to be.

The deed clearly indicated a *dwelling*. This wasn't a dwelling—it was a hole in the earth!

"There's been a mistake."

"Yes, ma'am," Gordie agreed. "You've inherited the Hellhole."

Edging closer, Maggie peered into the dimly lit chamber. In one corner someone had piled pine and juniper boughs. Two or three chunks of old tree bole were scattered about for tables. Close to the entrance, a crudely built fireplace dominated the west wall.

"There has to be a mistake." Maggie shook her head, refusing to believe the cruel twist of fate.

"No, ma'am, no mistake." The man's eyes swung back to the sagging door. "It's all yours."

Well, this was too much. Maggie's frustration boiled over. While Gordie was trying to be respectful, she could see he found it all amusing. "How do you know so much about this mine? There *could* have been a mistake!"

He touched the rim of his tattered hat courte-

ously. "Forgive me, ma'am. You're right. I only
know what I've heard, and around these parts,
stories have been known to be blown out of proportion."

"Stories?" She straightened. "What stories?"

He squirmed visibly, finding the topic uncomfortable.

"What stories?" she asked again.

"Just stories," he said. "You're bound to hear
everything imaginable if you stick around long
enough."

Huddling deeper into her cloak, Maggie tried to
imagine what the stories related to. By now she
was afraid to speculate.

The miner's hand moved reassuringly to the
flask he kept in his left coat pocket. "It's a harsh
land," he said more to himself than to her. "You
might want to think about returning to England."

Within the past few days he'd heard of a young
man committing suicide in a fit of insanity, and another couple of prospectors found dead, wolves
having feasted on their carcasses. Five others died
in a fire that swept the hilltops. It wasn't a fitting
place for women and children. If she were smart,
she'd leave now.

Maggie's eyes returned to the primitive lodging.
"I can't go back to England. For one thing, I don't
have the money."

"Ma'am, I'll be happy to take you and the boy
back to camp." He recognized the trapped look in
her eyes. Didn't blame her—on the contrary, he
sympathized.

"No," Maggie sighed. She couldn't do that either.

Well, it was her life. He'd done what he could; he showed her to the mine. No panic-stricken look was going to influence him, though he did feel sorry for her. She had a hell of a mess on her hands.

"You'll want to keep your gun close by," he said. Bears were always a threat, not to mention other wildlife. "You do have a gun?"

"No, but that's all right. I don't know how to use one."

No gun? Stuck atop a godforsaken mountain, and she had no gun. Wonderful. Still, it wasn't his problem, and he wasn't going to make it one.

Clearing his throat, he prepared for a quick departure. "The shelter isn't much, but it's dry. The animals won't bother you as long as you keep the door shut." As far as other miners, they treated a woman with respect. That was the code of the land.

"Oh . . . yes, thank you. We will." He could count on that. Taking a deep breath, she drew Wilson close to her. Things wouldn't be so bad, once they adjusted to the poverty, the isolation—the wretchedness.

She brightened. Why, within the week she would have a crew hired, and she and Wilson wouldn't feel so lonely.

"Well, this should be a bit of adventure, shouldn't it, Will?"

Wilson's suffering gaze fixed on the sagging

door. His frail frame shook in the biting wind. "It's a cave, Maggie. A *cave*."

"Be good for you, son. Toughen you up," the miner predicted.

Maggie squeezed Wilson's shoulders reassuringly, determined to be strong. After all, Gordie had been kind enough to bring them up here. They had no right to ask anything further of him.

"Thank you again for your kindness, Mr.—" She paused, waiting for him to officially introduce himself.

"T.G. Manning, ma'am." He tipped his hat again. "T for Terrence, G for Gordon. Most folks just call me Gordie."

She smiled, a courageous little smile that made him feel like a heel. "I'm Maggie."

"Yes, Maggie Fletcher. Wilson told me."

Taking another deep breath, she smiled again. "Thank you again for your assistance."

Gordon waved her gratitude aside. He hadn't done her any favors; she'd realize that soon enough.

He turned and was about to leave when his conscience hit him and hit him hard. He couldn't leave them like this. They deserved to know.

Turning back, his eyes wouldn't quite meet hers. "You should know—some people say the mine is haunted." There, he'd said it. It was up to her what she wanted to do about it.

"Haunted?" she echoed lamely.

"Yes, but like I said, folks tend to blow things out of proportion." No sense making a big deal out of it. He just thought she had a right to know before she decided to stay.

Wilson looked up at Maggie, slack-jawed.

She managed to find her voice. "Do you believe those stories?"

"About a ghost living in the mine?" He didn't answer immediately, realizing he'd never wasted any time thinking about it. No, he decided, he didn't believe the stories. Whatever was disturbing the equanimity of that mine, he was certain, wasn't a spook.

"Just stories, ma'am. I wouldn't give it another thought." Of course, she couldn't avoid the subject once she discovered there wasn't a man in a hundred-mile radius who would work the mine, but he wasn't about to tell her.

"Did you hear that, Maggie?" Wilson whispered hoarsely. "He said a *ghost* lives in our mine!"

Maggie patted his shoulder. "He also said it was purely speculation," she said brightly.

"Well, I have to be going on." Before he left, T.G. made sure they had enough food and water to last the night. After this, they were on their own.

"You'll be fine," he assured them one final time as he felt their eyes riveted to his back.

"Sure, we'll be fine," Maggie agreed. "It'll be fun."

Absolutely T.G. thought. A genuine circus.

With a friendly wave, he started down the mountain, sporadically glancing back over his shoulder to find them staring bleakly after him.

He gave another wave, and they hesitantly waved back.

Hell, Manning, he thought as he stepped up his pace. *When will you learn to mind your own business?*

Chapter 4

It got dark early. That was what T.G. hated about winter.

He could take the cold; he was used to it by now. He hadn't minded it when he came to Colorado five years ago, and he didn't mind it now.

The only thing he minded was that it got dark early.

Swigging from the flask, he made his way back down the mountain, trying to erase the boy's face from his mind. The girl's too, for that matter. They shouldn't have come all the way from England to claim a useless mine without knowing the dangers.

He'd seen more stupidity since he'd been here than he could shake a stick at. It was amazing the way people acted at the mention of gold.

He took another swig from the flask. The boy looked scared. Couldn't blame him. The Hellhole should scare anyone in their right mind.

But they would be all right. The dugout was dry, and he'd made sure they had plenty of wood before leaving. Come morning, Maggie Fletcher would begin the process of hiring a crew, and she'd find out what she was up against. She wouldn't be around long after that.

Another vision of Maggie flashed through his mind.

She was a handsome woman. Citified and domesticated. That was her, all right. Citified and domesticated. A woman beyond his reach. Oh, she'd been grateful when he carried her out of the land office, but he'd seen the way she looked at his scruffy appearance—as if she wasn't sure she could trust him.

Looking down at his whiskey-soaked jacket, he chuckled. What was there not to trust about him? Until five years ago, he'd been considered a prize catch.

Phoenix women had clambered for his attention. More than one distressed mama actually shed tears when he failed to court her daughter.

As he lifted the flask back to his mouth, he lost his footing, stumbling.

Quickly righting himself, he giggled, *Careful, old man.* The liquor made him clumsy. He couldn't fall and break his neck, could he?

Who'd care? he thought, laughing outright now.

Sure. Jenny would be upset, but she'd get over it. His kid sister didn't even know where he was, let alone worry about him. Hadn't kept track of him for years. She was in Phoenix being a dutiful wife to her husband, good old reliable Joe. Together they had respectfully produced three strapping heirs in just under four years. Pop was probably real proud of them.

"And he'd consider me a flat-out disgrace," he acknowledged, taking another drink.

Loose rocks gave way beneath his heavy boot as he tilted the flask way back to his mouth. He was getting drunk, and he didn't care. If he fell and broke every bone in his body, there'd only be one man who'd care.

That, of course, would be Mooney Backus—the man who held his gambling debts.

How much did he owe Mooney now?

A fair chunk, he'd bet. Back years ago, he'd have been worried about owing a man money and then suddenly finding himself unable to pay it back.

Yessir, he tipped the flask again, there'd been a time when he'd have stayed up nights trying to figure out how to repay it.

But back then, he'd been honorable. Honorable and full of himself.

Hell, no use crying over spilled milk. He had no one to blame for his problems but himself. He could have stayed home, become the town doctor, married Mary Porter, and produced, damn, maybe four heirs to Pop's fortune.

Mary's papa wasn't exactly a pauper. The old man would have given him fifty acres of prime farmland—no, more like two hundred and fifty—in order to spare his daughter the agony of spinsterhood—but that wasn't what he'd done.

No sirree, not T.G. Manning. T.G. Manning

struck out for Colorado, where he'd sunk every last penny he had in a gold mine that produced squat.

Diddly-ass, squat.

Bringing the flask back to his mouth, he took another long drink. Not particularly bright of T.G. Manning, but when a man had gold fever, he wasn't too bright.

From the day James Wilson Marshall discovered the first gold nugget in a ditch that channeled water from the river to the sawmill, gold had enriched and ruined men's lives. That afternoon of January 4, 1848, forty-five miles east of Sutter's Forbes in Sacramento Valley, changed the course of history.

And put a pretty damn good dent in T.G.'s life.

But that was neither here nor there. Tipping the bottle back to his mouth, he took another drink. The money was gone, Pop had given up on him ever taking over his practice, Mary had been spared spinsterhood when she married the depot clerk, Pete Wiler, and any day now, T.G. would be dead.

Mooney Backus wasn't long on patience.

Three days ago, Backus's thugs had delivered an ultimatum. Gordie had exactly two weeks to come up with twenty-five hundred dollars.

As he said, he'd be dead any day now.

He caught himself again as his boot slid in the loose dirt, the rocks spilling down the precipitous incline. The liquor was going straight to his head. He should have eaten something today. He'd thought about it, just never got around to it.

The trail started to blur. Shaking his head, he tried to focus on the path. There was a hundred-foot drop on either side of him. One slip and he'd save Mooney the trouble of coming after him.

Concentrating now, he slowed his pace. The wind whipped his frayed coat. His hand came up to hold his hat in place as a lone coyote howled at the moon.

The flask found its way back to his mouth, and he drew deeply on it, weaving now. He was drinking too much. A man ought to have more pride than to drink himself into a stupor. If he could think of a reason, he'd quit.

One moment he was walking, and the next he felt himself hurtling down the mountainside. Panic-stricken, he tried to catch himself, but he was too far gone this time. He tumbled end over end, arms and legs flailing wildly.

Liquor came back up in his throat and he choked, hitting the ground hard. Sliding down the mountainside, he snatched for a handhold, his life flashing before him.

All the things he could have been, and wasn't. The women he could have loved, and didn't. The things he should have said, and hadn't. A child he might have held. Everything flashed through his mind except gold, the one thing that had dominated his every waking thought for the past five years.

I'm sorry I failed you, Pop; take care of yourself, Jenny; kiss my ass, Mooney—all flashed through his mind.

Basics dispensed with, his thoughts turned to the immediate. His whiskey; he was spilling it. He could hear the metal flask pinging against the rocks, spraying its contents over the rocky ground.

Miraculously, his hand snagged something and latched on.

Silence closed around him as he lay, afraid to move a muscle, panting, praying whatever it was would continue to support his weight.

A coyote howled at the moon, its cries fading into emptiness.

Using his free hand, T.G. slowly felt around, determining that he was on the edge of a mine shaft, or maybe a deep precipice.

His scraped and bleeding fingers explored the uneven ground. Sweat beaded his forehead as he touched the small outcropping of rock he was lying on.

Damn.

If he moved, the rock would fall, plunging him to certain death.

He thought about yelling, but was afraid to risk even that slight movement. Besides, no one would hear him. Not at this hour.

Flat on his back, he watched a cloud drift across the moon, temporarily obscuring it. The first snowflakes of the season started to swirl as a cold wind buffeted the hillside.

Minutes, then hours dragged by. T.G. lay motionless, his eyes fixed to the sky.

At times he trembled; at others he thought about home, his sister, Jenny, Pop.

Maggie Fletcher entered his mind toward morning. He didn't know why. Maybe because he realized it would have been nice to have loved a woman like her.

He prayed, offering his anguished soul up to God. The next breath he cussed, railing at fate that he was too young to die.

If God would only let him live, he'd straighten up. He'd give up drinking; he'd get a job. Maybe even think about going home—yes, he'd go home.

He'd give up chasing worthless dreams. He'd make something of himself. He hadn't always been this worthless; it was the gold. It did something to a man.

As dawn streaked the sky, Gordie wearily opened his eyes. Every joint in his body ached from precariously clinging to life.

But he'd made it through the night.

Now if he called out, someone might hear him and come to investigate. Hope flickered anew.

Easing his eyes sideways, he saw where he was. Alongside a chasm two feet deep and a foot across.

Sitting up, he stretched, trying to ease the pain in his stiff joints. Coming to his feet, he irritably knocked the dust off his hat.

Shitfire, he needed to get a life.

Chapter 5

Wrenching the door open, Maggie looked out into the morning. A blast of arctic air nearly blinded her.

Munching on a pickle sandwich, she focused on the mine's boarded entrance, determined not to be beaten by her circumstances. Sure, there were problems she hadn't considered, but problems were meant to be solved, weren't they? And the ghost? She'd have to see that to believe it.

Even if there was one, the Fletchers came from sturdy stock. Her father had never taken no for an answer, and everyone said she had a lot of Wilson Fletcher Sr. in her.

Breathing deeply, she watched the sun come up over the mountain. The pine-scented air was bracingly pure. Snow had fallen during the night, lightly coating the ground. Early September and it was snowing already. What would January bring?

Leaning against the doorsill, she sighed. Surrounded by such loveliness, it was hard to be pessimistic about the future.

The Hellhole wasn't that bad. Thanks to Aunt Sissy's money, she could hold on a little longer. Why, in the time it took to say, "What am I doing here?" she'd have the mine operating at full speed.

Ghost or no ghost, the men of Hoodee Doo camp would welcome new employment opportunities. The big companies couldn't offer the caring, family-oriented workplace she intended to give her crew. Wilson's college nest egg would be growing—

Oh, shoot! Who was she kidding? The living conditions were deplorable.

Vile, dirty, cold, and horrible.

She'd be lucky to hire a monkey crew if the Hellhole's reputation was as bad as Gordie Manning indicated.

Tossing the last of the sandwich away, she shut the door. Rubbing the goose bumps on her arms, she hurried back to the fire.

"Wilson!" She eyed the tuft of russet burrowed beneath the blanket as she swung a pot of water over the flame to boil. "Rise and shine! We enroll you in school today!"

"Freezin'," Wilson complained in a muffled voice.

"Get up, slug bug! Sun's up!"

A jumbled thatch of reddish hair poked out of the blanket, followed by a pair of disgruntled eyes. "I'm stiff as a poker."

"We'll have to do something about that draft," she agreed.

"Draft," Wilson exclaimed. It was more like a *hurricane* whistling underneath the door. Throwing the blanket aside, he stared at the blocks of ice that had formerly been his feet. "I'm crippled," he announced.

"No, you're not," Maggie assured him cheerily as she stirred oats into a pan of boiling water. "The circulation will return once you're up and around. Hurry now, you don't want to be late your first day."

It was close to eight-thirty by the time they wound their way down the mountain and located the school. The weathered, one-room shanty sat two blocks up from the land office.

The homely young teacher, Miss Perkins, greeted Wilson warmly and had the children bid him a hearty welcome.

The schoolroom was dimly lit and drafty. Twelve desks, the teacher's platform, a blackboard, and a large potbellied stove crowded the interior. Along the back of the room, heavy coats, knit hats, and warm mittens hung randomly on pegs. Nine pair of children's galoshes, and one pair of adult's, formed muddy puddles along the wall.

Miss Perkins smiled. "We're just about to work on our geography, Wilson. Please take a seat."

Geography. Wilson's heart sank. His *worst* subject.

"Miss Fletcher, you're welcome to stay and visit the class this morning," Miss Perkins invited.

"Thank you," Maggie said. "I can't, but I will another day."

Wilson sized up the room full of strangers, praying that feeling would return to his feet. He was going to look silly dragging them across the wooden floor.

"Psst," a big kid in the third row jeered. "Four eyes—over here!"

Placing her hands on Wilson's shoulders, Maggie firmly steered him to a seat closest to the blackboard.

"Can you see clearly from here?"

Removing his glasses, Wilson wiped a film of steam away with the handkerchief Maggie had stuck in his pocket earlier. The other kids were staring a hole in him. He could feel their eyes drilling into his back.

Hooking the rims back over his ears, he squinted up at the blackboard. "I can see."

"Good." Maggie squeezed his shoulder reassuringly. "I'll be back to walk you home." Leaning closer to his ear, she whispered, "Don't be nervous; the first day is always the hardest."

Wilson nodded, his eyes glued to the colorful world map covering the blackboard.

Geography.

On his first day.

Gee whiz.

"Your best bet's to post it on that thar board, lady."

Maggie thanked the elderly prospector and

walked on. After tacking the notice on the public information board, she stood in front of a saloon, waiting for takers. She had carefully compiled the handbill while Wilson ate his breakfast. It read:

Wanted: Sturdy young men with strong backs willing to work long hours in exchange for fair wage. Contact Maggie Fletcher, proprietor of the Hellhole.

The notice went up at exactly 9:02 A.M.

At 10:18 A.M., she dug in her purse for a pencil. Returning to the board, she amended the poster to read:

Wanted: Men willing to work for competitive wage. Must be honest and hard working. Age no factor. Dinner provided. Contact Maggie Fletcher, proprietor of the Hellhole.

Returning to the board at 11:26 A.M., she scribbled:

Wanted: Anyone willing to work. Wage negotiable. Two square meals a day. Contact Maggie Fletcher (woman standing in front of the saloon), proprietor of the Hellhole. P.S. Thank you.

Men came and went, pausing in front of the board long enough to read the advertisement. One or two looked in her direction.

Several laughed.

Others snorted.

But no one approached her about the job.

1:43 P.M. Marching back to the board, she scrawled:

Hello? *Anybody* out there? I am *willing* to pay *above* average wages, expect you to work no more than forty hours a week, and promise to provide three delicious meat-based meals a day.

What more do you want?

Maggie Fletcher (the woman who's been standing in front of the saloon for hours now!), proprietor of the Hellhole.

2:35 P.M. Desperation set in. Pacing back and forth, Maggie observed Hoodee Doo's male population with growing resentment.

What's wrong with these people? There had been no less than two hundred men who had read that handbill and walked away. Family men, men who could certainly use the money!

She had been as generous as her funds allowed. She wasn't made of gold! What more did they want?

"Might as well save your energy. Ain't nothin' you're offerin' likely to entice 'em, ma'am."

Maggie looked over to see the elderly prospector she'd spoken to earlier sitting on the sidewalk steps, whittling.

"Is *everyone* employed?" she asked. "Doesn't *anyone* in this camp need a job?"

"No, ma'am." The old man leaned forward and

spat. Wiping tobacco juice on his coatsleeve, his eyes returned to the small deer he was carving. His crippled hands worked the wood slowly and lovingly. The carved figure was intricately fashioned with delicate details.

Maggie came over to sit beside him. She watched him work for a moment before she spoke. "That's very nice. Have you been carving long?"

The old man sat forward, spitting again. Wiping his mouth, he nodded. "Pert near all my life."

"You're very good at it." She'd never seen an image so lifelike. The doe's supplicating eyes immediately drew her in.

"Ain't no one gonna work your mine," the prospector predicted.

Maggie's thoughts unwillingly returned to the problem at hand. "The men can't *all* have jobs."

"Nope, lot of 'em looking for work. But they don't wanna work for you."

Maggie couldn't imagine why not. She hadn't been in town long enough to make enemies.

The old man held the carving out to study it. "It's the mine."

"The Hellhole?"

"Yep, Butte Fesperman won't let no one come near it."

"Who's Butte Fesperman?"

"The ghost who's living in your mine."

"Oh, that's poppycock. You mean to tell me that grown men would actually refuse to work for me because someone thinks the mine is haunted?"

"Yep." He spat again.

"Poppycock."

He looked, frowning. "What's that?"

"What's what?"

"That thar poppycock. You a cussin' woman?"

"Oh, my ... no," Maggie stammered, embarrassed now. "I wasn't being vulgar. Poppycock means nonsense, empty talk ... you know."

"No, cain't say as I do. Never heared the term before. Folks say you come from one of them foreign countries. They talk like that over there?"

"Well, some—but I don't think poppycock is especially English."

"Yeah? Well, it's a new one on me."

Maggie watched as he painstakingly shaped the animal's hind leg.

Drawing her knees to her chest, she rested her chin, watching the men come and go, their incredulous laughter getting on her nerves. "Do you believe in ghosts?"

"Ain't never seed one, but I allow they could be some." Chappy was smart enough never to say never.

"Well, apparently everyone around here thinks there are." She sighed. "I have a problem."

"Yep, guess you do."

"What should I do?"

The old miner gave it some thought. What would he do if he were her? Hard to say. Rumor had it she had to work the mine. She needed the money, bad.

"Heared tell thar's some Chineymen over at Silver Plume. They might could help ya."

"How far is Silver Plume?"

"Oh . . . day, day and a half ride from here."

A day and a half ride! Maggie didn't own a horse, and she couldn't leave Wilson alone.

The old miner seemed to read her thoughts. "I got a jackass—she ain't pretty, but she'll get you there."

"It isn't that—I don't care what the animal looks like. It's my brother; I can't leave him unattended."

"The boy's old enough to take care of himself, ain't he?" He'd seen the two of them walking to school this morning. The boy looked capable of seein' to his own needs.

"Wilson is sensible, but I wouldn't leave him alone," Maggie said. He didn't know a soul in Hoodee Doo. He would be terrified among all these strangers.

"Well, ole Widow Noosemen will help you out." He held the carving out for final inspection. "She'll look after the boy till you git back."

"I can't pay her much for her services."

Handing her the carving, the old man smiled. "That's all right. Widow Noosemen's service ain't worth much, but she'll see to the boy."

"Ole Widow *Noosemen*," Wilson groaned as he and Maggie walked up the mountain late that afternoon. He didn't want to know Widow Noosemen!

She was probably one of those old people who smelled funny.

"I'll only be gone four days, Wilson. Chappy Hellerman told me there are some Chinamen in Silver Plume who might be willing to work. I've already spoken to the Widow Noosemen, and she has agreed to let you stay with her until I get back."

"But, Maggie—"

"No buts, Wilson." Maggie hated to disappoint him, but there was no other way. "Widow Noosemen is very nice, and I appreciate her kindness." The widow even refused Maggie's money, saying it was her Christian duty to help out. "You know I've tried everything I know to hire workers, but no one wants to work for us. Maybe if I go far enough away, I'll find *someone* who's never heard of the Hellhole." It was their only salvation.

"How you gonna get there? Walk?"

"No, Chappy has graciously offered to let me borrow his mule."

"Gee whiz."

"I'm sorry, that's how it is. I'll be back as soon as I can. With any luck, we'll have our crew, and maybe some nice Chinaman will even teach you to speak Chinese."

"Gee whiz."

Trudging up the incline, Wilson supplied all the logical arguments. Maggie couldn't go off and leave him: someone might steal him, he might get hurt, he could fall off the mountain and no one would ever find him, an elk could eat him, he could lose his glasses and go blind, Widow Noosemen might beat him.

But in the end, Maggie held her ground. First light tomorrow morning, she was going to Silver Plume.

Surely to goodness they hadn't heard of Butte Fesperman over there!

Chapter 6

Jiminy! Maggie couldn't believe news traveled so fast! Even the *Chinamen* had heard about Butte Fesperman. Another week had gone by, and she still didn't have a crew.

Lifting an egg out of the skillet, Maggie called Wilson again. "Hurry up! Breakfast is getting cold!" As she sliced bread, her mind raced with plan three.

The women. That's where she'd go. Hoodee Doo women enjoyed a certain amount of independence. Miners, it seemed, were starved for the sight of the lovelier sex, so women were revered and seldom hampered by propriety.

The camp ladies were mostly shopkeepers' wives who enjoyed certain refinements within their own social realm. They might welcome a break in their monotonous routine. After all, a woman could mine gold just as easily as a man, or better.

She'd just go to the women, explain her plight, and offer to pay them a man's wage to help her.

Of course, they wouldn't be able to work the

mine forever, but they could at least get the work started. They had little else to occupy their time but a few frivolous efforts that Maggie had prudently avoided by saying her obligations to the mine prevented her from joining in the fun.

The ten respectable ladies of Hoodee Doo, it seems, had formed a Social Club, Study Club, Ladies' Bicycle Club, and a Monday morning sewing circle.

The camp's other twenty-three women—commonly referred to by the ten respectable women as harlots, prostitutes, trollops, strumpets, drabs, hussies, harridans, fancy women, painted ladies, soiled doves, sluts, chippies, wantons, and girls on the line—were slightly less industrious, since they worked long hours serving drinks on their backs at Careless Ida's red-light district crib house.

The twenty-three frail sisters didn't attend the Social Club, Study Club, Ladies' Bicycle Club, or the Monday morning sewing circle because the ten poker-faced uppity do-gooders, as the frail sisters commonly referred to the ten respectable women, didn't invite them.

But in general, the women left each other alone. As long as the ten respectable women's husbands stayed clear of the twenty-three crib-residing floozies, any serious trouble was avoided.

Men, Maggie was finding out, got lonely, too. During her recent journey to Silver Plume, she'd witnessed an incident that left her both amused and sad. A woman's bonnet had been found lying in the middle of the road. No one seemed to know how it got there, but it caused quiet a stir among the miners. Three or four had nabbed the saucy little bonnet with its ribbons, bows, and laces and erected it on a Maypole in the center of town.

Their shenanigans turned into a near-riot as the other men, looking for an hour of diversion from the cold streams and damp mines, poured into camp to join in the fun.

The bearded, booted roughnecks were so hungry for female companionship they staged an impromptu dance around the bonnet, joking and laughing as they took turns dancing with the lovely Miss Bonnet.

Maggie watched the good-natured fiasco from her hotel window, wondering if Gordie Manning were ever as eager for female companionship. Her thoughts were surprising, and she wondered why she'd thought them in the first place.

She'd seen the red-headed miner on her trips into camp, but they hadn't directly spoken to each other since the night he'd taken her and Wilson to the Hellhole.

Drawing her knees to her chest, she grinned, admitting that with a little cleaning up, T.G. Manning would be downright handsome. She had never seen eyes so remarkably blue, nor hair more fiery red, or a chest so broad and manly. The young men who had courted her had been mere boys by comparison.

She couldn't imagine why he had given up on life. He looked to be in excellent health—too thin, perhaps, but a few good meals would remedy that. He had no zest about him, no anticipation of that next strike the other miners exuded. He seemed to be a man with no purpose.

From what she could tell, he had no claim. She'd seen him in camp at different hours of the day, and he never seemed to have a reason for being there. He visited with other miners fresh from the diggings, sometimes loitering for hours.

Wilson's voice dragged her back to reality. "Couldn't we wait until it warms up?" he complained, unhappy about being pulled from his bed before daylight.

"Just eat. We have to hurry."

He cracked one eye in the direction of the front door. "It isn't even day yet, is it?"

"Just barely, now hurry and eat, grouch."

Directly after breakfast, they set off. "You'll be a little early, but I want to be the first one at the store this morning," she explained as they descended the narrow trail. She didn't want to miss talking to a single woman. The moment the school bell rang, the mothers headed for the store to exchange the latest gossip.

She planned to be there waiting for them.

"I don't like school, Maggie, nobody likes me," Wilson complained as he hurried to keep up with her. "The girls talk mean to me, and the boys call me four eyes and bat boy."

"Bat boy?"

"Yeah, 'cause I'm blind as a bat. Butch Miller tried to make me eat *bugs* yesterday."

"Why?"

" 'Cause that's what bats *eat*, Maggie." Gee whiz.

"The moment we start making money we're going to get those new glasses," she promised. He'd needed stronger lenses for years. Aunt Fionnula was a miser when it came to doctors. She thought the less you saw of one the better.

"Why do I even have to go to school? You could teach me at home—Willie's mom teaches him at home."

"Willie's mom doesn't have a gold mine to run. Colorado's different than England."

"You don't have to run the mine. You're trying to get someone to run it for you, aren't you? When you do, then you could teach me at home, huh, Maggie?" Then he wouldn't have to be humiliated by Butch Miller anymore.

"I can't, Wilson. Money is extremely tight, and I'll have to help no matter who I get to run the mine." She gave him a quick hug. "Besides, it'll do you good to be around children your own age. You'll make friends. The others will warm to you."

"They won't. They're mean. Butch Miller took my sandwich yesterday and threw it down the privy hole. I was starving all day!"

"Did you tell Miss Perkins?"

He looked aghast. "No! Butch would'a creamed me!"

Oh, Maggie wished she knew how to fight! She would teach Wilson how to hold his own against bullies like Butch Miller!

"If Butch Miller takes your sandwich today, you tell Miss Perkins, you hear?"

Wilson sighed. "I can't."

"Well, for heaven's sake, why not?"

" 'Cause he'll just take my apple, too."

Depositing Wilson on the school steps, Maggie hurried on to the mercantile. She bought a half pound of sugar, three apples, half a pound of tea, and a spool of white thread before the women started to arrive.

The more she thought about her plan, the more she warmed to it. *Women* working in the Hellhole. Not only would they enjoy the added income, they could take pride in the fact they were lending a sister a helping hand.

One by one, the women came into the store, their conversations ranging from diaper rash to peach butter.

When the most recent gossip, innuendoes, and rumors were adequately "oohed" and "ahhed" over, they started to browse.

Maggie approached each one singly, striking up a friendly conversation.

"Hello! My name is Maggie Fletcher."

"I don't know anybody."

Maggie blinked. "Pardon?"

"I don't know anybody to work your mine."

"Oh—well, thank you."

* * *

She moved to the dry goods table, still looking over her shoulder.

"Hello! My name is—"

The woman sorting through the bolts of calico never looked up. "Maggie Fletcher."

"Yes." Maggie smiled. "I'm the new owner of—"

"The Hellhole."

"Yes, that's right, and I'm—"

"Looking for a crew."

"Yes—do you—"

"Know anyone who'll work for you?" The woman laughed. "Lordy, no."

"Well, nice talking to you."

"Hello, my name is Maggie Fletcher."

"Nice to meet you."

"Have you ever considered a job outside the house? The pay is good, and it can be arranged for you to be home when school lets out."

"I have a job: five kids and a lazy husband."

"Yes, but haven't you ever wanted to stretch—do something on your own?"

"No. Never."

"Well, nice talking to you."

"I'm Maggie Fletcher."

The young mother turned and smiled. "I know, dear. Welcome to Hoodee Doo."

"Thank you. I was wondering if you could possibly help me?"

The young woman's smile never lost its vigor. "I'm afraid not."

Maggie frowned. "You don't know what I want."

Lifting a spool of ribbon, the woman waved to the clerk. "I'll take two yards of the lavender, Edgar!"

"Nice talking to you."

"The same, I'm sure." Maggie moved on.

"Think about it. The pay is good, and I'll arrange to have you home before your family even realizes you're gone. You don't believe those silly ghost stories, do you?"

"Certainly not!"

"That's what I thought. The moment I saw you I said, Maggie, this is an intelligent, hardworking woman who you would be honored to call an employee."

"Well, thank you. I certainly would try to be."

Maggie's face lifted. "Then you'll help?"

The lady drew back, affronted. "Do I look like I've lost my wits?"

Snatching up a tin of peaches, Maggie moved on.

Coming out of the store a few minutes later, Maggie lifted her pendant watch and noted the time. Exactly nine o'clock.

Blowing her bangs out of her eyes, she sighed. That didn't take long.

"No luck?"

She looked up to see Chappy sitting on the bench, whittling.

"No." She glanced in the storefront resentfully. "They must think I'm a fool."

"Well." Chappy calmly inspected the humming-bird he was carving. "Wouldn't feel too bad. I could have told you they wouldn't be interested. Women are considered bad luck in a mine."

"Really?" She walked over to take a seat beside him.

"Yeah, known men to set fire to a mine if a woman had been in it."

"Why, that's silly."

"Might be, but you won't find many miners who'll agree with you."

"Well, guess it doesn't matter." Maggie leaned back, soaking up the sun. She didn't have the slightest idea what plan four was. "The women didn't want to work anyway."

"Got their hands full taking care of the family."

"I guess so."

Chappy chuckled, getting a kick out of the little girl from England who didn't know beans from apple butter. "Don't know much 'bout miners, do you, sissy?"

"Nothing," Maggie admitted.

"Well," he said, a foxy note creeping into his voice now. "You might ought to learn. A pretty little thing like you will be wanting to take a husband someday. Might need to know what he'll be looking for."

"And what might that be?" Maggie asked, not

really interested. From what she could tell, a woman's only prerequisite to catch a man around here was that she was breathing.

"Well now, the Frenchies thinks it's got something to do with a woman's legs."

"A woman's legs?"

"Yep, the dark girl with a large leg will get fat at thirty, and lay in bed reading novels until noon."

Maggie looked at him, sneering.

"Yeah, and the brunette with the slender limbs, now she'll worry a man's heart out with jealousy."

Maggie examined her own legs as Chappy examined the bird's progress.

"Now, the olive-skinned maid with a pretty rounded leg is sure to make a man happy.

"The blonde woman with big legs will degenerate by thirty-five into nothing more than a pair of ankles double their natural size and afflicted with rheumatism. The fair-haired woman will get up at the crack of dawn to scold the servants and gossip over tea."

"So, a man wants the olive-skinned maid?"

"No, the light, rosy girl with a sturdy, muscular, well-turned leg is the one men want. But if he's lucky enough to find a red-haired little gal with a large limb he'd better pop the question quick as he can." Chappy's eyes twinkled with devilment, aware he was confusing her.

"What about a red-headed man? Do the same rules apply to him?"

"You know any red-headed men?"

"Maybe," she answered evasively.

There were only two in camp. Young T.G. Manning and seventy-year-old Webb Henson. Wonder which she'd noticed?

"The short lady should have a slender limb, and the tall lady should possess an ample one." He handed her the finished bird. "Think you can remember that?"

She nodded.

Chappy ambled away, satisfied any man would be proud to claim that one. Red-headed or not.

Chapter 7

Maggie had a problem. Wilson wasn't supposed to know it, but he did.

He might only be eight years old, but he had a big mind—adultlike, actually. Almost old, adult-like.

And his adultlike mind told him Maggie had a problem.

She'd done a good job hiding it, but she didn't fool him. He saw how red and swollen her eyes were every morning. She kept saying she was coming down with a cold, but if that were so, she'd already have come down with it.

And she blew her nose a lot lately.

No, Maggie couldn't fool Wilson; she was worried. Worried sick 'cause she couldn't get anyone to work that ole mine.

She'd tried real hard. She'd gone everywhere there was to go, done everything there was to do, but nothing worked. Nobody liked the Hellhole. Everybody thought a ghost lived there.

Wilson walked to school with a heavy heart.

Maggie said it was okay for him to walk by himself this morning. He appreciated that. He liked it when Maggie treated him like an adult. She did most times, except lately, when she couldn't think of anything but ghosts.

He didn't know if he believed in ghosts.

Maybe he did; he wasn't sure.

Most everybody else did, that was for sure. Maggie wouldn't be having such a hard time getting workers if they didn't. If he were a man, and Maggie asked him to work in the mine, he'd do it, whether he believed in ghosts or not.

Because Maggie was nice, and even better than that, there were some things a man just ought to do.

Swinging his dinner pail, Wilson made his way down the mountain. He bet that giant would work in the mine. He didn't know why Maggie hadn't asked him to.

She probably just forgot.

Hunching deeper into his coat, Wilson pretended he was smoking a cigarette. The crisp, cold air formed a perfect vapor for his favorite make-believe game. He played it every day when no one was looking. When he grew up, he was gonna smoke for real. Smoke and cuss and spit tobacco and look mean, because that's what men did.

Exhaling, inhaling, exhaling, inhaling, out, in, out, in, Wilson watched the air take on fascinating shapes as he enjoyed his pretend cigarette.

It was easy to play like he was smoking because it was freezing cold. Colder than a well digger's ass in January, Gwendolyn would say, but he wouldn't know about that. He didn't know any well diggers.

Sucking in a deep breath, he blew out a long, heavy draft. He was a heavy smoker. Very, very heavy. Not good for you, heavy.

Puff, puff . . . pufffffffff . . . Delicious cigarette. Delicious tasting.

His foot struck something and he stumbled, nearly pitching face-first into the ground. He caught himself in the nick of time, mad because he'd just 'bout knocked the cigarette out of his mouth.

His face brightened when he spotted the giant sprawled beside the path, snoring.

"Mr. Giant!" he called, happy to see a familiar face. He hadn't seen the giant in a long time! "What're ya doing?"

When the giant didn't answer, Wilson veered off the path to get a closer look at him. Maybe he was sick.

Wilson stared down at T.G., relieved to see his large chest rising and falling in a normal pattern. Yes, it was the giant all right. He was sleeping out here in the freezing cold.

Wrinkling his nose, Wilson sniffed, recognizing the smell. The air was sharp with liquor. Poor giant; he had a bad problem. Edging closer, he gingerly nudged the giant's side with the toe of his boot.

Rolling over, the giant cupped his hands under his cheek and snored on.

Spying the giant's discarded flask, Wilson reached over, picked it up, and shook it.

Empty.

Unscrewing the cap, he took a deep whiff, then put the lid back on and tucked it carefully away in the giant's left coat pocket. The giant would feel better without it, but it would be disrespectful of him to discard something that wasn't his.

Wilson stared at the sleeping giant, absorbed with his hands. They were big. Really big. There was hair on his knuckles. *All* of them. It was curly red hair, but lighter than what was on his head.

Dropping onto his belly, Wilson strained to get a better look up the giant's nose. Yep. Some up there, too. Yuk.

He jumped back as the giant stirred in his sleep. He'd better go. The giant would be mad if he woke up and found a kid looking up his nose.

As the whiskey gradually loosened its hold, Gordie moaned, straining to sit up.

Where was he?

What day was it?

Was it day or night?

A shaft of light perforated his eyelids and he groaned. Day. Fading back to the ground, he fought the rising bile in the back of his throat. He hated to puke—damn, he hated to puke.

As the wave of queasiness ebbed, he cracked an eye open. Both eyes flew open when he saw the kid standing over him. Struggling to sit up again, he groaned, gritting his teeth against the pain.

"Better wait a minute, Mr. Giant. You don't look so good."

Sinking back to the ground, Gordie murmured, "My name is T.G." He didn't know where the kid got the idea he was a giant. "Call me T.G."

"Sure, Mr. Giant, I can do that." Now that he'd gotten to know him, Wilson sorta liked the giant. He wasn't scary or nothing anymore. "How 'bout me calling you Gordie? That'd be better, huh? And you can call me Wilson 'cause that's my name!" He grinned.

Making another futile attempt to sit up, Gordie wilted again.

"Don't feel so good, huh, Gordie?"

"Shouldn't you be somewhere, kid?"

"I'm walking to school by myself this morning. Maggie said I could."

"That's good." Holding his head, Gordie tried to silence the throbbing anvil being pounded inside it.

Wilson stood by and watched patiently. Boy, the giant looked sick. Really sick. Wilson remembered the last time he'd been sick, and it hadn't been fun.

He hovered protectively over Gordie.

Aware of his close scrutiny, T.G. growled. "You're going to be late for school."

"It don't matter. I only go because Maggie makes me. I hate school."

Gordie didn't say anything, just sat there looking real sicklike.

"Want to know why I hate school? 'Cause the kids don't like me."

"Have you done something to make them not like you?"

"No. Honest." He hadn't done nothin'.

"Yeah, well, that happens. Don't worry about it, it'll work itself out." He rubbed his head. "You better run along or you'll be late."

But Wilson hadn't explained his side. "The girls talk mean to me, and Butch Miller steals my sandwich every day."

"And you let him?"

Wilson made a hmmpph sound. "I can't *stop* him."

Rubbing his shoulder, Gordie sat up. Damn, he'd slept outside again. He'd be lucky if he didn't have frostbite. Sunlight danced off the heavy layer of early morning hoarfrost.

Resting his hands on his knees, Wilson looked him right in the eyes. "Feelin' better?"

"Yeah, just ducky. Just go away."

Wilson suddenly thought about Maggie and all the trouble she'd been having. Why, he bet she *had* forgotten to ask Gordie to help her run the mine!

Excited now, he realized how he could help! He'd just take Gordie home with him; that's what he'd do. He'd surprise the britches right off Maggie!

T.G. lazily scratched his beard, yawning.

Wilson sized up his physical stature and decided he looked good and strong. Strong as a bull. Fit as a fiddle. Tight as a drum, and all that other stuff people always said. He'd make a good gold miner.

He could mine a bunch of gold and then Maggie would be happy again; she wouldn't cry anymore.

Yet Wilson wasn't a fool. He knew he'd have to be pretty crafty to trick Gordie into coming home with him. He'd be a good worker, all right, but it seemed as if he didn't like work.

Wilson had noticed that the night he'd brought him and Maggie up to the mine. Maybe that's why Maggie forgot to ask him to help her.

Gordie was a little uninspired. Probably because he didn't have anything to do but drink out of his little flask and sleep outside on the ground. Even Wilson knew that wasn't motivating.

Well, he'd just have to fool him into going to the mine with him. Once he was there, Maggie could ask him to work for her. She was good about talking people into doing things they didn't want to do. She called it tact, but Wilson called it browbeating.

But Wilson liked his idea a whole lot and decided to follow through with it. "Gordie?"

T.G. looked up, having forgotten the kid was there. "Yeah?"

"I'm not feeling so good," Wilson clutched his stomach. "I'd better not go to school today."

Gordie frowned. "What's wrong with you?"

"My stomach hurts."

"Well, run along back home." Rolling to his feet, Gordie stood up, squinting against the bright sun. "You seen my hat?"

"You was sittin' on it."

Reaching down, Gordie picked up the battered cap and dusted it off.

"Guess you'd better walk me home, huh, Gordie?"

Wincing, Gordie glanced down at him. "Walk you home?"

"Yeah." A ray of sun glinted off the rim of Wilson's glasses. "I'm feeling sick."

"You'll be all right."

Grabbing his middle, Wilson bent over double. "Noooo, I think you're gonna have to walk with me, Gordie, 'cause I'm real sick."

"Wilson ..." T.G.'s head was killing him!

"*Really sick*, Gordie. Honest. It must've been that cigarette I smoked."

Gordie shifted his stance, annoyed. "You've been *smoking*?"

"Yeah—don't tell Maggie." It was a white lie; only the black ones counted.

"Good Lord, kid." Gordie glanced around, trying to think of a way out. The last thing he wanted was to walk the boy up the mountain. The day was starting off on the wrong foot.

"You gotta come with me, Gordie. Maggie'll be mad if anything bad happens to me."

"Look, kid, I didn't take you to raise."

Wilson peered up at him. "You don't want me to walk home by myself, really sick, do you?"

Actually, Gordie didn't care, but he was beginning to suspect he didn't have a choice. If the kid was sick, he'd have to walk him home. His head felt like a punching bag.

"All right, let's get it over with."

Wilson's face lit up. "You'll do it? You'll walk home with me?"

"I said I would. Let's go."

"Okay ... just a minute." Wilson motioned for him to lean over.

Eyeing him warily, Gordie refused to comply. "What?"

"Lean over."

"Lean over? Why?"

"Just *lean* over." Boy, adults could be a pain.

Gordie hesitantly bent over.

Wilson set to work sprucing him up. "Do you have a comb?"

"A *comb*?" One eye cracked open. "Do I look like I have a comb?"

No, he sure didn't look like he had a comb. "Never mind, I'll use my fingers." That's what Maggie did.

Wilson carefully fluffed Gordie's hair and knocked the crumbs out of his beard. He had to get him more presentable or else Maggie wouldn't want him. She didn't like messiness, 'specially bad messiness.

Knocking the dust off the back of Gordie's coat, Wilson took his handkerchief out of his pocket, spit on it, and was about to wash Gordie's face when a big hand with curly red hair on the knuckles blocked him.

"Don't even think about it, kid."

He could've used a full bath, but Wilson knew he wasn't smart enough to fool him into that. He'd just have to make sure he stood downwind of Maggie.

Gordie watched Wilson's performance, puzzled by his actions.

When Wilson finished, Gordie didn't look any better. He could'a used a lot more sprucing up.

T.G. returned his critical look impassively. "What are you doing?"

Wilson shrugged. "Nothing."

"Obviously, you're trying to accomplish something."

"No, I'm not." He grinned. "Wanna stay for dinner? Maggie cooks real good." If he stayed for dinner, that'd give Maggie more time to remember to ask him to help her work the mine!

T.G.'s stomach rolled at the thought of food. "I'm not staying for dinner."

"Well, you can think about it."

"I'm taking you home, then I'm leaving." The kid didn't look sick to him.

"Okay." Turning, Wilson walked off, casting a sly look over his shoulder to make sure Gordie followed.

Boy, and adults thought kids were a pain.

Chapter 8

After supper that night, Maggie rinsed the last dish and laid it aside. With a tired smile, she recalled how T.G. had eaten with such appreciation. It was a treat to cook for someone other than herself and Wilson.

She was surprised when Wilson showed up with T.G. in tow. By the reserved look on his face, she got the feeling it was not Gordie's idea. It seemed Wilson bumped into him on his way to school and somehow managed to convince him that he was feeling punky.

Gordie had been coerced into accompanying the boy home. With very little coaxing, Maggie persuaded the visitor to stay for dinner. After they finished eating, Wilson's usual robust health returned, and he pressured his new friend into a game of stickball.

Stickball turned into mumblety-peg. Gordie showed Wilson how to hold the knife just right, so that with a flick of the wrist, he could stick the blade into the ground. Maggie never knew there were so many positions from which a knife could be thrown.

Late in the day, Maggie looked out to see the tops of two red heads, one big and one small, disappearing over the hill. Seems the fish were biting.

Maggie grinned, grateful to T.G. for taking the little boy fishing. Wilson needed a man's influence. Papa had died when her brother was barely old enough to toddle. He had never known his father.

Late in the afternoon, T.G. and Wilson returned bearing an impressive string of trout, which Maggie rolled in cornmeal and fried, and they all enjoyed for supper. It turned out to be quite an extraordinary day.

Lord knew, Gordie Manning was anything but ordinary. In England, she would have thought twice about taking up with someone who cared so little about his personal appearance, but T.G. was somehow different. She knew it the moment he carried her out of the land office. She wasn't sure of the role he'd play in her life, but she knew he had one.

And he wasn't all that bad—only his physical appearance needed attention. During both dinner and supper he proved to be an interesting conversationalist, and his table manners were impeccable.

One really did have to wonder what lay beneath Gordie Manning's disreputable facade.

Maggie would have liked for him to stay awhile

and talk, but he seemed uncomfortable with the situation. The moment he swallowed the last bite of fish, he bolted for the door like a jackrabbit.

Hastily downing the last of his milk, Wilson ran after him, explaining over his shoulder that Gordie was going to teach him how to tie trout lures.

T.G.'s unexpected visit created a pleasant diversion. Maggie had seen him nearly every time she went into town, but they rarely took the time to visit.

She had to admit she knew little about men. Maybe T.G. would find her more interesting if she had something interesting to talk about.

Social opportunities were scarce as hen's teeth at Aunt Fionnula's. Mildred and Gwendolyn worked hard to attract eligible suitors, but they rarely did.

And to be honest, by day's end Maggie was too tired to worry about a social life. Pickle sandwiches, a glass of cold buttermilk, and a good dime novel went a long way to curb her interest in the opposite sex.

She spent hours sitting in bed, reading about Calamity Jane, Deadwood Dick, and Kit Carson. When she tired of dime novels, she'd pretend to be Meg in *Little Women* by Louisa May Alcott.

Then on to *Journey to the Centre of the Earth, From the Earth to the Moon,* and *Twenty Thousand Leagues Under the Sea* by Jules Verne.

She loved them all.

Untying her apron, she laid it aside, then knelt

beside Wilson's pallet. He was already fast asleep, exhausted from his busy day. Lifting a bare foot, she gently tucked it back beneath the blanket.

Gazing down on his cherubic features, she was once again assailed by doubts. Had she done the right thing? Colorado, for all its beauty, was a harsh land—maybe too harsh for a such a small boy. They had arrived weeks ago, and she had yet to find one person to work the mine.

Emotions surrounding the Hellhole ran high and were coupled with deep-seated suspicion. It was useless to try to persuade the residents of Hoodee Doo there were no such things as ghosts. Years of skepticism and unexplainable events surrounding the mine had convinced them otherwise.

Maggie had no explanation regarding the strange goings-on. Nothing unusual had happened the few times she'd ventured into the mine—no odd cave-ins or peculiar lights or bizarre singing—none of the various incidents men swore had happened.

Restless now, she moved to the door for a breath of fresh air. A full moon bathed the mountain. Loneliness washed over her.

Leaning against the doorsill, she thought about England and the life she left behind. She was content there—comfortable. If Aunt Sissy hadn't left her the mine, she might have stayed forever. For what purpose was her life uprooted in such a disrupting manner? If she couldn't find anyone to work the mine, what good would the gold do her? She couldn't work it herself. She knew nothing about mining.

Her mind drifted to Aunt Fionnula, and she was consumed with guilt. Had she received the letter Maggie wrote, expressing her deepest apologies for leaving the way she had?

How hurt and disappointed she must be for having such an ungrateful niece. Wilson wasn't to blame for their abrupt departure; he was only a child. The responsibility for their rash actions lay squarely upon her shoulders. She only hoped Aunt Fionnula could find it in her heart to forgive her.

A twig snapped, and Maggie's hand flew to her heart, startled.

A deep voice came to her from the shadows. "Didn't I tell you to keep your door closed at night?"

"T.G.?" She shaded her eyes against the bright lantern rays. "I thought you had gone."

"Sorry, I didn't mean to alarm you." T.G. appeared from the shadows, removing his hat. "Evening, ma'am."

"I didn't expect to see you again so soon." Opening the door wider, she smiled. "Come in."

"No, ma'am. I just came back to check on Wilson." Now why was he lying? He knew Wilson had pulled a fast one on him. The boy was no more sick than he was, but he'd suddenly had an inexplicable urge to see Maggie again.

"Wilson?"

"Yes. Is he okay?"

"Oh . . . yes." She looked embarrassed. "He's fine."

A strained silence lapsed between them.

Twisting the brim of his hat in his hands, Gordie searched for a mutual topic. He didn't know what got into him, coming all the way back up the mountain at this time of night.

"Nice night—not so cold," he ventured.

Rubbing her arms, Maggie gazed at the star-studded canopy. "You think so? I haven't been warm since I got here."

"It don't get cold in England?"

She grinned. "You know anything about England?"

"No." His knowledge of other countries was limited. "I've heard that it's pretty, though."

"Very pretty."

Once again silence reigned.

"Wilson asleep?"

She smiled, reaching for a wrap. Why, he was lonely! "Wilson was asleep five minutes after his head hit his pillow." Stepping outside, she closed the door.

She settled the woolen shawl around her shoulders as they fell into step.

"I'm glad you stopped by."

"I apologize. It's late."

"Not too late."

They walked for awhile, mindful of each other's company.

"I wanted to tell you, you're a good cook. Haven't tasted food that good in a long time," he observed casually.

She blushed, unaccustomed to praise. "Just plain old fish and corn bread. Nothing special."

What was he doing here? Gordie wondered. He hadn't a clue. For the first time in years, he was suddenly conscious of his appearance. How long had it been since he'd bathed? Lord, he couldn't remember.

The breeze caught her lemony scent in the crisp air, and he was flooded with shame. If he were going to come up here, why didn't he take the time to clean up first?

"What did you say those sweet things were?" He'd been embarrassed eating so many, but she'd continued to pile them high on his plate.

"Blackberry scones. I brought the jam all the way from England."

"You carried jam all the way from England?"

She nodded. "I picked, washed, stemmed, and put up thirty-two quarts of blackberries last summer. I wasn't about to leave all of them behind." She had confiscated six quarts from Aunt Fionnula's pantry and packed them away in her bag between her underwear and Sunday blouse before leaving.

"You been here long?" she asked.

Time had lost all meaning for T.G. How long had he been here? "I came in '88—I guess that makes it just about five years."

"I guess gold brought you here?"

"No." He grinned. "Actually, it was a train, but I came in search of gold."

"Oh, you," she laughed, relieved to discover he had a sense of humor.

A cloud shadowed the moon, and it seemed colder.

"Are you warm enough?"

"Fine, thank you. And you?"

"Fine. Could snow before morning."

"It sure feels as though it could."

"Snow comes early to the mountains."

The conversation began to lapse.

"You're sure you're not too cold? We can go back."

"Really, I'm fine. Thank you."

"The 'quarters' warm enough?"

She laughed, recognizing the tongue-in-cheek tone. "Well, actually, there's a crack under the door big enough to throw a moose under. We're losing a lot of heat."

"I'll take a look at it tomorrow. Meanwhile, stuff a blanket in it."

"In the door?"

"In the crack."

"Oh . . . thanks. I will."

"So, you're doing okay?"

"Gordie—"

"My name is T.G."

She glanced over. "Do you want me to call you T.G.?"

"That's my name."

"All right."

They walked for a few minutes more.

"You were saying?" he prompted.

What had she been saying?

"I asked if you were doing okay and you said—"

"*About* to say I was, but that isn't the truth," she admitted.

"Something wrong?"

"I can't find anyone to work the mine—but then you know that, don't you." He had watched her try to hire a crew and fail for weeks now.

His tone held a note of humility. "I don't stick my nose in other people's business, Miss Fletcher."

"If I have to call you T.G., you have to call me Maggie."

That would be hard. Maggie was too personal, and the last thing he wanted was to get too personal.

"You do know why no one will help me, don't you?"

"Yes, ma'am, I know why."

She sighed. "Well, you did warn me the mine was haunted."

"That I did."

"But you also said you didn't believe in ghosts."

"I don't, but everyone else does. That's the problem."

Pausing, she dusted a seat on a fallen log, and they sat down.

Gazing at the mountain, she said softly, "I'm in trouble, Gordie. I've been everywhere, tried everything, and I can't find one single person who will work the mine. I heard of a group of Chinamen over in Silver Plume. I hired Widow Noosemen to look after Wilson, and I borrowed an old prospector's mule and rode clear over there. Took me two long days over, and two long days back. The Chinamen just laughed at me. Even they had heard of the Hellhole."

A smile touched the corners of T.G.'s mouth. Chappy had told him all about her escapade.

"Then I got this bright idea to ask the camp women to work in the mine."

T.G. kept quiet. He'd heard about that, too.

"They thought I was crazy. I didn't know women were considered bad luck in a mine." Sighing, she leaned back, staring at the moon. "Guess I shouldn't be burdening you with my troubles, but I don't know what else to do. What money I have won't last forever. I *have* to get that mine operating."

When he still didn't answer, she glanced over at him.

"What would you do?"

"Me?" He laughed. "You're asking the wrong person."

She cocked a brow. "Why? You're intelligent."

The compliment bought a rush of color to his face. Him? Intelligent? She was kidding now.

"You've worked in mines, haven't you?"

"I've staked claim to several, ma'am, but as you can see, my success has been limited." An understatement, to be sure.

"But you know a lot about mining, don't you?"

"Not a lot."

"But some—you know what needs to be done."

He looked away. "I know enough to recognize when it has me whipped."

"Poppycock—nonsense," she amended quickly. Their eyes met briefly in the moonlight. "You're not the kind of man who gives up that easily."

"No disrespect intended, but you couldn't know that."

"I am an excellent judge of character."

He found that amusing. "Trust me, ma'am, you're wrong about this one."

He was down on himself. Down on his luck, but most of all, down on his pride, Maggie concluded. Underneath he was a good man. She could see that; all she had to do was make him aware of it.

"Why don't you work the mine for me?" She hadn't thought about it before, but why not? He was strong, capable, and knew about mining. "I'll hire you to run the mine. You can operate it any way you see fit."

"I'm afraid not. I've been gainfully unemployed for awhile, and I like it that way."

He didn't appear to have a home. "How do you live?"

T.G. stifled a laugh. He wouldn't live much longer. Mooney's thugs were after him. "A few odd jobs here and there. An occasional, semi-worthless claim. I get by."

"But I could make you rich."

Rich. The word had been a millstone around his neck for years. He wished he'd never heard of it.

Rich—a catchword for fools and dreamers. Down-and-out, dirt-poor: that was reality.

"Thank you, but I'm not interested, Miss Fletcher. I appreciate the offer, and I regret your circumstance, but I'd be of no use to you." He stood up, pulling his threadbare jacket closer around him. "I've got to be going."

Maggie stood up, facing him. "I beg you to reconsider. You came here with a dream. Apparently, that dream hasn't worked out. I'm offering you a second chance."

He looked down at her. For some crazy reason, he wanted to hold her. She looked very embraceable.

"Another chance, Gordie Manning, to realize your dream." She pointed to the mine. "Right now, the Hellhole's got *me* whipped. I'm asking—no, I'm begging you for help. You don't believe in ghosts, you said so yourself, so that shouldn't stop you. Work the mine for me. Whatever gold it yields will be half yours."

"Miss Fletcher—" There were things she didn't know about him.

She lifted her hand. "No, I mean it. If you'll supervise the work, whatever the mine yields is half yours."

He turned away. "I don't want your money."

"It wouldn't matter if you did." She took his chin and turned his face back to meet hers. "I'm desperate. See? I can't go back to England, and I don't have enough money to stay here.

The only chance Wilson and I have is buried in that mine."

"The mine could be worthless—most likely is," he argued. Would be, she could be assured, if he worked it.

"Maybe, but it could be there, Gordie. More gold than you've ever dreamed of. Think about it. Another chance. A fresh start. A chance to realize your dream."

For a moment, hope flickered in his eyes. It faded just as quickly.

"If you can't find anyone to work the mine, what makes you think I can?" His reputation wasn't the best. Other miners knew of his problem. No one would take him seriously if he attempted to run a crew.

Maggie was relying on instinct now, but instinct told her she was on solid ground. "Because you're a man who doesn't want to give up his dream, and I believe in you."

"Believe in me," he scoffed. "Why would you believe in me?" He was the epitome of disgrace. The past year he had either drunk or gambled away everything he owned. He'd done nothing to deserve her confidence.

"Sorry, I can't help you." Turning, he started to walk away.

"Say you'll think about it," she called, refusing to give up. He could do it. She knew he could.

"Sure, I'll give it some thought." In another hour he planned to be so drunk he wouldn't remember his name.

"And you'll let me know?"

Lifting his hand carelessly, he dismissed her. Sure, sure, he'd let her know.

Chapter 9

Snow fell early on the Rockies that year. Late in September pristine, undefiled powder drifted down from the sky in thick, wet flakes. It piled onto the crudely built log hut Hoodee Doo called a hotel. The primitivelike structure, which sat on a hillside overlooking a deep ravine, was joined row on row, sharing a common wall with the other buildings. Elegant it wasn't.

Each room was about the size of a clothes closet, with one, dirty paned window. A crude bedstead made of planks, with small poles as slats, dominated the small space. A mattress and pillow stuffed with meadow grass discharged a dry sound when lain upon. An old blanket, a chipped washstand with a fragment of a mirror above it, and a bar of claybank soap completed the dismal setting.

Crawling off the cot, T.G. reeled to the washstand. Fumbling for the tin pitcher, he dumped the contents over his head. Shuddering, he threw back his hair in an effort to minimize the icy jolt.

Cracking an eye open, he stared at the sagging ceiling.

God, another day.

Jerking the towel off the washstand, he dried his face. Where was he this morning? He knew without asking. Another cheap room. Another seedy hangover to compound the misery.

Brother, he was one sorry son of a bitch.

Catching his image in the mirror, he leaned closer. A stranger stared back at him. Long dirty hair, matted beard, bags underneath his eyes. Not a pretty sight.

For no particular reason Maggie Fletcher came to mind. If things had turned out differently, he might have married a woman like her. She was pretty, smart, spirited. There wasn't a woman in Hoodee Doo who could hold a candle to her.

She had spunk. He used to like that in a woman. He'd seen the way she fought to get a crew. Even watched her become the laughing stock of camp. He'd turned his back on the unkind remarks, closed his ears when they ridiculed her perseverance, but he still admired her. Lord, how he admired her.

A smile touched the corners of his mouth. What a pair the two of them would make. She refused to give up; he gave up too easily.

Pounding sounded at the door and, spinning around, he dropped the towel.

"Open up, Manning! We know you're in there!"

Mooney's thugs.

Grabbing his pants, T.G. hopped on one foot,

trying to get them on, his eyes searching for his boots.

"Manning!" The racket got louder. "Open up!"

T.G.'s head throbbed as he dropped to his knees, frantically searching under the bed. Where were his damn boots?

Grabbing his shirt off the chair, he yanked it on, all the while gravitating toward the window. Wherever the hell he was, he hoped it wasn't far to the ground.

Lifting the window pane, he managed to throw a leg over the sill before the door crashed open. Two beefy-looking characters rushed into the room, snaring him by the shoulder before he could jump.

"Not so fast, Manning."

T.G. moaned as a fist slammed into his stomach, then another. He was hit in the face. His bottom lip split, and he tasted blood.

A knee found its mark, sending him sailing across the warped floor.

Yanked back to his feet, he felt a meaty knuckle connect with his nose. A swift knee smashed to his groin, followed by a right hook to his chin.

A left, then another fast right, and the floor came up to meet him.

Sprawled flat on his back, Gordie stared up at the double images floating above him.

"Mooney's gettin' impatient," a gravelly voice reminded.

"Yeah, he wants his money, Manning."

A boot smashed into T.G.'s rib cage, knocking

the wind out of him. Rolling to his side, he tee-tered on the brink of unconsciousness.

"It ain't nice to borrow money and not pay it back."

"Yeah, it ain't nice, Gordie. How many times you got to be told that?"

A sharp blow to his back sent an excruciating pain spiraling up his left shoulder.

"This is your last warning. Either pay up, or you're a dead man."

Turning, the two stalked out of the room, slamming the door behind them.

Shifting to his side, Gordie squeezed his nostrils to stem the stream of blood gushing from his nose. He lay for a moment, trying to clear his head.

As his vision gradually returned, he spotted his boots, crammed upside-down onto the bedposts.

Hell, he thought. Now I find them!

Maggie answered the knock at the door later that morning to discover Gordie, hat in hand, standing on her doorstep. For a moment she didn't recognize the stranger before her. He was cleanly shaven, freshly bathed, his hair newly cut, wearing a new pair of red flannel drawers, an open neck, blue woolen shirt, blue jeans tucked into new leather boots, and a brand-new hat. Only the color of his hair gave away his identity.

T.G. Manning had been transformed into one handsome, respectable-looking man. The transformation nearly took Maggie's breath away.

He also had a humdinger of a shiner, a deep

slash across his cheekbone, and a wad of cotton stuck up his right nostril.

"Morning, Miss Fletcher."

"What in the world happened to you?" Taking his arm, she ushered him through the doorway. Grabbing a dish towel, she wet the end, then went to work cleaning away the remnants of blood circling his cuts.

T.G. was uncomfortable with her sympathetic clucking. It was bad enough she had to see him this way. It was bad enough he had to show up at all, and he sure didn't like her making a big fuss about it.

She stepped back, fixing her hands on her hips, frowning. "Have you been fighting?"

"No, ma'am, I haven't been fighting." Unfortunately, he'd never thrown a punch.

Taking the towel out of her hand, he set it aside. "Maggie, I've come here to say something, and I'd appreciate it if you let me get it said."

Uncrossing her arms, she waited. "All right."

"I've thought about your offer, and I've decided to accept."

Maggie felt faint with relief. It had been days since they talked, and she had given up on him accepting the job. "You'll work the mine for me?"

He nodded. "I'll run the crew for you."

"That's wonderful!" Far beyond her wildest hopes!

"*Run* the crew," he stressed. "I don't intend to work in the mine."

She thought that an odd declaration, but she wanted him on any terms.

"All right. What about a crew?"

"I think I know where I can put one together."

"I've tried everything," she warned. "I even borrowed Chappy's mule again and rode clear over to Squatter's Ridge yesterday, but to no avail."

"I know all about that, but there's one place you haven't tried. There's a woman over near Piety Hill who will help us out."

"A woman? Women are bad luck in a mine."

His look was purely impersonal. "You really think our luck can get any worse?"

She frowned. He had a point. "I guess not. Who do you have in mind?"

"Moses Malone. She and four other women have been working a worthless claim over at Piety Hill. I can't say for certain, but I imagine they could use the money. If you have no objections, I'll talk to Moses this morning."

"Objections? Of course I don't have any objections. How soon can she start?"

"I'll have to see." He stood up, looking as though he had something more to say.

She looked back at him expectantly. "What?"

"You should know . . . Moses and her crew have done hard time."

Maggie gripped the edge of the table for support. "For what?" Murder? Mayhem? Worse?

"You name it. They're no church choir."

Women ex-convicts. How desperate was she?

That desperate.

"Will I be endangering Wilson?" She wouldn't permit that for any amount of gold.

"No, the women are loners. They'll stay to themselves."

"Do they know about the mine?"

"About the ghost?"

"Yes . . . him." Butte Fesperman.

"I can't imagine anyone who doesn't," he conceded.

Sighing, Maggie lifted her hand to her temple. It was sink or swim time, eat or be eaten. "I'm desperate, Gordie. Do whatever it takes to get them."

"Which brings me to the next question. What can you afford to pay?"

"Nothing, but I'll match any wage around." If there was no gold in the mine, she was sunk.

"Not good enough."

"Well . . ." She started to pace, anxious now. "I don't know—what should I offer?"

"That depends on your funds."

"They're low—I was counting on the mine producing right away, which it hasn't."

"It might take as much as a share of the profits. You'd better hope the mother lode's in that damn mine."

The mother lode darn well *better* be in that mine, Maggie agonized. Her profit was dwindling fast.

"Do whatever it takes," she said. "I need a crew. Will you need money to buy a horse?" It seemed he had to walk wherever he went.

His face colored with embarrassment. "I . . . uh . . . it would speed things up."

"All right, I'll provide whatever you need."

Walking to the door, he opened it. "I should be back before dark." He looked competent and self-assured—a far cry from his former self. What happened? The answer lay in those cuts and bruises.

"Gordie?"

He turned. "Yes?"

"What made you change your mind?" He'd been so adamant about not taking the job.

"I need the money."

She knew it took a good deal of courage for him to admit that. Smiling, she said quietly, "Then I guess you'll want to get started right away."

"Yes, ma'am. Soon as possible."

He started to walk out the door when her voice interrupted again. "I want you to know, I don't care why, I'm just glad you're doing it."

He looked up, his eyes meeting hers. "Don't be; I'm no bargain."

Something deeper than a smile shone in her eyes now. "Isn't that for me to decide?"

Walking out, he closed the door behind him.

Chapter 10

"But Maggie! It's only a chicken! It don't eat much!"

"Wilson, take the rope off that chicken's neck and turn him loose, immediately!"

"You *said* I could have a pet," Wilson reminded her sullenly.

"One pet, Wilson, not an entire zoo." Balancing the wash basket on her hip, Maggie sidestepped a raccoon, squirrel, two rabbits, a stray hound dog with its ribs showing, and a rooster. The animals had ropes around their necks and were staked to the ground in front of the dugout.

Wilson was suddenly hell-bent on acquiring yet another pet.

"He lays eggs!"

"*He* does not lay eggs."

Wilson bent over to examine his latest acquisition. Straightening, he called back expectantly, "He can wake us up!"

"Turn that cock *loose*." Jamming a clothespin in her mouth, Maggie marched to the line to hang the wash out to freeze dry. All she needed was another mouth to feed—even if it was a chicken's! Their cupboard was as empty as last year's bird's nest.

Maggie realized she was on edge this morning. Gordie had been gone for over twenty-four hours. He said he'd be back by dark. She stayed up long into the night, waiting. She wanted to believe he'd be back, prayed that he would, yet images of the dented flask he carried in his left coat pocket colored her faith. T.G. Manning had no obligation to her, and by all indications he cared nothing about himself.

Why should he be concerned over two strangers from England? He was a full-grown man, and he didn't want to be bothered with an eight-year-old boy and seventeen-year-old girl. He seemed to like his life the way it was.

She knew all that, and yet she'd lain awake most of the night listening for him to return. Toward dawn she accepted he wasn't coming. And she had given him money to buy a *horse*.

The rooster set up a terrible squawk as Wilson slipped the rope off his neck and set him free.

Feathers fogged the air as the bird ran around in circles, flapping its wings and screeching. In a burst of energy, he charged Wilson, sending him shrieking around the corner of the dugout.

The remaining hostages bolted for cover, their tiny legs jerked from under them as the ropes around their necks yanked them to a screeching halt.

"You're going to get spurred!" Maggie called as

Wilson raced headlong around the dugout hounded
by a reddish white blur.

At the height of the ruckus Gordie arrived, followed by five women, all carrying picks, axes, and
shovels.

With an exclamation of relief, Maggie dropped
the wet shirt she was about to hang back into the
basket and ran to meet him. It took concerted will-
power to keep from flinging herself into his arms.
She deliberately slowed her steps as the odd assort-
ment of humanity approached.

"Hi."

Gordie took off his hat. "Morning."

Wilson rounded the house again, the rooster
bearing down on him hard.

"The trip over to Piety Hill took longer than expected," Gordie apologized. The pass between Fi-
brin and Muncie was blocked by mud slides. It had
taken him over half a day to shovel a path through.

He looked tired this morning, his eyes red and
whiskey-soaked. Demon rum, most likely, had
caused the delay, but then Maggie wasn't his
judge.

Instead, she smiled gratefully and said, "I'm
glad you're back." Her eyes switched to the
women, and she swallowed. A church choir they
certainly weren't.

"Maggie Fletcher, Moses Malone," Gordie introduced.

Maggie recoiled as she faced the rawboned Eskimo who looked mean enough to whip a weasel.
Dressed in men's boots, faded overalls, and a

heavy bearskin coat, Moses Malone's squat, two-hundred-pound, five-foot frame was intimidating.

Moses's eyes skimmed Maggie impartially. "Heard you're looking for someone to work your mine." Her voice was whiskey-deep, her hair styled with a butcher knife. The uninspired salt-and-pepper locks hung in dirty strings below the flaps of a dingy yellow wool hat. Her features were ageless. She could have been thirty or sixty.

"Yes," Maggie said, unhappy about the sudden squeak in her voice. "I understand you might be interested?"

Moses looked around. "Might. For a price."

Maggie glanced at Gordie, then back to Moses. "If you'll help me, I'll give you a third of the profits."

Moses's eyes shot to Gordie. "A third?"

"A quarter," he corrected. "That was the agreed amount."

Maggie's mind was busy trying to add and subtract. Half to Gordie, a quarter to Moses . . . that left a quarter for Maggie and Wilson. Not exactly the fortune she'd envisioned, but enough, if the mine proved bountiful.

Moses locked eyes with Gordie in a silent duel. After a while, she turned and said over her shoulder, "A quarter of the profits."

The women, having exchanged a series of harsh looks, nodded. A quarter of the profits.

Moses turned back to address Maggie. "You know about me and my crew?"

"Yes . . . somewhat."

"Couple of prostitutes, bank robber, an ax murderer, and I'm just damn mean," Moses said.

Definitely not your typical mining crew.

"Got any problem with that?"

"No," Maggie swallowed. "Ma'am."

"Manning says we work for him."

Maggie glanced at Gordie. "He's the boss." Thank God.

Wilson rounded the corner again, flinging his arms, screaming.

Moses threw him a prudent glance. "The boy has a rooster after him."

"I know. One of them will give up eventually." Maggie grinned. "How soon can you start?"

"Tomorrow."

"Thank goodness." Money would be coming in now. "I'll have breakfast waiting."

"We fix our own breakfast." Moses's eyes drifted to the mine.

Holding her breath, Maggie wondered if she knew about the ghost.

"We use our own equipment."

That was okay, since Maggie didn't have any. "All right."

Eyes still fixed on the Hellhole, Moses acknowledged, "If there's gold in there, we'll get it."

Maggie didn't doubt that. This woman was downright scary.

As Wilson rounded the corner again, Gordie reached over and plucked him to safety.

* * *

Five o'clock the next morning Maggie's crew arrived. They looked like fifty miles of bad road.

When Maggie asked to be introduced to the other women, Moses told her they were there to do a job, not to socialize. Names didn't matter. Folks called them the shady ladies and Maggie could do the same if names were important to her.

Armed with picks, axes, shovels, and lanterns, the women went to work at 5:07 A.M.

Day one passed without incident. At exactly five P.M., the women came out of the mine and snaked their way back down the mountain.

Maggie watched them go, wondering how the day had gone, but she wasn't brave enough to ask. If they *had* encountered Butte Fesperman, *he* would have been the one on the run.

Day two dawned. Five A.M. the women returned. After a short meeting Gordie dispersed them into the mine. As the parley broke up, his eyes touched Maggie's briefly before he turned and walked away. As far as she knew, he had yet to enter the mine.

Maggie knew he was uncomfortable around her and wondered why. She'd done everything she knew to make him feel at home. At times she wondered if he even liked her.

Day three came and went.

Day four.

Gordie showed up each morning to issue the women their orders. By daylight he disappeared again, Lord only knew where.

Maggie had no idea where he ate or slept, but

his appearance was improving. He didn't look nearly as scroungy as before, and he shaved every day now. He was really quite a handsome man.

Sighing, she shook out a rug, praying gold would soon be found.

Gordie Manning was beginning to look good to her.

Week two.

Placer deposits, small hollows in the streams, began to show up. Gold dust, flakes, and nuggets were found scattered though the sand and gravel downstream from the Hellhole.

"That's encouraging, isn't it?" Maggie exclaimed when Gordie told her the news.

"It's going to take a lot more than flakes and dust to meet the payroll," he warned.

"Still, it's encouraging." She smiled. "Maybe we're getting somewhere."

"Maybe, but the easiest way to find gold is to get yourself a burro and turn it loose."

Taking three loaves of bread out of the oven, she set them on the table to cool. "A burro?" She laughed. That's all she needed, another animal.

"Laugh if you want, but there's been many a prospector who's hit pay dirt because of his donkey."

"Now what could a donkey possibly have to do with finding gold?"

"Whiplash Johnson tells the story about how his donkey got away from him one afternoon. When he finally caught up with it, the animal was standing next to an outcrop of gold."

"Gordie," she chided, wondering if he really believed such stories.

"Go ahead, laugh. Spineless Jake Henshaw swears his mules ran away and when he found them, they had taken shelter from a storm behind a huge outcrop of black rock. While Jake waited for the storm to blow itself out, he got to looking around and what do you think he found?"

"Gold."

"Not right away. He chipped a few samples out of the rock and talked a friend of his into having them assayed."

"Know a lot of men who've found water, gold, and silver with a dowser stick."

She gestured to the simmering pot of stew she'd just taken off the stove. "Stay to supper? There's plenty."

"Thanks, but I have to be going."

"There's corn bread in the oven," she tempted. It would be so nice to have adult company at the table tonight.

"No, but I appreciate the offer."

Maggie wasn't going to let him see her disappointment. "Maybe next time."

"Maybe next time."

"Gordie, where do you live?" The question had nagged her for weeks. He came and went like the wind.

"Here and there," he said vaguely.

"Is it far from here?"

"Why do you ask?"

"Well." She sat down to rest for a minute. "I was thinking it might be easier if you were to live closer. I mean, the women come so early in the morning, it would be much easier for you if you didn't have to get up so early."

His eye searched the small quarters curiously.

"Not here," she said.

"Where?"

"I thought maybe you should take our portion of what we've mined and purchase a tent. That way, you could be nearby if I needed you for anything."

"We've only mined enough to pay the shady ladies' wages to keep them going."

"Didn't you find a good-size nugget a couple of days ago?"

"Yes, but it hasn't been assayed yet."

"Then go into camp and get it assayed. Then buy a tent." She got up to stir the stew. "And while you're at it, stop by the store and pick up some salt and baking soda for me. We're getting low."

We're getting low. *Our* portion of the gold. The correlations made T.G. uneasy. "Anything else?"

"No," she smiled. "That's all."

For now, she added under her breath as the door closed behind him.

"Apple pie?" she called from the doorway the following night.

Gordie glanced up from his task of honing knives.

"It's just coming out of the oven!"

"Don't care much for apples," he called back. "They give me the hiccups."

She frowned. *Hiccups?*

"Biscuits and rabbit?" She stood in the doorway the next evening, shading her eyes against a fading sun.

Gordie glanced up from loading the sluice box. The day's diggings were brought out in large carts and sifted for gold. "Fried?"

"No, boiled with dumplings."

"Like my meat fried. Much obliged, though."

Sighing, she closed the door.

"Blackberry scones and fried chicken!" she sang out the next night.

Getting to his feet, Gordie dusted the dirt off his pants. "Give me a few minutes to wash up."

"Take as long as you like!"

Grinning, she slammed the door. "Wilson, pick up your shoes. We're having company for supper."

Chapter 11

"Boy, mining's hard work, huh, Gordie?" Wilson rested his elbows on T.G.'s shoulder, watching as he checked the day's work.

"Pretty hard," Gordie agreed absently. He tightened his grip on the knife handle to still the trembling in his hand.

"You smell better'n you used to."

"Thank you."

"You don't stink or nothin'."

"I appreciate that."

"And you look better. I didn't like your beard."

"Well, I guess I needed a change."

"It's cleaner this way," Wilson explained. Shifting his stance, he got more comfortable.

"What're you doing now?"

"Cleaning a crevice."

"Why you doin' that?"

"Because a little piece of gold might have been overlooked."

"Gold?"

"Yeah."

"We found gold already?"

"Not in any quantity yet."

"But soon, huh, Gordie?"

"I hope so."

"How much gold is in the crevice?"

"I don't know if there's any, but we clean them once we've worked an area. It's called coyoting."

"Coyoting?"

"Yeah, coyoting."

"That's a funny name."

"Yeah."

"How come?"

"How come what?"

"How come they call it coyoting?"

"I don't know, they just do."

"Who calls it that? Moses?"

"Moses and the other miners."

"How come?"

T.G. paused, pretending to hear something. "Listen, I think Maggie's calling you."

"Huh, uhhh." Gordie was trying to trick him again. Maggie *said* he could come out and keep Gordie company, long as he didn't ask a bunch of questions.

Wilson looked back at Gordie charitably. "Aw, you're just teasing again, huh, Gordie?"

"Yeah, just teasing, Wilson."

Hopping off the ledge, Wilson trailed T.G. deeper into the shaft.

"How come you're in the mine this afternoon? You don't like to come into the mine, huh, Gordie."

"I'll only be here a few minutes." T.G. could already feel his breathing quicken, and his head getting lighter.

"You afraid of the ghost?"

"No, Wilson, I'm not afraid of the ghost."

"I haven't seen him, have you?"

"No—are you sure Maggie isn't calling you?"

Wilson listened for a moment. "No, she's not. Honest. Where's Moses?" Wilson had taken an instant liking to the Eskimo. Although Maggie forbade him to get in anyone's way, Wilson still found time for daily visits.

Moses was nice, even sharing part of a fish with him for lunch one day. It was *raw*, but Wilson ate it anyway 'cause he didn't want to hurt her feelings. But, boy, he'd spat, and spat, and spat on the way back to the dugout.

He didn't like them whores and murderers as much because they never talked to him. Just Moses was nice.

"Moses went home," T.G. said.

"How come?"

Holding the lantern higher, T.G. inspected a heavy beam. "Because it's time for her to go home."

Switching subjects completely, Wilson launched into a review of his day. "Thursday Matthews almost ate lunch with me at school today, but she changed her mind and said she was gonna eat with Prudy Walker, but *maybe* she would eat with me on Wednesday, or maybe on Friday—she'd just have to think about it."

"Well, maybe she will," Gordie mused.

Wilson sighed. "Who knows?" Women were a mystery to him. "She thinks I talk too much."

"Can't imagine that."

"Gwendolyn thinks I talk too much, too."

T.G. was having a hard time following the conversation. The walls were closing in on him. His breathing was more calculated now.

"You *know* who Gwendolyn is?"

"A classmate?"

"Noooo," Wilson scoffed. "She's not a classmate, she's Aunt Fionnula's girl—you know, Aunt Fionnula—the woman who let me and Maggie live with her 'cause our parents got killed on that train?"

"I'm sorry, I didn't know about your parents, Wilson." That would explain what Maggie was doing so far away from England without family.

"Oh, it's all right. I'm not sad anymore. Maggie says Mama and Papa are up in heaven, singin' with the angels and walking on streets of gold. That's nothing to be sad about, huh, Gordie? Maggie says they're real happy, and we shouldn't wish them back. That would be selfish of us."

"Yeah, I think she's right, kid."

Wilson cocked his head cagily. "You think Maggie's pretty?"

Slipping the blade of the knife inside a crack, T.G. pried a piece of quartz loose. "She's okay."

"She can cook good, huh?" He'd seen the way Gordie enjoyed her meals, and the funny way he looked at her when her back was turned. Outright

stared at her bottom twice; he'd seen it. He didn't
think Gordie was supposed to be looking at her
bottom, but there was still a lot Wilson didn't
know.

A smile lifted the corners of T.G.'s mouth.
"She's a good cook." He was putting on weight
from the meals she was preparing for him on a regular basis now. Even more worrisome was the
knowledge that he looked forward to those hours
with her. It had to stop. He didn't need a woman to
complicate his life further.

"I'll bet ole Mildred was madder'n a wet hen
when we left," Wilson said. "She *really* liked
Maggie's cooking." She really liked *food*, period.

T.G. was lost again. "Mildred?"

"Yeah—Aunt Fionnula's daughter."

"I thought Gwendolyn was Aunt Fionnula's
daughter."

Wilson gave him another magnanimous look.
"She is. So is Mildred. Aunt Fionnula has *two*
daughters."

"Oh," T.G. said, as if he'd finally made the connection.

"Bet Aunt Fionnula was real mad, too."

T.G. glanced up. "Why would she be mad?"

" 'Cause Maggie did all the work! Aunt
Fionnula made Maggie work real hard, cookin' and
cleanin'—and then she took all our money and
wouldn't give it back to us." He peered up at T.G.
in earnest. "She just ought to have her butt kicked
clean up between her shoulder blades for doin'

that, huh, Gordie?" That was an *awful* thing to do to orphans.

"But she was happy you and Maggie inherited the mine?"

"I don't think so—but I don't know. We didn't tell her."

"Your aunt doesn't know you're here?" It was none of T.G.'s business, and it wasn't his nature to pry into anyone else's, but he was intrigued by the boy's disclosure.

"Well." Wilson was pretty sure Aunt Fionnula did know. Maggie said she was going to write her a letter telling her how sorry they were for sneakin' away. "You'll have to ask Maggie about that."

A thump at the back of the mine suddenly caught T.G.'s attention. Halting the discussion, he cocked an ear, listening.

"What?" Wilson whispered. "You hear something?"

"Shhh," T.G. warned, listening intently now.

A low rumble centered at the back of the mine. Dirt and loose rock showered down through the uneven cracks of the timbers.

Wilson started coughing. "What's happening, Gordie?"

"Come on, son." Taking the boy's hand, T.G. began propelling him toward the shaft opening.

"What's wrong, Gordie? Is it the ghost?"

"Keep walking, Wilson." Glancing over his shoulder, T.G. moved the child swiftly through the mine. Bedrock showered down on them, hindering their progress. The ground began to vibrate, and walls began to crumble.

"Run, Wilson!"

Breaking into a run, Gordie impelled Wilson toward the entrance. A loud roar followed on their heels as they burst clear of the mine.

A thunderous explosion rocked the ground as dirt and rock came crashing down. Dust obliterated the fading twilight as the entrance to the mine sealed shut.

Shaken, T.G. clasped Wilson tightly to him, stunned by the unexpected onslaught of destruction.

Was it possible Butte Fesperman was about to show his hand?

Chapter 12

Maggie finally knew what hell was like; she had had five weeks of it.

"Why?" she agonized as she stood beside a pale-faced Gordie, viewing the latest catastrophe.

"It just happened, Maggie!" Wilson was still upset over the experience. "Me and Gordie was just talkin' and all of a sudden we heard this funny noise and Gordie said, 'Run, Wilson!' and I did!"

Maggie looked at Gordie expectantly.

"I don't know what happened. The timbers were shored-up properly. I checked them myself." Kneeling before the pile of rubble, he examined it for color.

Maggie shut her eyes, sick at heart. It would take days to get the mine going again. "Now what?"

T.G.'s eyes firmed with resolution. "We dig."

It took all of them—shady ladies, Wilson, Maggie, and T.G.—working twelve hours a day to extricate the rubble from the mine entrance. The

front province of the tunnel had collapsed. After
days of digging, they managed to clear the biggest
part of rubble away from the opening.

It was hard, backbreaking labor. The women
swung picks, axes, and hammers, sweating like
men in the cold temperatures.

Even Wilson did his part, lugging heavy buckets
of water from the stream to slake their thirst.

Gordie was steady, working alongside the
women, giving orders when needed, a strong back
where necessary.

Maggie wasn't surprised by his quiet leadership.
It was just one more facet about him that intrigued
her.

She had a growing need to prove her own worth,
but by the end of the week, she realized she was
no match for his strength. He discovered her late
one evening sitting behind the dugout, trying to
hide her emotions.

"What's wrong?" Concern filled his voice as he
knelt beside her.

When he saw her pale features, worry quickly
turned to alarm. "Are you sick?"

"No, of course not. I just needed a few moments
alone, that's all." With all the confusion lately,
heaven knows she'd had little of that.

"Are you sure?" His eyes reflected his doubt.
She wasn't one to slip away and be gone for hours.

She shook her head, smiling. "I'm fine, silly."

He was still unconvinced. She had been acting
strangely all day.

"Wilson sick?" Gordie turned to look over his

shoulder. He could have sworn he'd seen the boy forcing worms down his latest acquisition, a blackbird with an injured wing.

"No, Wilson is fine. We're both fine," she insisted. "I just wanted to be alone."

"What then?" he asked, exasperated. Inscrutable women drove him nuts!

Sighing, she turned her hands, revealing the huge watery blisters filling her palms.

"Blisters?"

She nodded. "I don't know what to do for them."

"Maggie." Reaching out, he gently took both her hands in his. "Why didn't you say something?"

She gazed back at him trying to keep her lower lip from trembling. "I've ... never had ... blisters."

"Well, you do now." He smiled at her, and she immediately felt better. She hadn't known he knew *how* to smile. The realization did wonders for her sagging disposition.

"Where's your salve?"

"I don't have any."

"Damn it, woman." Lifting her into his arms, he carried her down to the stream.

Wilson, sitting on his heels, looked up and saw Gordie disappearing over the hill carrying his sister. Dropping a grub, he sat up straighter. "Hey—what's the matter with Maggie?"

"She's got blisters!"

"Oh." Sinking back to his heels, he crammed

another worm into the bird's mouth. Blisters. He
had 'em all the time.

Kneeling beside the stream, Gordie dipped
Maggie's palms into the icy water. The crystal
clear liquid bubbled and danced musically over the
jagged rocks. Leaving her side, he was back momentarily carrying a tin of salve Moses kept in a
leather rucksack at his nearby campsite.

Liberally coating her palms with the thick ointment, he gently bandaged them with a layer of
clean, white cloth.

Maggie watched him tend her wounds as gently
as he would a child's. Something akin to love
stirred within her heart.

When he was through, he unconsciously continued to hold her. "Better?"

Nodding, she smiled, embarrassed he'd had to
take care of her again. He undoubtedly thought she
was a world-class weakling. "I'll bet you think I'm
something—upset over some silly blisters."

His eyes avoided hers as he admitted to himself
that, yes, he thought she was something. Something so good, so perfect, she wouldn't be in his
life very long.

Setting her aside, he put the lid back on the
salve tin and stuck it back into the sack.

Maggie was determined to hide her swelling
frustration with him. The moment he sensed he
was getting too close, he retreated into his shell.
Was it just her, or women in general that frightened him?

"Will you be working the mine tomorrow?" she

asked. Now that the entrance was passable again, there was a lot of work to be done.

"Moses can handle it."

"I suppose, but because of all the delays, I thought you might be working with her."

Maggie thought it was strange that T.G. rarely entered the mine. He did so only at the end of the day, and only long enough to review the women's work.

"No, that's Moses's job."

She squirmed around to look at him as she talked. "Yes, but if you were working, too, it might go faster."

They had already lost a week, and winter would be upon them soon. She couldn't imagine what he did all day. He didn't have another job; he was around too regularly for that. He swore he didn't believe in ghosts, but something kept him out of the mine.

"I agreed to run the crew for you," he said. "Nothing was mentioned about me working inside the mine."

"Well, tarnation! Why not? What's wrong with going into the mine?"

"I don't want to. Moses and her crew can bring the diggings out, and I'll work the sluice boxes— day and night, if necessary, but I'm not going into the mine any more than necessary."

"Of all people, T.G. Manning, you would be the last person I'd think of being a scaredy-cat," she fussed. Who'd ever heard of a foreman of a mining crew refusing to enter the mine?

T.G. turned away, unaffected by her scorn. She could think whatever she liked. He agreed to oversee the mine, not to work it.

"A sissy!" Maggie taunted in a surprising spurt of annoyance. "Sissy, sissy, sissy!"

She was going to replace his apathy with enthusiasm if it killed her!

Springing to their feet, they butted noses.

"You're calling *me* a *sissy*?"

"Yeah, a big one."

His eyes glittered dangerously.

Hers flashed back just as intensely. "You don't scare me, T.G."

"I could if I tried."

"Truth is, you are a *scaredy*-cat."

Their eyes locked in a poisonous duel.

"You don't know what you're talking about."

"Then tell me why you won't go into the mine," she goaded.

"Because I won't. That's all you need to know."

"Yes, you will."

"No, I won't."

"Yes, you will!" They were practically shouting now.

"One of us has to be in there," she reasoned. "We can't let Moses do all the work."

"That's why she has a crew."

"It will go faster if you're in there helping. That's what I'm paying you for."

"No," he contended. "You are paying me to run the crew."

Tenacity stormed through her. "Then *I'll* just

have to be there and get in everybody's way, because I don't know squat about gold mining!"

Bending from the waist, he politely gestured for her to be his guest.

She turned away, disappointed in him. "You *are* a sissy."

"Think whatever you want." Let Mooney slit his gullet; he'd been out of his mind for ever taking this job.

He was about to walk off when she reached and latched onto his coattail.

"All right," she conceded. "We'll both help—at least long enough to get the operation running smoothly again." Sighing, her eyes shifted to the hated mine—and she was beginning to hate the thing. It was a curse! "The ghost isn't likely to appear to both of us, if that's what you're worried about."

Modesty filled his voice now. "That's not what I'm worried about."

"Then for heaven's sake, what is? We're wasting precious time!"

The time for honesty was at hand; T.G. knew it, yet he continued to fight against confessing his problem.

"Well?"

"Well." He stripped off his hat, scratching his head. Damn, she was pushy. Too pushy. His hand instinctively slipped to his left pocket in search of the flask only to find its familiar comfort missing.

"Gordie?"

"All right, damn it. I'm claustrophobic."

She gasped. Terminally ill. She knew it. The first man she was ever interested in, and he was dying.

"Oh, Gordie ... how long ... ?"

A muscle flexed tightly in his jaw. "Four and a half years."

"*Four and a half* years." So little time left for a man who was still young and vital.

"I'm so sorry," she murmured, prepared to do anything to make what time he had left bearable. "When did you find out?"

He glanced up. "Four and half years ago."

Four and a half years ago.

"At first I didn't know what was happening." Now that the truth was out, a weight was lifted from his chest. The snake was out of the pit. "Every time I went into a mine I felt like I was suffocating."

"Oh," she soothed. *A horrible lung disease.*

"One day, it got so bad I blacked out. My partner hauled me in to see a doctor, and that's when I learned the truth."

Her heart ached. *Consumption.* "It must have been dreadful."

"No. Embarrassing as hell."

She gazed back at him, longing to cradle him to her breast. God love him; he was so brave—so sensitive. He was dying, and *he* was embarrassed.

Meeting her stricken gaze, he suddenly realized that she misunderstood. "Maggie."

"Yes?"

"Do you know what claustrophobic means?" It

was a relatively new term in medicine. He had been fortunate enough to be diagnosed by a gifted young doctor who had recently completed his training in Boston and knew of the latest medical advances.

Maggie felt faint. She wanted to be strong in his hour of need, but she was hampered by a delicate constitution. "No," she admitted hesitantly, hoping he wouldn't find it necessary to go into detail.

"It means a fear of tight places."

Nodding in total understanding, she sighed benevolently. That would make the grave even more dreadful.

Cupping her chin in his hand, he said, "I am not dying. I *faint* when I'm in a mine because I have a fear of being closed in."

It took a moment for his words to register. When they did, Maggie was giddy with relief. "*That's* what's wrong with you? You're afraid of tight places?"

He looked away, humiliated. "Isn't that enough?" He'd squandered everything he owned for a mine he couldn't work. Failure turned to despair; despair to desperation. Five years later, he was not worth the lead it would take to blow him away.

"Well, all you had to do was say so," she chided. "Then you're *really* not afraid of ghosts?"

"Afraid of Butte Fesperman?" He laughed. "No."

"While we're on the subject, *who* is this Butte Fesperman?" She'd heard the name until she was sick of it, and yet she hadn't the faintest idea who he was.

T.G.'s eyes returned to the shaft, recalling various accounts of the feud. "Almost thirty-six years ago, Butte Fesperman and Ardis Johnson both lay claim to the Hellhole. Seems Butte stole the mine from Ardis while Ardis was gone into town for supplies and other things."

"Other things?"

He looked away. "Other things."

"Oh," she said, getting it.

"The story goes, Butte was trying to bluff Ardis and the sheriff off the property when he blew himself up."

"How did he do that?"

"The stories vary, but apparently it was a blunder on Butte's part. Some say he never intended to kill himself, only to trick Ardis."

"But if Butte was dead, the mine would have returned to Ardis."

"It did, but from that day on, no one has been able to work it. Legend has it, Butte Fesperman lives in the mine and isn't about to let anyone near his gold."

Maggie laughed. "That's absurd. And now, Butte is supposedly in the mine, aimlessly roaming around, locked in some deep, black void forever?"

"Worse. He's locked in the Hellhole forever."

She glanced back to the mine. "I don't believe a word of it."

"Me either, but others do." He'd always considered the stories improbable.

She crossed her arms, thinking of the agony she'd gone through to hire a crew. "People can't conceive that this 'ghost' has been blown out of proportion—that it's only silly folklore that's been handed down from generation to generation and no one's thought to question whether or not it's just a figment of someone's highly active imagination?"

"It looks that way."

"Poppycock."

His brows raised at her expression.

"Rubbish," she amended. Turning away, she muttered, "Hoodee Doo men are a disgrace." She glanced over her shoulder protectively. "Present company excluded."

Scooping up the leather rucksack, he followed her up the hill.

"How do you figure?"

"They've sent a bunch of *women* to do their work."

Chapter 13

Quartz mining is different from placer mining. If a man pans for gold, he stands in an icy stream for ten to twelve hours a day, scooping dirt and gravel into a pan. Holding the pan underwater, he'll rotate it gently, tilting it slightly to let the loose dirt float off.

Stirring the lighter matter, called "slickens," he'll pick out the larger pebbles and gravel, allowing the heavy gold particles an opportunity to settle. He'll continue to work the pan in such a manner until he can see what remains in the bottom.

If he's lucky, he'll see color; if he isn't, he'll begin the process all over again. A man will go for years suffering from rheumatism, back trouble, sore hands, sore feet, yet the wild, get-rich-quick light in his eyes won't dim.

Quartz is gold found in veins or lodes, housed in shafts or tunnels, and often in solid rock. At times it's necessary to blast to reach the source. Once the quartz ore is broken up by blasting or digging, it's hauled to the surface and separated from the gold.

Quartz mines are the stuff miners dream of, for in these mystical passages and caverns the mother lode is hidden.

The mother lode: a place where an incredibly fortunate discoverer can scoop out pure gold by the shovelfuls, a place so fertile that it might contain more gold than all the other mines put together.

That's what drives the miners, the search for that one vein that will make them unbelievably rich. Seldom do they pause to consider that gold is easily found but hard to gather in any quantity.

The Hellhole is a lode mine. Once the diggings are brought out of the mine they are scooped into long flumes and sent to the bottom of the mountain. There they are washed in sluice boxes—long troughs, sometimes in several sections, from fifty to one-hundred feet long, designed so water can run through them. Riffle boxes, which have false bottoms with cleats to arrest the flow of water and mud, are used to let the gold and heavier particles sink into the shallow boxes.

It is excruciating, backbreaking work. Moses Malone and her crew didn't seem hindered by their sex. Two of the women stood beside the sluice box with hoes and shovels, keeping the dirt stirred up as it washed down the trough. Two more shoveled in material at the head of the sluice as

the other two hauled dirt from the mine in wheel-
barrows.

Maggie ceased trying to help; she only got in the
way. But she could cook, toting large pails of
beans and piping hot loaves of fresh baked bread
to the mine daily. To vary the menu, she fried pans
of rice with tomatoes, onions, and chili powder;
baked pans of beans flavored with salt pork and
thick, rich molasses; made crusty brown peach pies
from canned peaches, and piping hot skillets of
cinnamon-fried apples.

The shady ladies consumed the meals without
comment.

As she cooked, Maggie thanked the Lord that
Aunt Sissy hadn't left her a mine in the Klondike.
Two years ago, the newspapers had been filled
with stories about the big gold strike in Dawson
City. Overnight, the area around the Klondike
River had exploded. Men from Canada, England,
Germany, France, and Turkey stormed the area,
some coming from as far away as Australia, Af-
rica, and China in search of gold.

Maggie glanced up as Gordie came into the dugout. She smiled, relieved that he seemed to be
more comfortable around her lately. He stayed for
every meal now.

"Hi!"

"Hi."

"Seen Butte Fesperman?" It was getting to be a
standing joke between them.

"Not today."

"Finding any gold?"

"Nothing to get excited about."

Pouring water into the washpan, he started to clean up for dinner. "Something smells good." He scooped water with his hands and flushed the grime from his face.

"Slumgullion," she verified. Poor man's hash, her mother used to say.

"It would be nice to have some fresh meat," she mused. They'd had very little the past few weeks. Just a few rabbits and fryers the neighboring miners had brought them. Fresh vegetables were unheard of, and fruit was as scarce as hen's teeth, unless you were fortunate enough to get a few cans of peaches at the store. Next summer she was going to plant a garden, a big one, and can everything she raised.

She put a towel in T.G.'s hand as he blindly fumbled around the washstand. Lifting his head, he smiled. "Thanks. I'll see if I can scare up some for you."

She smiled, happy to see the way his face had filled out lately. A healthy glow replaced the earlier gray pallor.

"You think you can?" Fresh venison, or a plump, wild turkey would be delicious.

Taking the lid off the skillet, she stirred the hash. "I was just thinking: I'm glad Aunt Sissy's mine isn't in Dawson City. Have you heard what's going on over there?"

"They say things are pretty crazy." He pulled out a keg and sat down, making a conscious effort to avoid looking her way. When she stirred a skillet, parts of him responded. The way her bottom shifted back and forth, in a come-hither fashion, stirred up feelings he would just as soon stay dormant. His life was better now. He had a tent over his head and three solid meals a day. Enough gold was coming out of the mine to keep Mooney off his back, and the mine kept him so busy he hadn't been to the gaming halls for weeks. At this point, the last thing he needed was a woman to complicate matters.

Taking a pan of biscuits out of the oven, Maggie shut the door with her hip.

T.G. deliberately looked the other way.

Setting the pan on the table, she brushed a lock of stray hair from her eyes. "You know what I heard at the store this morning?"

In spite of himself, he did look up, and something hit him like a freight train. The front of his britches suddenly lost a lot of their former roominess.

"What did you hear?" he asked in as normal tone as possible.

"I heard that picks and shovels are going for twenty-five dollars apiece in Dawson City. Nails, ten dollars a pound; flour *seventy-five* dollars a sack; a can of tomatoes, *eight* dollars. Salt's worth its weight in gold, and eggs are two dollars apiece. Can you imagine?" She wouldn't be able to survive a day!

"They say the miners are paying the prices. Chappy Hellerman was telling me the sourdoughs have to feed their mules bacon because hay is running five hundred dollars a bale nowadays."

"What's a 'sourdough'?"

"An old prospector."

Well, the prices were ludicrous, but nothing astounded her anymore.

"How is Chappy?" She hadn't seen the old prospector around the past few times she'd been in camp.

"He's staked a claim over near Cherry Creek. Word has it, he's found a few good-size nuggets."

Her hands brushed his as she handed him a warm biscuit. Their eyes unwillingly drifted together. "There's blackberry jam if you like."

Blackberry jam wasn't on his mind. "Thanks— I'll wait until you make scones again."

Her eyes seemed hesitant to move on, her breathing imperceptibly more shallow. "Guess I should call Wilson. The biscuits are getting cold."

The front of his britches burgeoned miserably, but he couldn't look away. "He's just outside the door—Maggie, I had to cut the rope on the skunk. Wilson was upset, but if his luck ran out, you wouldn't be able to live with the smell that close to the dugout."

"No, you did the right thing. I've told him as much." It was a miracle the skunk hadn't turned on them already. It was as if Wilson had all of the animals under a spell.

Look the other way, T.G. agonized.

Don't you dare look the other way, her eyes admonished. *And stop looking like a whipped pup. I know how hard you're trying. You haven't had a drink since you started work—I know that. I've seen the way your hand shakes and how hard you have to fight some days to keep it together. I've watched you hand over your hard-earned money to those two wretched thugs every Friday night. I see you paying for your mistakes.*

Each day I watch for the missing flask to reappear in your left coat pocket, and when it doesn't, I'm proud of you. You hear me, T.G.? Of course you don't, but I'm saying it anyway.

I know it's hard—how easy it would be to slip back into your old comfortable ways. It's easier not caring. Bad habits are like old shoes: they're hard to throw away.

I stand at the door at night, lonely. Your tent is so close, and yet it might as well be a million miles away.

If it were up to me, I would make the first move, but I'm a woman and I can't. Mother said that men don't like forward women, and I desperately want you to like me.

It could be only my imagination, but I see the same hunger in your eyes I know is in mine. Yet you hold me at a distance.

Is your lack of interest because I'm so much younger than you, that I have a small brother to raise? Do you dislike children? Are you afraid of responsibility? You don't seem to be. You work as hard or harder than any man around.

Then again, maybe it isn't interest I see in your eyes, only idle curiosity.

Darn it, Maggie! You care! You care whether or not he looks at you with more than idle curiosity. You're deeply attracted to him!

The revelation wasn't even mildly disturbing. Actually, it was fascinating. She *was* deeply attracted to him; maybe it went even deeper than attraction. She had never felt anything remotely like this about another man.

"Butter?" she asked.

T.G. looked away first. "Thanks."

One hour—thirty minutes, hell, ten would do it at Paradise Nell's, he conceded, and I'd rid myself of this agony.

The plan had only one fallacy: he wasn't interested. Maggie had taken control of his every waking thought, but this time he was not going to set himself up for a fall. And the last thing she needed was to tie up with a thirty-year-old loser. . . .

The front door flew open, and Wilson burst in on a draft of cold air, dragging a bobcat on a leash. "Hey, Gordie, look what I just found!"

Maggie and Gordie bolted toward the door, scrambling over each other in their haste to clear the room.

Overturned kegs and the pan of biscuits clattered to the floor as they darted through the open doorway.

"Huh," Wilson said, mystified. "Wonder where they're going in such a big hurry?"

Chapter 14

"Don't *ever* do that again!" Maggie was still shaking from the lynx encounter. "You're going to get somebody killed!"

"But Maggie, he's not very big! He wouldn't hurt nobody!" Now she'd gone and let Gordie scare the cat off with a *gun*—it wasn't fair! She *said* he could have a pet, but she got all excited when he tried to bring one home.

"It was a *bobcat*, Wilson. A wild animal. He has to hunt for food; when he grows up, he won't know that you're not his supper."

"I could train him. He likes me a lot! When he grows up, he won't be mean, honest, Maggie! I'll teach him to be nice!"

"You can't have him."

"Well, *shit*," Wilson said disgustedly.

Maggie gasped. "Wilson Douglas Fletcher!"

"*What?*"

"Where have you heard such language!" It sure wasn't around here! Miners were notorious for foul language—they'd honed it to a fine art—but

Gordie kept a tight leash on his rhetoric, and the women guarded their tongues when Wilson was nearby.

Wilson peered up at her. "Is 'shit' bad?"

"Yes, very bad. Don't say it again. And while we're on the subject, young man, your English is terrible lately!" He had always been an exceptionally bright, articulate child. Since coming to Colorado he was quickly picking up speech patterns that were appalling.

"Butch says 'shit' all the time. He says it every time he throws my sandwich down the shitter. He says, 'Say good-by to your ass 'cause it's going down the shitter next!' "

"Wilson! Stop that this instant!"

" 'Shitter' is bad *too*?" *Nothing* suited her lately!

Maggie started off in a mad huff toward the door. "Get into the house, I'm washing your mouth out with soap."

"Soap!" Wilson wailed.

"Yes, soap!"

"I won't say it again, I promise!"

"I know you won't, young man!"

Wilson whooped, and kicked, and yelled as she caught him by the ear and marched him straight into the dugout.

Shitter, indeed!

"Pass me the goddamned beans."

They were sitting at the supper table that night when he did it again. Maggie's fork clattered to her plate.

She glared at her brother, her pupils pulsating.

Silence seized the table.

Gordie lowered his head, staring at his plate as if it suddenly had vital safety instructions written on it.

"Please," Wilson added when the air started to palpitate.

"What did I tell you about using that kind of language?"

Wilson tried to think. *What* language? He'd asked for the beans! What's wrong with saying beans?

Shoving back from the table, Maggie motioned him toward the sink.

"What? What'd I say *now*?" Wilson's eyes shot to Gordie for help.

Keeping his head low, Gordie kept out of it.

Latching onto Wilson's ear, Maggie hauled him to the sink, verbally castigating Butch Miller every step of the way.

He was turning sweet, innocent Wilson into a common foulmouthed hooligan!

A full moon glittered atop the frozen ground later, as Maggie opened the door and looked out. Plagued by remorse, she stared at the small figure swathed in a heavy blanket, sitting on the log, his revered pets gathered about him for support.

Emotion formed a tight knot to her throat. She was such a failure. *Mama, I'm trying*, she whispered, consumed by the need to talk to someone who understood—anyone.

Maybe she was too young to raise Wilson properly. She didn't know the first thing about nurturing a child; that was all too apparent. In the past, she had relied on Aunt Fionnula's insight; now there was no one but herself to lean on. And her wisdom was running on empty.

Settling her cloak around her shoulders, she stepped outside the dugout and closed the door.

The moon lit her pathway as she strolled to the log. When she approached Wilson, she was met with a frostier reception than the cool October night.

Undeterred, she sat down, nodding hello to the animals. A raccoon stared up at her with inquisitive eyes.

One by one, she acknowledged the other animals' presence. "Hello, Edgar, Pudding, Jellybean, and of course, a good evening to you, Selmore." She sat for a moment, enjoying the night.

Wilson refused to look at her.

After a while, she reached over and pulled him onto her lap. He was getting awfully big for such an action, but he wasn't too big yet.

He set up an indignant protest, but she held him firmly to her until he gradually settled down.

They gazed at a sky ablaze with stars. Just the two of them, the way it had been for a while now.

"Bet you can't find a big fat cow."

Studying the sky, Wilson solemnly pointed to what he thought looked like a big fat cow. Their father played the nonsensical game with them from the time they were infants. The frivolous diversion never failed to win a smile, or mend an unintentional slight.

"Bet you can't find a skinny pig."

Maggie's eyes searched the sky studiously. "How skinny?"

"Real skinny."

After a while, she pointed to a configuration of stars just to the left of the Milky Way. "There, the scrawniest pig in the whole universe."

"No, it isn't."

"Yes, it is."

"Bet you can't find a fish wearing a hat."

"What kind of a hat?"

"A *miner's* hat."

"Pooh, too easy." She pointed out a clump of stars to the right of the moon. "Right there—plain as day. A silly-looking fish wearing an even sillier-looking hat."

"The kind Moses wears?"

"Even sillier."

Giggling, they played the game a while longer as the moon climbed higher in the frosty sky.

Nestling deeper against her warmth, Wilson forgave her. He was going to try and do better. He'd never say "beans" again. Sadness touched his voice now. "I miss Papa."

Resting her chin on the top of his head, she hugged him tightly. "Me too, Wilson. And Mama."

"Yeah, and Mama, too," he echoed wistfully. "Sometimes it's hard to remember what they look like. I think real hard about Papa, but sometimes I just can't see him."

"You were very young when he died."

"What *did* he look like, Maggie?"

"He was very handsome, just like you'll be someday."

"Will I look like him?"

"I bet you will," she said. "Exactly like him."

They sat for a moment, recalling happier times.

"Wilson, I'm sorry I've been so hard on you lately."

He sighed. "I didn't mean to say bad things."

"I know you didn't. We haven't been in church for awhile, but you know the Good Book tells us not to take the Lord's name in vain."

"I didn't!"

"You did."

"When?"

"When you asked for the beans tonight."

" 'Beans' is taking the Lord's name in vain?"

"No, 'goddamned' is taking the Lord's name in vain. It's blasphemy, and you shouldn't do it."

Wilson was immediately repentant. "I'm sorry— Butch says it all the time."

"Well, maybe no one has told Butch that he shouldn't. The Lord says we are in the world, but not of it—and that means we are to be especially aware of what we say and do."

"But sometimes we mess up, huh, Maggie?" He'd heard about a lot of people that had messed up—real bad—since he'd been here.

"Many, many times, but that should only make us try harder to be the very best that we can be."

Wilson thought about that for awhile. "Gordie messes up sometimes."

"Yes," Maggie whispered conspiratorially. "Sometimes he does—real bad."

"But he's gettin' better, huh, Maggie? He doesn't smell like whiskey anymore, and he's real clean now—why, he even shaved off his beard so's he wouldn't get snot in it anymore."

"Wilson, there you go again. Your language is slipping."

"Well, that's what he said." He didn't know a more refined way to tell her.

She laughed, hugging him. "Well, I agree, he is getting much better."

"Maybe he just needs someone to take care of him, huh?"

"Yes," she said softly. "Maybe he does."

"He's a real good worker."

"Very good. We're lucky he's working for us."

"Why doesn't he like to go into the mine?"

"Because he has something called 'claustrophobia,' which means he's uncomfortable in closed places."

Neither spoke for a moment.

"How 'bout we ask him to marry us?" Wilson suggested.

Maggie blinked. "Marry us?"

"Yeah, you like Gordie, don't you?"

"Yes," she admitted. "I like him a lot."

"Well, I think he likes you too, so why don't we just keep him. He don't have no home, 'cept that old tent. I bet he'd like for us to marry him."

"Well, I'd like to think he'd like that, but I don't think he would."

"Why not?"

"I think he's sort of used to living alone. I think he likes it better that way."

"Want me to ask him?"

"No! Under no circumstances are you to ask him that, Wilson."

"Why not? He'd say if he likes us or not. He always answers whatever I ask him. He's real good about that." His face brightened. "I'll even ask him if he wants to marry us, how about that?"

Scooping him off her lap, she hastily stood up. "It's late; you need to be in bed."

Helping him gather his pets, they began to herd the animals back to the dugout.

As they passed Gordie's tent, they noticed his lantern was extinguished.

"Gordie's asleep," Wilson whispered.

"Yes, I see that."

Wilson shot a shrewd glance in her direction, recalling an earlier conversation he'd had with Butch on the playground today. Butch claimed to know everything that went on between a boy and a girl when they got bigger and how babies were made. Boy, he'd be eating soap for a month if Maggie had heard that!

Well, Wilson didn't believe a minute of it.

Gordie wouldn't do anything like that to

Maggie; Maggie wouldn't let him. She'd box his ears good if he even tried.

Just the same, he was gonna ask Gordie about it. Gordie would tell him if there was any truth to it.

Chapter 15

"Bellyache. Bad." Moses stood in front of Gordie's tent early the next morning, sick as a dog.

"All of you?"

The Eskimo nodded. "Bad whiskey." The shady ladies had hung one on last night. Whooped it up too much.

T.G. didn't like the sound of that. A day's delay wouldn't hurt, but he had hoped to wind up the week on a promising note. So far, only enough gold to get them by was coming out of the mine.

"Loaded cart in mine."

"You left a cart in the mine?"

"Yes."

"Can't you bring it out?"

"No bring out today." Moses grabbed her seat. "Go now." Turning, she trekked off, doing the green-apple quick step.

Dumping the wild turkey he'd just shot on the ground, T.G. glanced at the mine. Damn. The women had left a loaded cart in there. If they were

160

too sick to work, that meant he had to go in after it or cause even further delay.

Damn. He broke out in a cold sweat just thinking about it.

"A turkey!" Maggie rejoiced as he deposited the bird on her doorstep a few moments later.

"It's been hanging around the shaft. I thought it would look better on your table."

"I'd say!" Taking the game from him, she held it up for inspection. "He's nice and plump! We'll have him for supper." She looked up, grinning. "I'll even make dumplings."

Gordie smiled, and she noticed his eyes were uncommonly blue this morning. "I'll be looking forward to that, ma'am."

"Not half as much as I will," she teased, enjoying the way he immediately flustered up.

Settling his hat jauntily back on his head, he started off for the mine.

Maggie called after him, "Where're the shady ladies today?"

"Sick."

"All of them?"

"All of them," he confirmed grimly.

Wilson came out of the dugout carrying his dinner pail. When he saw a limp turkey dangling from Maggie's right hand, he frowned.

"Unh-unh," she tsked before he could set up a loud protest. "Turkeys are not put upon this earth as pets. They're meant—for other purposes."

Wilson's eyes flew to Selmore, who was still safely tied to the stoop.

"With the exception of Selmore," she allowed. Leaning forward, she tapped her cheek. "Big kiss."

Grumbling, Wilson gave her the perfunctory peck. With a sympathetic look toward the deceased bird, he stepped off the porch, whispering to Selmore, "I hope it wasn't anybody you knew."

Standing at the entrance to the Hellhole, Gordie tried to see inside. The narrow chamber stretched incessantly down the tight corridor.

Undoubtedly, the cart was sitting at the furthest point of entry.

Kneeling, he lit the lantern, trying to control the tremor in his hand. This was insane. All he had to do was locate the cart and push it out. He wouldn't be in the mine for more than ten minutes.

Straightening, he took off his hat, wiped the sweat from his forehead with his shirtsleeve, and put the hat on again.

Taking a deep breath, he picked up the lantern and entered the mine.

The damp, musty smell assaulted his senses as he hesitated at the entrance. The cart was nowhere in sight.

Edging deeper into the tunnel, he jacked up the lantern wick, flooding the shaft with light. Sweat rolled down his temples even though the temperature was warmer inside the mine than out.

Lantern glare played along the walls exposing shored-up timbers and overhead leakage. Water stood in shallow puddles on the mud floor.

Rounding a corner, Gordie lifted the beam

higher. The familiar tightening in his lungs warned him that in a few minutes he would be struggling for breath. Light flickered off the walls as his leaden feet picked up tempo. Where was that damned cart?

Taking a left fork, he moved through the tunnel, his breathing more strained now.

Rounding another corner, panic nabbed him. The walls closed in and his lungs battled for air. Rationality fought with phobia but, as usual, terror won out.

Whirling, he started to run. Hell with the cart— had to get out—now! Gasping for breath, his left foot tangled with his right and the lantern went flying. Diving headfirst, he managed to trap it inches before it smashed to the floor.

Struggling unevenly back to his feet, he leaned against the wall, sweating in earnest now.

"Heh, heh, heh."

T.G.'s head shot up. "What?"

"Somedays it jest don't pay a man to git outta bed, does it, Buddy Boy?"

Cocking an ear, T.G. listened, hearing nothing but his own ragged breathing.

"Tee, heh, heh, heh."

"Who's there?" Lifting the lantern, T.G.'s eyes searched the darkness. The light danced along the cracks and crevices revealing nothing. Someone snickered—he heard it.

"Snort, snort, snigger, chortle, tee, heh, heh!"

Jerking the light back, Gordie ran it along the

walls more deliberately. "Who's there? You're trespassing on private property!"

"I know—mine."

Nailing the beam directly on the voice, Gordie hit pay dirt. What he saw made his blood run cold.

Perched on a ledge, a man, small of stature and sporting a long, slightly singed white beard, lifted five fingers and waved at him.

Stunned, Gordie's heart hammered. Lowering the lantern, he tried to think. He hadn't had a drop of whiskey in weeks. It had to be his imagination. The damned thing was playing tricks on him!

Waiting a moment, he lifted the light again, moving it back to the perch.

Grinning, the figure on the ledge devilishly wiggled five fingers, waving at him. Smoke rose from his tattered clothing, shrouding the apparition in a smoldering vapor. He cocked his head. "Yo? Hello?"

Lowering the light again, Gordie sweated. He'd lost his mind; claustrophobia had turned to delirium. He was deranged, loco—gone nuts.

"Yes, you see what you see, Buddy Boy. It's me. Shine that light over here. I want to get down and my eyes ain't the best."

As Gordie searched for his voice, the man became impatient, bellowing. "Hey! You deaf? I said shine that light over here!"

The light shot up and over. Grinning, Butte hopped down off the ledge. "Thank ya. That's better."

Aghast, Gordie watched the little old miner walking toward him.

"Butte Fesperman here. How ya doin'?"

Mesmerized, Gordie reached out to shake hands when Butte quickly drew back. "Wouldn't do that if I was you, Buddy Boy." He looked sheepish. "The hand's still a mite hot from the blast." Damn dynamite had ruint him.

Putting his hand at the small of his back, Butte stretched. "Rheumatism kickin' up on me again."

He glanced back to Gordie. "What's tha matter, boy? Cat got your tongue?"

"Who are you?" Gordie whispered. And what was he doing in the mine without a light?

The old man grinned. Putting his hands on his knees, he leaned forward. "Who you think I am?"

When Gordie didn't immediately answer, he leaned closer. "I'll give ya a clue. Boo."

Gordie started to edge backward, speechless now.

"Now, now, Buddy Boy—you ain't scairt of me, are you? Ain't you the one who's been blowin' off 'bout not believing in ghosts? Eh? That was you, wasn't it, Buddy Boy?"

"Butte Fesperman," T.G. murmured, unable to believe his eyes.

Butte bowed modestly. "In the flesh—oops—guess that ain't exactly the truth."

He suddenly straightened. "Say, where's them ugly women today? That one they call Moses? Lord *almighty*! That woman's so ugly, when she was born the doctor slapped her mother!"

T.G. was dumbfounded. "Does Moses know about you?" She hadn't said a word!

"Well now." Butte took off his hat and mindfully scratched his head. "I reckon she does—don't everybody?"

"Then she's seen you?" T.G. was relieved that he wasn't the only one losing his mind.

"Who, Moses?"

"Yes."

"No, she ain't seen me." When he saw T.G. was appalled, he added, "I ain't gonna show myself to nobody, just to you, Buddy Boy."

"My name is not Buddy Boy."

"Oh, I know that, *Gordie*." He put more emphasis on the nickname than T.G. thought necessary. "But that's what I'm gonna call you."

Why *me*, T.G. agonized. He didn't want this responsibility, and he sure didn't need the aggravation!

"Cain't say." Butte hefted himself back onto the ledge and got comfortable. "I haven't showed myself to nary a soul since the accident. Been mean as hell, causing all sorts of trouble with cave-ins and whatnots, but haven't showed myself to nobody." He grinned. "Not until today." A devilish twinkle danced in his eyes. "Now, why do you suppose that is?"

Gordie was powerless to say; he supposed it was just plain bad luck.

"Say, Buddy Boy, you're not breathing so hard. Ya feelin' better?"

T.G. realized his breathing had stabilized. When Butte appeared, the phobia had receded.

"That classtrefabio stuff? What is that?" Butte asked.

"How do you know about that?"

Butte shrugged. "I know everything."

T.G. inched backward, convinced he was imagining the encounter. It wasn't happening. The phobia was doing bizarre things to his mind. There was no ghost. Butte Fesperman had been dead almost thirty-six years.

"You leavin'?"

T.G. refused to answer. If he responded, he acknowledged his insanity. If he kept quiet, there was still hope he could pull out of it. He kept backing round the first corner, one boot behind the other, then another, then another.

Butte's voice pursued him down the corridor. "What's yore hurry? It gets lonely in here."

As T.G. rounded the last corner, he turned and broke into a run.

"I'm not kidding!" Butte shouted as Gordie burst out of the mine, white-faced. "It's depressing as hell in here!"

"There you are! I was worried about you."

Late that afternoon, Gordie glanced up to find Maggie coming toward him. Shoveling another spade of dirt into the sluice box, he continued working.

Pausing beside the cart, she shaded her eyes against the late afternoon sun. "Did you eat dinner?" Around one she had given up on him coming and put everything away.

"I wasn't hungry." Thrusting the shovel back into the cart, he hoisted another spade full into the box. Although it was cool, he was stripped to his waist, his shirt carelessly discarded on a nearby log.

For a moment Maggie could only stare. His body was *gorgeous*. Ridges of taut muscles glistened beneath a thin sheen of sweat as he rotated the shovel from cart to sluice box. His chest, coated in the same fiery mantle that covered his head, was broad, his rib cage brawny and well defined.

Maggie had never seen a half-naked man, but she was certain there could be none more remarkable than this one. For a moment, she wondered what other delights he was hiding from her.

The thought shamelessly intrigued her.

When T.G. felt her eyes on him, he glanced up again.

She continued to stare with an ambiguous smile on her lips. He asked shortly, "Did you want something?"

"I've lost Wilson."

Lowering the shovel, he looked at her. "You've lost Wilson."

She smiled. "Not permanently, but I haven't seen him in a while."

"I'm sure he's around somewhere."

"Have you seen him lately?"

Plunging the shovel back into the dirt, Gordie

went back to work. "He was here for a few minutes after school."

Maggie studied the setting sun with a worried frown. "That was hours ago. It'll be dark soon."

"He'll be along."

"Could you see if you can find him? The turkey's about ready to come out of the oven."

That was the thing about women; they were always interrupting. Whether they meant to or not, they interrupted—and usually at the most inopportune time. What the hell, his entire day had been one solid interruption, so one more wasn't likely to kill him.

"All right. I'll drop what I'm doing and look for Wilson."

Maggie decided to ignore the note of acrimony in his tone. "Thank you. Supper'll be ready soon."

Once he got a taste of her turkey and dumplings, his mood would improve considerably.

As she walked by him she reached over and lightly brushed her fingers across the thick mat of moist, carmine hair covering his chest.

Taken aback, he stepped aside as she continued on her way, that peculiar smile still brightening her face.

Ramming the shovel back into the cart, he marched over to the log and picked up the canteen. Walking to the stream, he knelt down and filled the canister with pure, cold mountain water, his gaze riveted on Maggie's backside as she made her way back up the hill. The touch of her hand backfired through his heated blood like a prairie fire.

Standing up, he pulled out the waistband of his pants and calmly dumped the canister of water down the front.

The icy jolt jerked his thoughts back into perspective, but it was considerably later when his lower district finally cooled down.

Chapter 16

"Wilson!" *Wilson, Wilson, Wilson,* T.G.'s voice echoed back from the mine.

"Wilson!" *Darn that boy's hide. Where is he?*

T.G. had searched everywhere he knew to look, but he'd still come up empty-handed. Wilson had been told a hundred times to stay away from the shaft; T.G. prayed this wasn't the time he'd decided to test his mettle.

Stepping closer to the entrance, T.G. admitted this had been the longest day of his life. Not once, but *twice* in one day, he was being forced into the mine. He wasn't sure he could do it again.

"Wilson!" Silence hung like a pall in the air.

T.G. didn't know why, but he knew the boy was in there. Sixth sense, or simple knowledge that it wasn't his day, sealed it. If anything happened to Wilson, Maggie would be heartbroken. That thought alone made up his mind. Lighting the lantern, he entered the mine.

"Wilson? You in here, son?"

Overhead, timbers creaked as he mechanically

171

put one foot in front of the other. *Butte could arrange for one of his cave-ins,* he thought. Having met the outlandish ghost, he couldn't deny that he was eccentric enough to wreak havoc—*What am I thinking? I didn't meet the ghost! The encounter was a figment of my imagination!*

His footsteps wavered as he listened to the sound of dripping water. *Plink, plink, plink.*

"Wilson, can you hear me?"

Maybe he *wasn't* in here. Premonition had led him astray more than once. Relief flooded him. There was no telling where that boy was—

"In here, Gordie."

T.G.'s heart sank as Wilson's muffled voice reached him. Turning, his eyes searched the jagged crevices. "Wilson?"

"In here, Gordie."

Running the light over the uneven clefts, T.G. tried to see where the voice was coming from. The boy was close. He could hear him clearly.

"Where are you?"

"In here."

Swinging the light around, Gordie checked the passageway jutting to the right. A bat darted up, disappearing between two ragged clefts.

"Wilson, what are you doing in there?" Wherever "there" was.

"Just sittin' here."

T.G. followed the sound, holding the lantern out in front of him. It was here he had encountered Butte earlier.

His eyes warily searched the blackness. "Come out, Wilson. Maggie's waiting supper for us."

"I can't come out, Gordie."

T.G. swore under his breath. He wasn't in the mood for games. The dampness seeped through his coat. His hand trembled as his breathing grew more labored.

"Wilson, get out here! Your sister's looking for you."

"I *can't*, Gordie!"

T.G. swung around and the light pinpointed a small chamber opening.

"Wilson?"

Wilson's voice came from inside the chamber. "Gordie, why do you keep sayin' 'Wilson'?"

"Why don't you stop asking questions and get out here?"

Dropping to his knees, T.G. crawled through water to get to the chamber. He realized why he wasn't overly fond of children. They were too much trouble. Women were interruptions, and children were too much trouble.

"Wilson, how did you get in there?"

"Crawled in, it was easy."

"Well, crawl out. That should be double easy."

"Unh-unh."

"Damn it, Wilson." Poking his head through the chamber opening, T.G. rammed his nose straight into something hairy.

Springing backward, he swiped at his nose, jarred by the putrid smell.

"Gordie?" Wilson called.

"Wilson, what in the *hell* do you have in there with you?"

"A bear."

Swearing, Gordie jumped to his feet, cracking his head on an overhead timber. An ill-tempered snarl split the air, and the hair on the back of his neck stood straight up. Backing warily away from the chamber, he called softly, "Wilson?"

"Gordie?"

"What?"

"Did'ja hear that?"

"What was that?"

"A bear."

A bear! There was a damn *bear* in there! "Wilson, get out!"

"I can't; the bear's sitting in front of the door."

T.G. tried to think. *Wilson was trapped in a chamber with a bear. What kind of bear? Big? Small? Did it matter? It was a* bear.

A bear, a boy, a tight chamber. Oh, hell. What a day.

"Wilson, listen. Now don't panic." He glanced around for something to distract the animal. How did a bear get in there? The opening was barely big enough for a child to squeeze through.

"Wilson?"

"Yeah?"

"Did you hear what I said?"

"Yeah, don't panic."

"Yes, stay calm."

"I have ta go to the outhouse. I have ta go bad."

"Oh, brother—you'll have to hold it—do you know anything about bears?"

"No, sir. We lived in England—I don't think they have bears over there. Leastways, none I've ever seen—but they might, 'cause I probably haven't seen everything in England yet."

"What's the bear look like?"

"Like he's real mean."

Black, cinnamon? Mama bear, cub—Gordie knew his luck wouldn't let it be a cub.

"What color is he?"

"Mmm, well, kind of black—no, maybe reddish brown—no, well, I don't know. My glasses are all fogged up."

"Hold on, Wilson, I'm going to have to find a way to get the bear out of there."

Wilson's voice came back urgently. "You'd better hurry, Gordie, 'cause I have ta go to the bathroom real bad!"

T.G. ran out of the shaft, returning a few minutes later carrying a pickax.

"Wilson?"

"Are you hurrying? I gotta go *bad*."

"I'm hurrying. Now listen. Where's the bear now?"

"Same place. Sitting in front of the door."

"He's just sitting there?"

"Yeah, looking at me."

T.G.'s eyes searched the cramped area, trying to think of a way to lure the bear out of the chamber. He needed bait.

"Wilson?"

"Yeah?"

"I'm going back to the dugout. Don't move—I mean it—*don't* move a muscle until I get back!"

"Gordie! I have ta go!"

"I understand, but I can't help you at the moment. Don't move. Don't do anything to antagonize the bear. Understand?"

"I have ta *go*, Gordie, *real* bad!"

"I'll be back in five minutes, Wilson. Five minutes." Whirling, T.G. sprang into action.

Racing back through the shaft, he dashed to the dugout. Maggie glanced up, smiling, as he blasted through the front door.

"Hi. The turkey turned out beautifully—" She gasped as he jerked the bird off the platter and sprinted off.

"No time to explain!" he shouted as he disappeared out the door again.

"T.G. Manning! Have you lost your mind?" The beautiful turkey she had labored over for hours—gone!

Stamping her foot, she marched to the door and slammed it behind him. Beans for supper *again*.

Dashing back to the mine, Gordie tore down the narrow passageway, juggling the hot turkey with both hands.

"Wilson!"

He could hear crying coming from the chamber now.

"Wilson!" T.G. shouted, panic-stricken. "What's wrong?"

The bear let out another death-defying roar that ricocheted off the walls.

"Wilson!"

"What?"

"Are you hurt?"

The sobbing increased, more intense now.

"Are you *hurt*?" Had the bear attacked him? Sweat beaded T.G.'s forehead, rolling down his armpits now.

Wilson mumbled something he couldn't make out and cried harder.

Damn! Gordie glanced around helplessly. Ghosts, bossy women, and bawling kids threatening to mess their pants. He couldn't take much more.

Desperate now, he tore into the meat, laying a trail of turkey. If the bear took the bait it would lead him out of the mine.

"Better spread it thick, Buddy Boy. That's a *big* bear in there. *Tee, hee, hee, hee.*"

T.G. closed his eyes, swearing. Not again.

Looking up, he found Butte sitting on an overhead ledge, swinging his stubby legs in a carefree manner. Lifting his hand, Butte wiggled five fingers, waving at him.

Ignoring him, T.G. tore off a drumstick and crawled through the water to the chamber entrance.

"Okay, Wilson, I'm back. Everything's going to be all right—where's the bear now?"

"Sittin'—*sniff, sniff*—in—*sniff*—front of the door."

"Okay, I'm going to try and lure him out."

"He won't come out," Butte predicted. "You'll have ta have a bigger turkey than that."

"He'll come out."

"No, he won't."

"Yes, he will."

"Who you talkin' to, Gordie?"

"Bet ya he won't."

"Just *shut up*! Okay?"

"Okay," Wilson called back, pained.

Placing his index and middle finger in the center of his tongue, Gordie whistled.

The bear jumped, rearing to his hind legs.

Inside the chamber, Wilson shrank back in wide-eyed horror. The bear threw a huge shadow over the boy, saliva dripping from its jaws.

Whistling loudly, Gordie beat on the chamber, trying to get the bear out.

"Ain't no use. I put him in there, and he ain't coming out," Butte taunted. He got to his feet, dancing a lighthearted jig, having more fun than he'd had in ages.

T.G. thought his exhibition disgusting. "You'd do that to a child? That's pretty low, isn't it?"

"Shore! I'm bad!"

T.G. turned away. "You're more than bad, you're rotten to the core!"

"I'm sorry, Gordie!" Wilson sobbed harder. T.G. was talkin' mean to him—real mean.

Roaring, the bear whirled, dropping back to all fours as he got a whiff of the turkey.

Butte jumped up and down, having a whale of a time at T.G.'s expense.

"Here you go, boy. Come and get it." Gordie fanned the drumstick aroma into the chamber.

Growling, the bear sniffed, slapping out with his paw.

"Right here, boy." Shoving the meat into the hole, Gordie fanned it around, scenting the air.

"Right here, boy," Butte mimicked, clapping his hands with glee. "He's gonna tear yore head off, Buddy Boy! Yore gonna be blowing your nose out yore ear!"

The bear slapped out again, catching the back of Gordie's hand with its claws. Blood spurted.

Quickly retracting the decoy, Gordie held the meat on the ground within the bear's reach.

Roaring again, the bear sniffed around the chamber entrance, trying to capture the scent.

"That's it, boy—come and get it," Gordie coaxed.

"That's it, boy," Butte heckled. "Come and eat Gordie up!"

"Shut up!" T.G. blazed, sick of his interference.

"I didn't say anything, Gordie, honest!" Wilson agonized from the chamber. He was being as quiet as a church mouse!

"See what you're doing," T.G. snapped. "The kid thinks I'm talking to him!"

"I don't care."

Scrunching backward, Wilson watched as the bear suddenly dropped on his belly, trying to tunnel his way to the delectable smell.

"He's coming out, Gordie!"

"Better run, Buddy Boy. The bear's comin' after ya! *Heh, heh, heh.*"

Gordie waved the drumstick, keeping it within easy smelling distance.

The bear could barely maneuver his thick body through the tight opening. Gradually his head emerged, then his shoulders.

As the animal's back legs slid free, Gordie tossed the drumstick into the passageway and jumped into a crevice, nearly tripping over Butte.

Butte bristled. "Hey! Watch it thar, Buddy Boy! You caught my bunion!"

The bear quickly located the meat, devouring it. Lifting his head, he roared, his nose sniffing the air.

Loping forward, he found another chunk of meat, gobbled it down, and loped on. Gordie watched, hoping the bear's appetite held.

As the bear's fleshy backside disappeared down the corridor, T.G. quickly dropped back to his knees and crawled into the small cavern.

Wilson was huddled in the corner, crying.

"It's okay, Wilson. He's gone."

Lunging into Gordie's arms, Wilson clung to his neck. His frail body trembled as Gordie held him tightly. "It's all right, son. You're safe now."

"Bunch of ninnies," Butte sneered, reclining on a ledge above Wilson. "Boy, that was fun. Shame it had to end so fast."

When the boy's terror subsided, Gordie removed Wilson's glasses and wiped the dirt off them.

Hooking the wire rims back around his ears, he positioned them back on his nose.

"Gordie."

"Yeah?"

"I dirtied my britches." Wilson's face burned with shame as he waited for the recriminations. He was eight years old. Eight-year-olds didn't dirty their pants. And they didn't cry. But he'd done both.

But Gordie didn't say anything bad. He didn't even act like anything was wrong. He just said, "Come on, let's get you cleaned up."

Wilson stood on one foot while Gordie helped him out of his underwear. They pitched the soiled article into the corner, pretending to ignore the rancid smell.

"*Shew-eee!*" Butte held his nose, irritably fanning the air.

"How did you find this chamber, Wilson?"

Butte snickered. "He didn't, I found it for him."

"I was talking to Wilson." T.G. reminded him sharply.

Wilson looked up. "I hear you, Gordie."

"I wasn't talking to you, Wilson."

"Oh." He looked about to cry again.

"Yeah, kid, he was talking to me, only you can't hear or see me." Butte snickered. "Nobody but Gordie can see me—ain't that a cryin' shame?"

T.G. was losing patience. "Shut up—and keep your nose out of my business."

"Okay," Wilson said.

T.G. turned back to Wilson. "Now, why did you

crawl in here? I've told you repeatedly to stay out of the mine."

"I was lookin' for gold for Maggie. Guess that was kinda stupid, huh?"

"No, it wasn't stupid, but it was dangerous. I don't want you in here alone."

"I won't do it again if you don't want me to."

"Gordie, Gordie, Gordie. *He* wasn't alone. I was with him," Butte said.

"Shut up."

Wilson blinked back tears. "Okay—hey, look, your hand's bleeding, Gordie!"

"It's okay—the bear just grazed it a little."

Wilson looked at him imploringly. "Maggie needs the gold real bad—that's the only reason I was lookin'," he explained. "I won't do it again if you don't want me to."

"I don't want you to ever do it again. If you want to look for gold, you come and get me and we'll look together."

"Okay."

"It's dangerous in here—you could get hurt."

"Okay, I don't mind. I'll come and get you."

"It's for your own good, you know."

"Yeah, I know. I'll come and get you next time. I don't mind."

"Other leg—*other* leg!"

"Okay." Wilson obediently hiked his other leg.

"We don't have ta say anything to Maggie about this, do we?" Wilson's teeth chattered as Gordie helped him get back into his britches.

"I can't imagine why she'd want to know."

Wilson peered up at him, and Gordie swore he was getting a soft spot for the kid. He'd done well under the circumstances.

"Honest? You mean it can be sort of like our secret? Like we were best friends or something?"

Gordie fastened the top button on the boy's britches, smiling. "Yeah, something like that."

Later, as Wilson emerged from the chamber, he paused to wait for Gordie.

T.G. crawled out behind him, keeping a close eye out for the bear.

As he got to his feet, he ruffled Wilson's hair. "Can you imagine what would have happened if one of the women had run into that bear?"

Wilson laughed. They'd be upset, all right. Screaming and carrying on! *He* hadn't screamed. Color flooded his face when he thought of what he had done. *Least* he hadn't screamed.

Getting to his feet, Gordie knocked the mud off his knees. "I'm hungry. How about you?"

"Yeah, starving!"

"Let's see if we can sweet-talk that pretty sister of yours out of some dumplings."

"Yeah, and some turkey!" Wilson had smelled it cooking all day!

Gordie patted his head. "No, just dumplings." He'd have to break it to him gently about the turkey.

Wilson slipped his hand into T.G.'s, and the two walked out of the mine together. "Say, Gordie, I 'bout forgot."

"What's that, Wilson?"

"Maggie wants me to ask you something."

"Oh? What's that?"

"She wants to know if you'll marry her."

Chapter 17

"Marry me?" Maggie flushed a deep scarlet. "Did he *say* that?"

T.G. casually ladled beans into individual tin bowls. "I just wondered if you had a specific date in mind?"

Maggie might have been mortified at Wilson's audacity if she hadn't recognized the teasing note in T.G.'s voice. "I don't know what's gotten into that child!"

Carrying the bowls to the table, T.G. stayed neutral. "Naturally, I warned him I couldn't do anything right away." He looked up, his smile bordering on devilish now. "Not until more gold was coming out of the mine."

Blushing to her roots, Maggie poured coffee, longing for a hole to crawl into. She couldn't believe Wilson had repeated their conversation when she had specifically warned him not to!

Taking their seats at the table, they bowed their heads, and Maggie asked the blessing.

Reaching for the bowl of potatoes, T.G. spooned

185

a helping onto his plate. "Where was Wilson going
in such a hurry?"

"When he found out there wasn't any turkey, he
ate three biscuits, gulped down a glass of milk, and
ran out to assure Selmore his kinfolk did not die in
vain."

T.G. chuckled, recalling the bear's unexpected
feast. "He earned my respect today. Most kids
would have panicked faced with the situation."

Resting her elbows on the table, Maggie laced
her fingers together and gazed at him. Each day
brought a new awareness of him. "Thank you."

"For distracting the bear?" He shrugged. "Anyone would have done the same."

"No, for being you."

"Thanks." Avoiding her gaze, he handed her the
bowl of potatoes. "Can't say I've heard that recently."

Setting the bowl aside, she repeated, "Then
I'll say it again. Thank you for being you, T.G.
Why do you find it so hard to accept a compli-
ment?"

Having strong misgivings about the subject, he
slathered butter on a piece of bread. "You have a
lot to learn about men."

"Such as?"

"Such as, men don't want compliments."

Her brows lifted. "They don't?"

"This one doesn't."

"Nonsense. Everybody likes compliments." She
didn't know one person who didn't.

"I don't." He took a bite of beans.

"Really down on yourself, huh?" Picking up the bowl of potatoes, she spooned a helping onto her plate.

"I'm not down on myself, and I wish you would quit implying that I am." From the moment they'd met she had accused him of indifference. What right did she have to accuse him of anything? He was doing his job, minding his own business. That should be enough for anyone.

"Yes, you are."

"No, I'm not."

"Yes, you are."

Lowering his fork, he leveled his eyes at her.

Edging forward in her chair, she stared right back. "You are."

Jamming his fork into the potatoes, he took another bite.

She wasn't going to let him avoid the subject this time. He was quite proficient at hiding his feelings. "Tell me why you don't like yourself."

"Eat your supper."

"I'm eating." She slid a bite of potatoes into her mouth, gazing back at him. She was in a feisty mood tonight. "I know," she ventured. "You hate yourself because of your red hair."

Glancing up, he caught her grinning.

"That's it, isn't it? Rather be dead than red on the head."

Shaking his head at her nonsense, he reached for a second slice of bread.

"Yes, you hate your red hair. That's clearly the

reason you're so down on yourself." She picked up her cup and took a sip of coffee. "You're downright embarrassed because of it. No one in your family, other than old fat Aunt Fanny, has red hair, and you had to take after her." She smothered a giggle, loving the way she could frustrate him so easily.

Determined to resist her challenge, T.G. patiently spread butter over his bread, not appearing the least frustrated. "I don't have an old fat Aunt Fanny. My mother had red hair. My sister Jenny has red hair. And the color of *my* hair has nothing to do with my character. It so happens I like red hair."

"Mmmm, me too," she mused. "My father had red hair."

His features sobered. "Wilson told me about your mother and father."

Maggie nodded. "They were killed in a train derailment. They were on a holiday at the time." She met his eyes across the table. "What about your parents?"

She knew so little about the man she loved. And she did love Gordie Manning. Each day brought a clearer—if not understanding, then complete acceptance, of that love. He didn't love her—goodness, he was terrified of her, but he would love her someday—he would someday.

"Mother's dead. Pop's alive."

"Any brothers and sisters other than Jenny with the red hair?"

"No, only Jenny. She's married, with children of her own."

"Living where?"

"Phoenix."

"Phoenix?" She racked her brain trying to recall American geography. "Where is Phoenix?"

"In Arizona."

"You lived in Arizona?" Wasn't that the place with all the cactus?

"I lived in Phoenix most of my life. I went away to college for a few years, but eventually I went back there."

She grinned. "*You* went to college?"

"*I* went to college."

The conversation was becoming personal again, and he changed it. "There's a dance in camp tonight."

"Really?" Her pulse leapt with anticipation. Was he asking her to go? She would, of course. She would wear her blue dress, and do her hair in a French twist. For him, she would even dab on a hint of the lavender cologne Gwendolyn had given her for Christmas.

"You should go," he observed. "A young lady like you needs a social life."

"I'm not busy tonight," she offered, just waiting for him to ask.

When he didn't take the hint, she tried to help. "Where is the dance?"

He frowned. "Bonnie Blue's, I think."

"Bonnie Blue's?" Her smile faded. "Isn't that where the hurdy-gurdy girls are?" Maggie had never personally met a hurdy-gurdy girl, but she'd heard the other women talking about them. The women danced for a living at Bonnie Blue's. One dollar in gold per dance, twelve dollars for a bottle of champagne, twenty-five for whiskey, and fifty cents for a single drink.

"There are no hurdy-gurdy women at Bonnie's on Saturday nights. You can go without fearing recriminations from the camp biddies."

Toying with her food, she asked casually, "Do you go to Bonnie's often?"

"Not often. Would you pass the salt?"

She absently handed him the shaker. "So the dances are respectable?"

"As far as I know they are."

Maggie wondered. She had seen men dancing with each other in Silver Plume. She had also heard stories about Hoodee Doo men and how they made such a spectacle dancing with one another, half drunk and shamelessly disorderly during their Saturday night forays.

But it didn't matter. As long as T.G. was there to protect her, she wouldn't worry.

He handed the salt shaker back. "I'll watch Wilson if you like."

She glanced up. "What?"

"I'm not doing anything, I'll watch Wilson for you." When she still didn't seem to understand, he added, "While you go to the dance."

Shoving back from the table, she stood up, her hackles rising. "You're not going?"

"Me?" He laughed. "I hate to dance." Why would she think *he* liked to dance?

"Then why did you *ask* me to go?"

"I didn't *ask* you to go; I merely said you should go."

"Oh, really?"

He looked back mulishly. "Really."

Picking up the bowl of potatoes, she heaved its contents at him. Potatoes and onions hit him, sending him reeling backward on the stool.

Marching to the door, she jerked it open and slammed it shut on her way out.

Parting greasy onions out of his eyes, he stared after her, stunned.

A minute or two passed before the door opened again, and Maggie stuck her head around the corner. "You're not even coming after me?"

He brushed potatoes off the front of his shirt. "Hell, no."

Before he could say why he wasn't, she slammed the door in his face again.

When a knock came at the door that evening, Maggie was already in her nightgown.

"Want me to let Gordie in?" Wilson asked.

"Yes, and if wants to talk to me, tell him I'm busy."

Wilson's eyes appraised the cramped quarters. "Won't he know I'm lying?"

Crawling into her cot, Maggie jerked the blanket over her head.

Setting Jellybean aside, Wilson went to open the door.

"Maggie's busy," he relayed.

Looking over the boy's shoulder, Gordie's eyes traveled to the conspicuous hump in the middle of the bed. "I want to talk to her."

"She's busy," Wilson repeated.

"Doing what?"

Wilson really wished they wouldn't include him in their quarrels. His eyes gestured toward the bed. "She's real busy, Gordie. She can't talk right now."

Stepping around the boy, Gordie closed the door, holding his index finger to his lips. Tiptoeing to the bed, he lifted the cover and looked underneath.

Maggie stared up at him.

"Hello."

"Hello," she murmured, embarrassed he'd caught her fibbing.

"I hate to bother you, but the dance starts at eight. It's seven-thirty now, and it's more than a thirty minute walk to Bonnie Blue's."

"The dance?" she asked meekly.

T.G.'s eyes ran lazily over her. As a result, goose bumps raced up her spine. "The dance we talked about earlier today."

"Oh . . . that dance."

"Are you going to wear what you have on, or would you like to change?"

"Oh . . . I'll change, thank you." She noticed he

was dressed well. Clean denims, green-and-black checked flannel shirt.

"You look nice."

"I know. And you'd better appreciate the effort. Have you taken a bath in the stream lately?"

Shaking her head, she wondered *why* he had. The water was pure ice!

"Invigorating, I can assure you."

"You took a bath in the stream just for me?"

"Just for you," he confirmed.

"It'll only take me a minute to dress."

Nodding, he dropped the cover back into place. "Wilson, tell your sister I'll wait outside."

"What about me?"

"Guess you'd better get your dancing shoes on. We're going dancing."

"Oh, boy!" Wilson dropped Jellybean and ran to get ready.

A full moon hung overhead as they walked to the dance. Wilson walked up ahead, Gordie and Maggie lagged behind.

"You look mighty fetching tonight," T.G. told Maggie when she seemed unusually quiet.

"I feel very foolish about throwing those potatoes at you today."

"Why? I like potatoes."

Grinning shyly, she refused to look at him. "To eat, though, not to wear."

"Well, I was being an ass. I hope you'll forgive me."

Her smile widened. "You're forgiven."

The dance had already begun when they arrived.

The chandeliers above the dance hall burned brightly.

Wilson spotted a few of his classmates sitting together on the sidelines and reluctantly went to join them.

Offering Maggie his arm, T.G. led her to the dance floor where the musicians were just beginning a new round.

Bowing to one another, Maggie took Gordie's hand, and he twirled her gracefully around, then they moved across the room, passing each other twice before joining the other couples in a square.

Two forward four, one lady changes, then the couple crosses over, turning around, sashaying sideways. The men back up and the ladies dittod; side couple to the right, to the left, side couple goes the other way.

Side couple turn their ladies, ladies turn side couples, gentlemen turn side couples, all hands round, back again.

Breathless, Maggie collapsed into Gordie's arms, laughing as the dance ended. They danced the following five dances in a row, not even stopping for a cup of punch.

During the evening, they changed partners often. Maggie was surprised by the little tug of resentment she felt when she saw T.G. dancing with other women. And by the way he kept a close eye on her while she was in other men's arms, she knew he didn't like that either. She swelled with pride when she realized that he was jealous.

The last dance of the evening was a waltz. Several men approached Maggie, asking her if she would do them the honor of dancing the last dance with them. She refused graciously, waiting for T.G. As he approached, she didn't wait for him to ask. She quickly went into his arms without giving the other women a chance.

"Hello, belle of the ball," he teased, fondly smiling down at her. The fabric of his shirt made his eyes look as blue as a field of cornflowers.

"Thank you for bringing me tonight." She gazed up at him, her cheeks flushed, her eyes sparkling. "I've had a wonderful time."

"Wilson seems to be enjoying himself." Twice Gordie had seen him dancing with his friend Summer.

Gliding across the floor, Maggie realized that T.G. was an excellent dancer. He was full of surprises.

"Gordie Manning, you're good! Do you dance often?"

He smiled. "Only when I have to."

She feigned amazement. "Other women have thrown potatoes in your face?"

"I'm afraid they've thrown more than potatoes," he confessed, "but none have had your charming persuasion."

Wrinkling her nose, she made a face. "You smooth talker."

Laughing, he whirled her around the floor, holding her tightly. Maggie wished it could be this way between them forever. As the night progressed, the tempo began to change. The music slowed.

"I love this song," she confessed. "Do you know it?"

"I've heard it."

Softly, she began to sing "Jeanie with the Light Brown Hair," only she substituted Gordie for Jeanie, and red for light brown hair. Her eyes locked with his as they waltzed slowly around the floor.

In soft, whispery tones, she sang the words, for his ears only, in a voice as pure and sweet as a nightingale. Others around them faded away, and they were in a world of their own.

That moment, something changed between them; neither would ever be sure what, but something changed. They both were aware of it.

When he walked her to her door later, he said good-night, then turned in the direction of his tent.

Suddenly, he turned around. "Maggie?"

She looked up expectantly. "Yes?"

"I was wondering . . ." He hesitated briefly.

"Yes?"

"If it wouldn't offend you, I'd like to kiss you good-night."

There, he'd said it. She could laugh in his face and tell him to go home, but at least he'd said it. He had thought of little else but kissing her the entire evening.

"It wouldn't offend me," she returned softly.
"Actually, I've been hoping you would."

"You were?" Her response took him by surprise.

She nodded, smiling.

They stood for a moment, neither one certain of what to do next.

"Should I come to you?" she asked hesitantly.

"Oh ... no, of course not. I'll come to you."
Stepping back up on the stoop, he tried to position himself properly for their first kiss.

It was so damn awkward! His lips felt as big as rubber balls. He wasn't accustomed to asking a woman for a kiss, much less trying to be skillful about performing it.

With darting, chickenlike neck gestures, they hemmed and hawed around a few minutes, struggling to come to a meeting of the lips.

"Here ... turn your face this way ..."

"Sorry ... like this ... ?"

"A little to the left ..."

"Left ... ?"

"Too far ... back a little ..."

"Sorry ... this way ... ?"

"No, the other ..."

When it finally happened, Maggie felt a stab of disappointment. It wasn't much. Nothing at all like in her romantic novels.

After a few more unsatisfactory thrusts, T.G. finally aborted the attempt, realizing he was just too damn uneasy to make it worth her while.

"Well, see you in the morning," he murmured.

"Yes." She smiled, trying to hide her frustration. Was it her? Surely he could do better than *that*. "See you in the morning."

As T.G. walked off, he realized that no matter how lousy the kiss had been, he was still aroused. To a fevered pitch—hot as a pistol, loaded for bear, if he wanted to get crude about it.

Hot as a pistol. For Maggie Fletcher.

Chapter 18

Moderation was now a thing of the past. T.G. drove the shady ladies with a passion, working them long after the sun went down over the mountaintop.

Only a minimal amount of gold was being mined, but T.G. knew there was more, much more, buried deep within that black, abysmal creation called the Hellhole. Otherwise, Butte Fesperman wouldn't be so dead set on defending it.

On several occasions, T.G. was tempted to tell Maggie about his encounters with Butte, but stubborn pride always stopped him. He would have trouble buying the story if she were the one who had encountered the ghost, and she had no reason to believe him. Butte hadn't shown himself to anyone but T.G., and wasn't likely to. The less Maggie knew about the ghost, the better.

Yet Butte supplied daily interruptions. T.G. was glad the shady ladies weren't superstitious. Unexpected floods, unexplainable fires, collapsing timbers, strange noises, and obnoxious belching sounds occurred in the mine on a routine basis.

But T.G. was as determined as Butte. If the mother lode was in the Hellhole, he was going to find it. He had taken the job to save his own neck, now he was stubbornly determined to save Maggie's.

Moses approached him late Monday afternoon, out of breath. "Man at assay office say no can weigh gold for two weeks."

"Tell him we have to have it sooner."

"Told him. He say no."

T.G. paused, resting on the handle of his shovel. There wasn't another assay office around for thirty miles. Consequently, the one in Hoodee Doo was running weeks behind.

Lifting his hat, he wiped the sweat off his forehead. If he had a choice, he'd do business elsewhere. Sage Whitaker was as ill-tempered as they come. Miners were having to wait weeks to get their ore assessed, but T.G. couldn't wait weeks.

Smiling, T.G. winked at the sober-faced Eskimo, knowing she could talk a man out of his hide if she were inclined to do so. "Why don't you see if you can't sweet-talk Sage into cutting us a little slack?"

Moses returned his look stoically. "Diplomacy?"

He hadn't realized she knew the expression. Her English was broken at best.

"You know what diplomacy means?"

"Be nice until I find big rock."

He grinned. "Unless we can find another assayer, we're going to have to get along with Sage."

Moses trekked off to see what she could do about the situation.

Tossing a spade full of dirt into the sluice box, T.G. chuckled, wondering what sort of man would take Moses on. Most miners were so hungry for female companionship they'd marry anything in a skirt, but Moses would be a handful—

"Not for me, Buddy Boy. I'd take her on in a minute." Butte materialized, arms scissored behind his head, lazily reclining on the side of the cart.

"Do you know my every thought?" T.G. asked crossly.

"Yep. Downright unnervin', ain't it? Especially in view of what you've been thinking about that Fletcher woman lately."

T.G. was getting used to Butte's observations and sudden visits. They were daily now, and annoying.

"Thought you said Moses was ugly."

"Oh, she is. Ugly. But she's got possibilities," Butte allowed. "Winters get mighty nippy up here. That woman could provide some powerful bulk to a man in the dead of January." His hand flew over his mouth apologetically. "Did I say dead? Shut my mouth. Long 'bout January," he amended, still finding death a delicate subject.

T.G. shook his head in disbelief. Butte had time on his hands—a lot of it, and T.G. was his boredom target.

"You ever been in love, Buddy Boy?"

"Might have." T.G. had given up hoping Butte

was a figment of his imagination. He was real, excessively talkative, and a royal pain in the behind.

"Now, don't try to tell me you haven't, 'cause I know you have. Her name was Mary Porter, and she ended up marrying a boy by the name of Pete Wiler."

"Well, guess that saves me the trouble of telling you."

"Mary took your leavin' real hard at the time, but, actually, it was the best thing that ever happened to her. Take my word for it, Buddy Boy. She wasn't for you. Not enough fire in the ole boiler for your taste."

Taking his shovel, T.G. moved on downstream.

Butte tagged along. "Some other little gal got yore heart now, heh?"

"Not that I'm aware of."

"Liar."

"I said, not that I'm aware of."

"And I said, liar."

"Okay, so you tell me who has my heart now." T.G. felt like a fool even discussing the subject.

"That little gal with the fanny you find so fascinatin'."

T.G. bristled. "Have you ever thought about minding your own business?"

"Once, but decided there's no future in it." Trailing behind Gordie, Butte thought about the Fletcher woman. "Cute little bugger," he mused. "Shame she got mixed up in this hellhole of a mine." He laughed at his little play on words.

The woman never complained, even when the

going got tough. So far, she'd weathered loneliness, isolation, bitter cold, and powerful homesickness and still held firm to the belief that she could give her brother a better life here in Colorado. Had to admire a little gal with that kind of spunk.

"She deserves better," T.G. agreed.

"Who?" Butte baited. "Go ahead, say her name. You ain't got no secrets from me."

T.G. refused to be drawn back into the conversation.

"Sweet on her, are you?"

"No," T.G. denied.

"Are too."

"No, I'm not."

"Big liar."

"I admire her," Gordie conceded. "That doesn't make me sweet on her." She wasn't like most women. She accepted people for what they were, and with the exception of flinging a bowl of potatoes in his face, she was usually even-tempered.

"She throwed those potatoes in your face because she wanted you to take her to that dance Saturday night."

T.G. glanced up. "That's why she threw the potatoes?"

"You ain't got that figured out yet? Lord o'mighty. Where's yore brain, boy?"

Gordie rammed the shovel into a pile of dirt. "Why did I ever mention the dance in the first place? Women get upset over the damnedest things!"

"She had a right to get upset. She thought you was askin' her to the dance."

"Well, I wasn't. I merely mentioned there was one, and she should think about going."

"No, you shoulda never mentioned it to her if you had no intention of taking her."

T.G. grunted. "Well, hell, I *did* take her!"

"And had a dang good time, too, didn't ya?"

"I had a good time."

"But?"

"The last thing she needs is a man like me in her life."

"Cain't agree. You ain't no blue-ribbon prize, I'll grant you, but she could do worse."

"Look, do you mind if we just drop the subject?"

"No, I don't care." Didn't make him any difference.

But pretty soon he was heckling again. "Like to hitch up with her, wouldn't ya?"

T.G. didn't bother to answer. He'd learned the less he said, the quicker Butte would tire of badgering him and disappear.

"Oh, you'd like to all right, but you've got this idea you're not good enough for her."

"You talk too much, Fesperman."

"You ain't so bad," Butte assured T.G. Fact was, Butte was beginning to like him. Course, he didn't have much choice. They were stuck with one another. "You ain't necessarily anyone I'd choose for my daughter, but you've been behavin' yoreself lately.

"Quit the bottle, haven't you?"

"You tell me."

"You have—oh, you want to cave in ever now and then, but you haven't yet."

"That doesn't mean I won't."

"And you've never been one to prostitute yourself with women—cain't say as how I see the point, but reckon it's your life," Butte conceded.

Plunging the spade back into a cart, T.G. wondered exactly how much the old coot knew about him.

"Everything."

T.G. glanced up.

"I know everything about you. That's what you're thinking: 'How much does the old coot know about me?' The answer is, everything. Ain't that the shits?"

T.G. couldn't agree more.

"Yeah. Cain't do anything about yore thoughts, but I can shore read them."

"Then you should know that I don't like you, or anyone else, butting into my business."

"I know *that*," Butte chided as if he were dealing with some snotty kid. "I'm jest tryin' to tell you, you ain't as bad as you think."

"No." T.G.'s laugh was filled with irony. "I'm the epitome of success."

"Shoot, no, you ain't that neither, but you've had a run of bad luck. So what? You want to talk bad luck?" Butte could tell him a thing or two about bad luck. He'd invented it.

"I was sixty-two years old when I blowed myself up. *Sixty-two*, and not a penny to my name, but I ain't never considered myself worthless. Why, I'd worked one hopeless claim after the other—seen the elephant a hundred times, but always had the gumption to keep going. Didn't have a pot to pee in, or a window to throw it out of, but Butte Fesperman give up? Not on your life. Drank too much, yes, messed with the women too much, yes, got discouraged, yes, complained a lot, hell yes, but give up? Never entered my mind. I've lived through winters so cold I've seen horses froze solid standing up, and the horns on cattle freeze and burst off from the pith. I suffered through summers so hot you'd swear you was in hell. I've witnessed fires sweep entire towns and lay them out in ashes. I've seen grown men cry when everything they'd worked for went up in a sheet of flames.

"Hell, Buddy Boy, gettin' what you want out of life takes a powerful lot of effort. Nothin' worth havin' ever comes easy. Jest 'cause you left your sister to take care of yore father, deserted that little gal back in Phoenix, sunk everything you owned into a mine you found out you couldn't work 'cause of that phobia thing, why, that's sissy stuff. Stop beatin' yourself up. If that's all life's got to throw your way, consider yourself lucky."

T.G. listened quietly, his eyes turning to the top of the mountain. "That's the point, Butte. What kind of man gives up that easy?"

Butte scoffed. "Too hard on yourself. Ain't dead yet, are you? Never met a man who didn't have somethin' to learn, and wasn't the better for learnin' it."

T.G. would be thirty come spring. Thirty, flat broke, with the future of a salmon spawning upstream. He had nothing to offer a woman like Maggie. She was intelligent and pretty. She could have her pick of eligible suitors. What would she want with a broken-spirited miner like him?

"Well, look at it this way: you were decent enough to help her," Butte reminded him. "You cain't be all bad."

T.G. laughed caustically. "She didn't have a whole lot of choices, now did she? There wasn't anywhere else for her to turn as I see it."

Butte dipped his hands in the stream, enjoying the mild weather. Wouldn't be many more days like this one. Winter would set in, and deep snow would blanket the ground. It was a shame, actually. The Fletcher woman wouldn't be able to hold out until spring. She and the boy would be forced to return to England before the creamy white flowers burst forth from the dagger-sharp leaves of yucca plants.

"You sell yourself too short, Buddy Boy. Now take my gold—which you won't—but for right now, we'll pretend you will. You think you're going to find that gold, don't you?"

"I'll sure be doing my damnedest."

"Won't find it."

"I'll keep looking."

"You looking for it for Maggie's sake, or do you want it to save your hide from Mooney?"

"You tell me."

"Well, at first it was the latter, but now you're tiltin' more to the former."

"That just goes to prove you don't know everything."

Smiling, Butte gradually began to fade. "You still got a powerful lot to learn about women, Buddy Boy."

"Yeah," T.G. conceded. "But not from you."

Two nights later, Gordie knocked on Maggie's door. Unhooking the latch, she opened it, surprised to see T.G. up so late. She supposed he'd been asleep for hours.

"Did I wake you?" he whispered.

"No, I can't sleep." Opening the door wider, she invited him in. His eyes unwillingly sought the soft light filtering through her diaphanous nightgown. Flashes of lightning lit his face in quick successive portraits.

"Is it too late?"

"No," she whispered. "I'm grateful for the company."

Gordie stepped inside the dugout, closing the door quietly behind him. Wilson was asleep on his pallet before the fire, his arm gently curved around a kitten.

Moving to the fire, Maggie slid the coffeepot over the flame. Her hair was loose tonight, a dark auburn cloud swinging below her waist. Feeling his body respond, T.G. turned away, deliberately averting his attention.

"What are you doing up so late?" she whispered.

"I couldn't sleep either."

Seating herself at the table, she gazed at him. "Is something bothering you?"

Oh, yes. Something was bothering him, all right. He could feel its firm ridge pressing tightly between his thighs. Her breasts, small and firm, captured his eyes. The agony in his groin formed a tight, painful throb.

"Maggie, I've seen Butte Fesperman." He couldn't keep it from her any longer. Butte was getting reckless. Today, he'd caused two minor cave-ins, one trapping the shady ladies for over two hours before T.G. could dig them out. Moses was furious. She and the other women were getting tired of the hassles.

Maggie's mouth dropped open. "You've seen the ghost?"

"For days now," he confirmed. He watched her face for signs of belief. "I should have told you sooner, but I wasn't sure I believed it myself."

"But now you do?"

"I know it must sound crazy, but the ghost of Butte Fesperman lives in the mine—and outside. He roams wherever he wants, within a reasonable distance."

Maggie stood up, returning to the fire. Pouring two cups of coffee, she inquired softly, "And you believe you've talked to him?"

"*Believe?* No I don't *believe* I've talked him. I have talked to him. Every day. Sometimes two, three times a day. He's a pain in the bu—behind," he amended.

Maggie's features were detached, her expression unreadable. "Has he mentioned the gold?"

"Only to assure me I'll never find it."

Carrying the tin cups to the table, she set them down. Ladling two heaping teaspoons of sugar into hers, she cautiously voiced her thoughts. "Well, he's certainly entitled to his opinion."

"That's it?"

"Were you expecting more?" Her gaze never wavered from his face.

"You're not worried about having a ghost for a next-door neighbor?"

Lifting her cup, she took a sip of coffee.

"Maggie, we're talking about an honest to goodness *ghost*," Gordie reminded. "A spook—an apparition—I've *seen* him—talked to him." Fought with him, stumbled over him, cussed him. He'd been a thorn in his side for days!

She giggled, trying to hide her reaction behind the rim of her cup.

His eyes searched her face. "You think I'm nuts, don't you?"

"I didn't say that." She thought for a moment, then hurriedly reached for the sugar bowl. "Sugar?"

"No." Gordie picked up his cup and took a scalding swallow. She didn't believe him. She flat out did not believe he had seen and talked with Butte Fesperman.

Reaching over, she lay her hand over his.

"Gordie, we've been working hard lately. Why don't we take the afternoon off tomorrow? I'll fix a picnic and we'll find a nice place by the stream and enjoy the mild weather." She smiled encouragingly. "Doesn't that sound nice? The shady ladies can surely do without us for one afternoon."

"No, thank you." Shoving back from the table, he stood up. "Sorry I bothered you."

"Gordie . . ." Jumping up, she hurried around the table, realizing she had hurt his feelings. "I'm sorry . . . it's just, well . . . a ghost?"

T.G.'s eyes turned grave. "I saw him, Maggie. I've talked to him."

Her arms slipped around his neck. Sliding her fingers through the shiny mass of carmine hair lying next to his collar, she assured him softly, "If you say you saw him, then I believe you."

"No, you don't."

They stood in the dim light, uncertainty ruling the moment.

Something hummed inside Maggie, something mysterious and exciting. She knew T.G. was the cause of the reaction. She was also well aware of what happened between a man and a woman when passion ruled. On the surface, the lovemaking act was odd—and surely somewhat awkward on the first try, yet the mere thought of T.G. doing something like that to her was fascinating. Could a man really create unspeakable pleasures for a woman the way her dime novels hinted?

"Let's not argue," she coaxed. Edging closer, she whispered, "I need to ask you something."

When her voice adopted that tone it meant nothing but trouble. "Maggie, I have just told you that I've *seen* Butte Fesperman. Do you know what that means?"

"Have you ever made love to a woman?"

His brows knitted in a frown. "What?"

"Have you ever made love to a woman?" Her fingers dallied through his hair, touching his ears, the sides of his cheeks.

"There's a ghost in your mine." A ghost, he might add, who most likely was eavesdropping on this conversation.

"If I'm being bold, forgive me, but I wonder about this thing called sex." She gazed up at him. "You don't think I'm being forward talking about it, do you?" Of course, she was being forward. No respectable woman would dream of discussing sex with a man unless she were married, but she didn't consider herself indecent, only curious.

He took a mindful step backward. "Don't you have anyone else to talk to about this? Another woman?"

"No," she said thoughtfully. "I don't." There were no other young women her age around, and discussing the subject with one of the camp's married women intimidated her. "You think I'm a young, foolish girl who doesn't know the meaning of passion, don't you? But you're wrong. I'll be eighteen soon, and the subject is on my mind a lot lately."

"Nevertheless, I don't think I should be the one to discuss this with you." It wasn't the sort of thing a man talked about with a woman. No decent woman.

Maggie was fascinated by the warmth spreading through her lower regions. A delicious, inebriating warmth influenced solely by his presence. How did he do that? "Is sex as wonderful as they say?" she pursued.

He refused to let her probing eyes lead him astray. She was young and reckless and hadn't the slightest idea of the havoc she was wreaking inside him. "There's gold in the Hellhole. I'm sure of that now, but Butte isn't going to let us near it." He reached up and captured her wandering hand.

Their lips were inches apart now. "Don't do that."

"Why? You don't like it?"

"I like it, it just isn't proper."

"What would make it proper?" Feelings were blooming inside her, new, wonderful, completely illogical feelings she had to explore.

"Nothing would make it proper." He stepped back, the scent of her hair—honey and wild-flowers—affecting all rational thought.

"Would you kiss me?"

"Maggie," he warned, realizing the conversation was getting out of hand.

"Or perhaps," she brushed her fingers across his bottom lip, "make love to me—or would you find that too improper?"

"Extremely improper." He inched backward.

"Perhaps to some, but if you were only to ask," she murmured, covering the distance he had just created. "Gordie, I have this terrible ache when I'm near you that I don't understand ... perhaps you could help me understand it."

"Maggie ... where is this ache?" He could feel himself falling prey to her spell no matter how he struggled to fight it.

"Here ... between my legs," she whispered.

"Maggie," he warned, succumbing to agony now. Had no one taught her to hold her tongue concerning such matters?

"Do you know of the ache I speak?" she asked. Her eyes quietly implored his insight.

Touching her hair, he searched for the strength to serve him. "I know the ache, but this isn't something we should be talking about."

Her eyes grew more confused. "Why?"

"Because it isn't the way it's done."

"Then teach me how it is done. Do I ask ... or do you?"

"A kiss," he said softly, "or are we speaking of sex?"

"A kiss ... for the moment."

"Ahh, then I wouldn't ask for a kiss, I would take."

His smile, and the thickening of his voice told her all she needed to go on. Leaning closer, she whispered, "Then please take, for the ache is most unbearable."

Closing his eyes, he touched his mouth to the tip of her nose and conceded. "A kiss will do nothing to satisfy the ache, my innocent. It will only serve to make it more unpleasant."

"Please . . . the ache only grows stronger."

"One kiss."

"One kiss," she promised.

Gathering a handful of her hair, he lowered his mouth to hers, running the tip of his tongue along the corners of her mouth, touching, learning the taste of her. She tasted of sweetness, innocence, purity of heart. His own ache threatened to spill over and consume him.

Hearing her small whimper, he caught her closer, his mouth opening to hers.

And then there was nothing but the touch of her lips, the hunger of her hold, the bliss of knowing that no matter how hard he fought, he could not deny that he was falling in love with her.

As he left the dugout a few minutes later he realized the point of his visit had failed. She still wasn't aware that she was dealing with a ghost.

Chapter 19

"Let it slip out, didn't ya? Jest couldn't stand it, had to tell her about me."

"I could have mentioned it."

"*Mentioned* it?" Butte snickered. He'd witnessed that little smoochin' scene in the dugout last night. Buddy Boy had better watch his step, 'cause sure as shootin', the Fletcher woman was out to get him.

T.G. knelt beside the stream this morning, panning gold. Work inside the mine was proceeding at a snail's pace. "Does she believe me?"

"Well, now—" Butte squinted and scratched his mangy beard. "Want me to lie?"

"No." T.G. didn't have to be telepathic to know she didn't believe him. He saw the look in her eyes last night—the disappointment. Did she think he was hitting the bottle again? Could she believe he was seeing ghosts that weren't there?

"Now, Buddy Boy, she *wants* to believe you."

A tic in T.G.'s jaw gave away his thoughts. "But she doesn't."

"Well, now, I didn't say *that*. She's got some doubts—"

"She thinks I'm a worthless, gambling drunk who's seeing things that aren't there."

Butte cocked his head. "Which part ain't true?"

"Get out of here, Butte."

"No, not until I help ya."

"You can't help me."

"Oh, but I can. Now about the Fletcher woman. You ask if she believes you. The answer is, not exactly—she wants to reserve judgment until she fixes her eyes on me herself."

T.G. snorted. "Which will never happen."

Butte swung down from an overhead branch, dropping to his feet in front of Gordie. "Boy, Buddy Boy, you've got me pegged dead-center. I've done told you: no one but you is gonna see me, and no one, not even Moses, though Lord knows I've got an itch for that woman—is gonna get their hands on my gold."

"Is that your choice, Butte?"

"Is what my choice?"

"Is it your choice that I'm the only one who can see you?"

"Naw." He brushed dirt off his shirtsleeve. "I'd scare the shit outta anybody I could, but I'm limited."

"Why's that?"

"Why am I limited?"

"Yes—does that imply that others around you aren't?"

"Well," Butte said. "To be honest, I don't rightly know."

"Exactly where are you?" T.G. didn't want to ask, but he had been wondering about that. The mystery of death; Butte could tell him.

"Standing right here in front of you."

"No, I mean—where are you?"

"Oh, where am I? Well, I don't rightly know."

"You don't know?"

"Haven't a clue."

"Are you alone?"

"No, not alone."

"Then, there are others there with you—wherever you are."

"Oh yeah, lots of folks."

"What are these people doing?"

Butte looked around, his eyes scouring the area. "Well, now, there's a couple of 'em sittin' cross stream there. Then, over there," he pointed up the hill, "is another. Think that one must have somethin' to do with the Fletcher woman 'cause I see her hanging around a lot. And over there, sittin' outside the dugout, is a couple of kids."

T.G. felt foolish, but he looked in spite of himself.

"You can't see them."

"Why not?"

"Ain't no reason for you to see them."

"How do you know that?"

"I don't know—no one's said a word, yet they know what I'm thinking, and I know what they're thinking. It's real peculiar at first. Took some gettin' used to."

"Who are these people? Guardian angels?" T.G. asked, intrigued now.

"Must be something like that."

"Then there's a reason why I can see you?"

"Must be, or you wouldn't be seeing me," Butte agreed.

"You've been told this?"

"No, I haven't been told nothin'. Seems kinda dark where I am, and it's kinda light where they are . . . sorta peculiar," he mused.

"But you don't know where you are?"

"No, dadburn it! How should I know? I've only been here a few hours."

"Butte, you've been *dead* thirty-six years!"

"*Thirty-six* years!" He was floored. Scratching his beard, he frowned. "You shore 'bout that?"

"According to stories, you died in 1857. It's now 1893."

"Nooo."

"Yes."

"Noooo," he contended. "It cain't be!"

"It is, Butte. It's 1893."

"Well, I'll swan." Now he was confused. "I thought I'd only been gone a few hours." Now that put a whole different light on things. If he'd been here *thirty-six* years, where in the devil *was* he?

"You've been terrorizing the mine for over thirty years," T.G. told him.

"Me?" He knew he'd been acting up lately, but he had no idea it'd been going on thirty-six years!

"How long ago did you say the Fletcher woman staked her claim to the Hellhole?"

"She didn't stake a claim. She and the boy inherited it a few weeks ago—I thought you knew everything."

"I thought I did, too." Somebody had a sense of humor. "Few weeks ago, huh? Who'd she get it from?"

"Her aunt left it to her."

Butte suddenly peered over T.G.'s shoulder. "What?"

"Her aunt left it to her," T.G. repeated.

Butte shook off his answer, clearly talking to someone else now. "How do, ma'am." He lifted his hat respectfully. "Name's Butte Fesperman."

Listening for a moment, Butte nodded. "That right? . . . That a fact? . . . You don't say. Her aunt? . . . Well, now, that's interestin'."

T.G. rested on his haunches, looking up at Butte. "Who are you talking to?"

Butte ignored him. "No, ma'am, you're the first. . . . You don't say? . . . That where I am?"

He peered upward. "Yeah, I see the light. Whew! A mite bright, ain't it? . . . Yeah, I've noticed it before—couldn't miss it. . . . It's what? . . . *What?* . . . It *is*? . . . Well, I'll swan."

T.G. was losing patience. "*Who* are you talking to?"

"Hold on, Buddy Boy. This here is gettin' interestin'. . . . I have to do what? . . . Shoot no! It's mine!" he blustered a minute later. "Got myself blowed up over it! . . . Yeah? . . . Oh, *yeah*? . . . And if I don't? . . . Oh, yeah." His tone suddenly lost some of its brashness.

"Butte!" T.G. snapped. "Who are you talking to? Butte!" he demanded a moment later when Butte looked as if he were about to fade. "Don't go— what's going on? . . . Butte? Wait a minute—who were you talking to? . . . Butte!"

T.G. stood up, angry now. "Butte! Get back here! What is going on?"

"Sorry, gotta go, Buddy Boy. . . ." He disappeared in a vaporous puff.

"Butte!" T.G. shouted. But Butte was gone.

Slamming his gold pan to the ground, T.G. lit on it with both feet. Trouncing on it, he jumped up and down, venting his pent-up frustrations.

Up and down, up and down, he stomped the pan, mangling the tin and fouling the air with a string of epithets that made Butch Miller sound like a choir-boy. He'd had it! Cave-ins, floods, egotistical ghosts, Mooney Backus threatening to kill him, Maggie thinking he was seeing things, Maggie driving him up the wall with desire, wanting him to school her on sex, making him want things he had given up on having. Maggie and the damn gold, Maggie, Maggie, Maggie!

"Leave me alone, Butte! You hear me? I don't want to ever see your face around here again! Torment someone else! *You hear me, Fesperman? I've had it with you and your nutty ways!*"

Hammering the pan with the heel of his boot, he viciously ground it into the gravel bank.

Guardian angels roaming around, children sitting

next to the dugout, bright lights, ghosts talking to ghosts. Where did it end?

He'd given up drinking. He'd given up gambling. He'd given up giving up, all for Maggie Fletcher and this blasted mine called the Hellhole!

Rage burned out of control as he pounded the tin with the heel of his boot, cursing the day he was born.

A shadow crossed the ground, and he glanced up. Maggie was standing beside the stream, witnessing the fit of temper.

Bewildered, her eyes moved from his boots, to the throbbing vein in his neck, to his face splotched with anger.

Regaining his composure, he paused, his hiked foot in midair. "Yes?"

Smiling reluctantly, she murmured, "Dinner's ready."

Giving the tin one last stomp, he refused to look at her. "Okay."

She continued to stare at him as if there were something more that needed to be said.

But he wouldn't meet her stupefied gaze. "I'll be along in a minute."

"Are you all right?"

"Fine. Never better. First rate."

Sauntering away, she looked back over her shoulder to make sure he was coming.

Muttering under his breath, Gordie gave the mangled gold pan a swift kick, sending it skittering into the stream, and followed her up the hill.

* * *

After supper, Maggie left Wilson trying to braid the cat's tail while she stole a few minutes alone with T.G.

The scene this afternoon at the stream still bothered her. T.G. was behaving so strangely lately. She prayed that he hadn't resorted to drinking again. She refused to believe that he would risk Wilson's and her welfare for something so trivial and meaningless.

Even so, he continued to stand by her when it seemed they were fighting a losing battle. Any day now, she expected Moses and the shady ladies to walk out. There was barely enough gold coming out of the mine to keep them all going. And the constant interruptions were more than annoying; they were dangerous. Maggie was beginning to think they were an indication of something more sinister than just plain bad luck.

Pausing in front of Gordie's tent, she called softly, "Are you awake?"

A moment later the flap parted, and T.G. appeared in the doorway. Her eyes focused on his shirt, which was opened to the waist. He frowned when he saw her huddled against the biting wind. "Is something wrong?"

"Can I come in?"

Standing aside, he allowed her to enter the tent.

Hurrying to the small fire, she undid her scarf, permitting her hair to fall unrestricted around her shoulders. The effect was disconcerting to him.

Drinking in the sight of her young, ripe body, T.G. was painfully reminded of their differences.

She was young, with a great deal to offer a man. He was twelve years older, with nothing at all to give a woman.

"Where's Wilson?"

"Braiding Jellybean's tail."

"How can he do that?"

She shrugged. "Not easily, but it keeps him occupied."

Lifting her hands to the fire, she warmed her fingers. "It's getting so cold. T.G., I worry about you here, alone in this tent."

Stooping over, T.G. added another stick of wood to the fire. "I'm thinking it's time I moved back to camp." He should have left sooner, but he had stayed on because of her. Everything he did these days was because of her.

His acknowledgment of the inevitable brought a twinge of emptiness to Maggie. Without him nearby, life at the Hellhole would be indeed unbearable.

By now, T.G. knew her thoughts as well as he knew his own. Their eyes met across the firelight. "Nothing will change. I'll still be here every day."

"You won't be here at night. I'll miss our talks."

"We'll talk," he said kindly.

Neither was aware why it happened, or even how it happened, but she was suddenly in his arms again. Brushing a stray hair from her cheek, he smiled down at her.

"Am I funny?"

"No, you're not funny. I was thinking about the

look on your face today, when you found me at the stream. That was funny."

Her eyes clouded. "T.G., what was that all about?" All people lost their temper at times, but the incident that day had been more than a simple fit of anger.

"Butte Fesperman."

"T.G.," she complained. They weren't going to start that again!

"All right, don't believe me." He was willing to let it go for now. "What brings you out this time of night?"

Sighing, she rested her head on his shoulder, absently fondling the woolen fabric of his shirt. "You still insist there is a ghost?"

"I see him every day."

"You're sure it's Butte Fesperman, not just someone playing a trick on you?"

"It's Butte Fesperman."

Sighing, she lifted her eyes. "If that's true, why can't I see him? After all, I own the mine. If he wants to frighten someone, why not frighten me?"

The tent suddenly seemed very small. And she was suddenly too close. Her eyes were liquid warmth as she gazed back at him.

Holding her closer, he lowered his face in her hair, whispering. "Maybe he doesn't like to provoke beautiful women."

Her eyes drifted closed, relishing his nearness. It felt so right to be in his arms—*he* was so right for her.

"Does Butte Fesperman say why he appears only to you?"

"It has something to do with guardian angels and—I know how crazy all this sounds, Maggie—" It was beginning to sound crazy to him!

She held him tightly, desperately wanting to believe him, even though the thought of a ghost was distressing. If the old miner truly did exist, her future looked dim indeed.

Tilting her head, she looked deeply into his eyes. "Do you ever think of me? Especially after the other night when we kissed?"

He shifted, suddenly uneasy. What was she doing in his arms? He didn't remember inviting her there. "What kind of question is that? We were talking about ghosts."

"But we're not now. We're talking about you . . . and me . . . and kisses." She smiled up at him. "Do you ever think of me?" She'd thought of nothing but him for days.

"I'm thinking of you right now." His body had a mind of its own and was responding to her nearness. His blood was beginning to build with the same slow fever she always aroused in him.

"Then you feel the attraction, too?" She was both relieved and frightened by the revelation. If he felt the same magnetic pull that continually drew her, there could be no possible release from the sweet agony until both their thirsts were quenched.

"Yes, I feel it," he admitted. In spite of a foreboding premonition of disaster, T.G. pulled her closer with a force that would have been impossible to resist. He was tired of fighting feelings he no longer controlled. His voice dropped to a low, husky timbre. "I don't want this to happen, Maggie." Yet from the moment he first kissed her, he felt it was inevitable.

"Why are you so afraid of your feelings?" she chided. She wasn't afraid of hers—she raced to embrace them.

"My life was fine until you came along. I don't want to fall in love, Maggie. I have nothing to offer a woman."

She gazed back at him, aware of how hard he was fighting the attraction.

"Don't you think that's for the woman to decide?"

"No, it's what I've decided, and I don't want to complicate matters between me and you. You're young, beautiful, alive. You need a man who will match your spirit."

"I've found one."

"You're young and impressionable, Maggie. You know nothing about me."

"Then tell me about you, Gordie Manning. What are these thoughts you find so frightening?"

"They're foolish thoughts, and I'm a simpleton for thinking them."

"There's nothing simple about you," she assured him.

He hesitated, trying to sort through his confusion. "At night, before I drift off, I find myself wondering why you like sweet potatoes so much—or questioning your love affair with pickle sandwiches."

Laughing, she contentedly nestled deeper against the solid wall of his chest. He smelled of wood smoke and mountain air. "I was expecting something a little more romantic."

"That wasn't romantic enough?" He could feel his defenses starting to fall away.

"No. Try again."

"I'm not very good with romance." He held her closer. "What do you want me to say?"

"What's in your heart."

"I can't . . . not now, Maggie." Maybe he never could.

"Then say terrible things—brazen, shameless things."

A smile played at the corners of his mouth. "I don't think so. I am still a gentleman."

"Then tell me the sort of things a man might say to a woman when he wants her so badly he can think of nothing else."

He wanted to end his agony, but hadn't the strength. Now was the moment to set her aside and suggest that it was late, that she should return to the dugout.

That was what he should do; instead his mouth moved to the nape of her neck, languishing in her essence. He wanted to absorb her, draw her into his skin and never let her go. "If I were to say such things, let alone think them, I would be twice a fool."

Her eyes drifted shut, mesmerized by his voice.

The fire crackled, swathing them in a warm cocoon. "Then tell me what is in your heart."

"I wonder how you make your hair smell so good, or why your eyes turn the color of warm honey when you smile," he whispered. His breath fell softly upon her ear. She was like quicksilver in his hands, as he molded her tightly to his pulsating need.

"Mmmm, no one has ever said anything that nice to me before," she murmured.

Taking her hand, he eased it inside his open shirt. As her fingers slid into the mat of carmine hair, he heard her breathing quicken. Eyes locked with hers, he waited for her to bolt and run. By revealing the danger she incited, he planned to put a stop to her innocent flirtation.

But she didn't scare easily. Her fingers began to explore his bare warm flesh with light, feathery strokes. His thick mat of chest hair felt strangely erotic to her fingertips. She found the aching source of his urgency pressing slightly above the juncture of her thighs anything but frightening.

His voice was low and strained. "Your hands are trembling. Are you frightened?"

"Yes, I'm frightened."

"Of me?" He was quietly amused.

"Of me," she whispered. She leaned closer, whispering in his ear. "I like this. Why haven't we done it before?"

"I am trying to teach you a lesson," he whispered back, aware his tutelage was rapidly proving to be in vain.

"I would prefer you teach me other things."

He didn't want to fall prey, but demons possessed him now. "Such as?"

"Such as—" Her hand casually investigated the ridge of sinewy muscles along his rib cage, the width of his flat stomach, eventually coming to pause just a breath above his navel. Burnished red hair grew thicker here. Her voice trembled as she confessed, "What secrets lie," her palm rested lightly on his arousal, "here."

The pleasure of her hand nearly undid him. Passion, hot and unchecked, flooded him.

"Do I need permission to explore further, kind sir?"

Drawing her mouth roughly to his, he claimed her with a hot, elemental kiss. When her hand moved up to embrace his cheek, he moved it back. Releasing the buttons on his breeches, he eased her fingers to the source of her curiosity.

The ache inside her grew, demanding to be released as his mouth moved feverishly on hers.

Impatient, he released the tiny row of buttons on the front of her dress, baring her bodice. His mouth lowered to the bewitching swell of her breasts, eager to taste her sweetness.

Maggie was caught up by desire. Murmuring his name, she began touching him so intimately she thought she would die of shame. A desperate, reckless urgency seized her.

With soft, tiny whimpers, her mouth sought his in a desperate attempt to satisfy the awful need.

"No, Maggie . . . no," he whispered.

Sinking to the pallet, they exchanged hungry, unbridled kisses. He knew it was insane, that it would only complicate an already impossible alliance, yet the fire in his blood drove him.

"Hey! There you are."

Wilson's voice jerked them back to sanity.

The boy stood in the doorway, holding his cat. "What're you doing?"

Springing apart, Maggie bound to her feet, hurriedly fastening the hooks on her dress as T.G. rolled to the side of the pallet, fumbling with the buttons on his breeches.

Wilson's eyes moved from T.G.'s dishelved clothing to Maggie's flushed face. "You having a wrestling contest?"

Clearing his throat, T.G. glanced at Maggie. "Yeah, Wilson—a wrestling contest."

"Who won?"

Glancing at Maggie, T.G. admitted disgruntledly, "Your sister won."

Wilson's face lit up. "Honest, Maggie? You won!" He didn't even know she wrestled!

Brushing past T.G., Maggie pointed Wilson back out the doorway. "No, it was actually a tie."

Wilson didn't like the idea of leaving yet. He wanted to watch the rematch! "You going to give Gordie another chance?"

Leaving the tent, Maggie turned, winking over her shoulder at T.G. "Oh yes, he will definitely have another chance. When he feels up to one."

As the flap dropped back in place T.G. lay on his back, drained, staring at the ceiling.

When he felt up to one.

Chapter 20

"I know where that gold is."

They had had this conversation a hundred times. T.G. wished if Butte was a permanent fixture in his life, he'd get a new topic.

"Know exactly—could take you there in a minute, but I won't," Butte said.

T.G. grunted.

"You doubt me?"

"I don't doubt anything anymore."

"Yes, you do."

"Butte, I'm busy. If you want to argue, go do it with someone else."

"Can't," Butte admitted sullenly. "You know you're the only one I show myself to."

"Well, that's what happens when you limit yourself."

Butte sat back to watch T.G. work. The boy wasn't bad. He knew what he was doing when it came to mining. It was a shame his efforts would be in vain.

"What happened to you the other day?"

Butte sat up straighter, looking around him.

"Yes, I'm talking to you," T.G. established.

"You're talking to me?" Well, that was a good one. Gordie had never before initiated a conversation.

"Where did you go the other day?"

"When?"

"When you left in such a hurry. Who were you talking to?"

"Oh, that." Butte hopped on the cart ledge and stretched out. "Went courtin', Buddy Boy."

T.G. glanced up. "Courting? They do that up there?"

"Do what up where?"

"Court, wherever it is you are."

"Oh, well, not the kind of courtin' you're thinkin' of. By the way, sorry I didn't get around to checkin' on you last night. I was a little busy—anything happen between you and the Fletcher woman?"

Dropping his head, T.G. shoveled dirt faster into the sluice box. "You weren't around last night?"

Butte snickered.

"Damn it, Butte, a man has a right to his privacy!"

"Don't get bound up, Buddy Boy. I got other interests 'sides you, ya know. I had my own doin's last evenin' with one of my own kind. Met me a kindred spirit."

"I thought you hadn't met anyone."

"I hadn't, not until the other day. You know the

woman I said was hangin' around the Fletcher woman?"

"Yes."

"Found out her name. Sissy."

When T.G. didn't respond, Butte pressed him further.

"Name don't ring a bell with ya?"

"No—should it?"

"Sissy." Butte spelled it. "S-i-s-s-y."

"I know how to spell."

"S-n-i-d-e-l-y."

"Butte, I'm busy. Get away."

"S-i-s-s-y S-h-i-r-e. See any similarities with anyone you know?"

T.G. stopped shoveling. "Sissy? Maggie's Aunt Sissy? The one who left her the Hellhole?"

Butte slapped his knee. "Yore gettin' good, you are. That's the one!"

"*She's* up there?"

Butte slapped his knee again, cackling. "She is! She shore is!"

T.G. flat didn't believe him. Butte and Maggie's Aunt Sissy? He was putting him on.

"That's who you were talking to?"

"Yep. Spent the day with her—well, it mighta been a day. Time don't seem to have much meaning up here." Lying back, he gazed at the sky. "I shore wish I'd met that woman when I was alive. She's one of them—what's that new word they been sayin'? Corker? Yep, that's Sissy." He grinned. "A corker."

Shoving the empty cart aside, T.G. started on another one. "Did Sissy tell you she owned the Hell-hole?"

"Shore did, but I told her she didn't. Don't worry, we got it straightened out."

"She couldn't be too happy about you preventing her niece and nephew from getting the gold."

"Well, like I told her, that's my gold." Cocking his head, Butte studied T.G.'s profile. "Say, I'd never noticed before, but you remind me of someone—you any kin to Ardis Johnson?"

"No."

Butte sat up straighter, positive he saw a resemblance. "Looka there, why, you've got Ardis's eyes fer sure. You *are* kin to him. That's why you're up here tryin' to help that Fletcher woman get the gold!"

"I am not kin to Ardis Johnson." Gordie didn't know where he came up with his dumb ideas.

Butte eyed him dubiously. "Oh yeah? Where did you say you's from?"

"I told you, I'm not from around here."

"I think you are."

"I'm not."

"You are."

Gordie's patience snapped, and his temper flared. "I'm *not*. I lived in Phoenix until five years ago."

"Did not."

"Butte, did anyone ever tell you you were bull-headed?"

"Dadburn it! Ardis sent you up here for the gold, didn't he?"

"Ardis Johnson!"

Butte's eyes narrowed. "You know him?"

"No, I don't know him! I know *of* him. Everyone around here has heard stories about the row you two had going on."

Butte's disposition soured. "Blast that Ardis's rotten hide. If it weren't for him, I wouldn't be stuck here—wherever I am, forever."

"Give up the gold. Could be your greed's what's preventing you from moving on."

"Never." Scissoring his arms behind his head, Butte began humming a little ditty, then burst into song:

> *"I'm sitting on a big quartz rock,*
> *Where gold is said to grow;*
> *I'm thinking of the merry flock,*
> *that I left long ago:*
> *My fare is hard, so is my bed,*
> *My claim is giving out,*
> *I've worked until I'm almost dead,*
> *And soon I shall "peg" out.*

"I'm gittin' on yore nerves, ain't I?"

"Don't you have anything better to do than hassle me?"

"Nope, nary a thing.

> *"I'm thinking of the better days,*
> *Before I left my home;*

Before my brain with gold was crazed,
And I began to roam.
Those were the days, no more are seen,
When all the girls loved me;
When I did dress in linen clean,
They washed and cooked for me.

"Did I mention I was married once?"
"No."
"Was, but religion done us in."
"Religion?"
"Yeah. I was Catholic and she was Lucifer.

"But awful change is this to tell,
I wash and cook myself;
I never more shall cut a swell,
But here, must dig for pelf.
I ne'er shall lie in clean white sheets,
But in my blankets roll;
As oh! the girls thought I so sweet,
They think me but a fooooool."

The song faded away as Butte sat up, catching a glimpse of Sissy. "Say, there's Sissy. Fine-looking woman." He waved. "Afternoon, Sissy!"

He turned back. "It's my mine, you know."

"I believe you've mentioned that, Butte."

"It is, you know."

"You'll have to take that up with the new owner. I just work here."

"Maggie Fletcher? *Pfffffft.* She don't own the

Hellhole. I do." He hummed a few more bars of his tune, confident he had the upper hand.

"Everyone's wanting silver, but gold's what they need. Now, Buddy Boy, if we was to git ourselves over to that south Afreeca, we could make us billions. I hear tell they mined nigh on to nine billion dollars worth over there in the past ten years. Colerreta ain't done that good. It took pert near four hundred and seventy mines over in Cripple Creek to get a little over four hundred million." Butte laughed. "Pitiful, ain't it?"

"How much gold do you suppose is in the Hellhole, Butte?"

"In the Hellhole?"

"Yes. How much gold is in there?" Thirty-six years in the mine should have given him some idea.

Butte squinted up at him. "Is this here a trick?"

"No, just curious. How much gold is actually in the mine?"

"A lot. The mother lode, pay dirt, tons."

"And you know where it is."

"Exactly."

"But you won't say."

"I shore won't."

"Why not? What good can it possibly do you? You're dead."

Butte winced. "Don't need to get hateful."

"What good is the gold if you can't use it?"

"Ain't worth a ball of spit, but nobody else is gonna git it."

"It could make some people's lives a lot easier,"

T.G. said, thinking of Maggie and Wilson, and how desperately they needed the money. Maggie's funds were almost depleted now.

"Nobody ever made my life easy." Butte began to fade, tiring of the subject.

"Give it some thought," T.G. called. "Do something nice for once." *You old devil.*

Butte called back from a distance. "I heard that."

"Honest, Maggie! I *heard* him! He was talking to somebody, but when I asked him who he was talkin' to, he said, 'Nobody, and stop asking so many questions!' Then he walked off real mad-like."

Maggie ladled dumplings onto Wilson's plate, finding it increasingly difficult to defend T.G.'s odd behavior. She had caught him on several occasions mumbling, talking out loud, being argumentative with thin air. And this ongoing obsession concerning Butte Fesperman! Perhaps she should insist he see the doctor next time he passed through camp.

"Maybe he was talking to himself—people do that sometimes," she offered.

"Do they talk bad to themselves?"

"Sometimes," she acknowledged hesitantly. "Has T.G. been talking bad in front of you?"

Wilson nodded. "Real bad—but he didn't know I heard him."

Maggie frowned. "Where were you?"

"I wasn't hiding or anything," Wilson upheld. "I was just sitting on a ledge eating a biscuit when I heard him start yellin' and cussing, waving his shovel in the air and saying, 'Get away, a hole!' "

Maggie whirled on him sternly.

"I didn't say it!"

"You'd better not!"

"That's what *he* said, 'Get away, a hole!' " Wilson halfheartedly stirred his fork in the stew. "He couldn't have meant for me to get away, because he didn't know I was even there, and he's never called me an a hole, no matter how mad he gets."

"Sitting on a ledge?" Maggie asked, the implication of his words just hitting her.

"Yeah, in the min—" Wilson stopped.

Maggie's hand came to her hip. "In the mine?"

Developing an unusual preoccupation with his food, Wilson started spooning stew into his mouth, cramming it so full he couldn't answer back.

"Wilson, you are to stay out of the mine."

Wilson looked back at her, his cheeks round as a chipmunk's.

"They're blasting in there now, and it's extremely dangerous!"

Nodding, Wilson chewed emphatically.

Maggie sat down, unfolding her napkin. "And as far as Gordie's concerned, I wouldn't worry about his unusual behavior. He has a lot of things on his mind. It's your turn to say grace."

Swallowing, Wilson bowed his head. "Please help us, God. We're in trouble."

Maggie gave him a sideways look.

"And thank you for these good, nutritious dumplings. Even though we don't have any meat to go with them, dumplings are better than beans any day. Amen."

"Amen," Maggie echoed.

Wilson reached for his fork. "We're not doing so good, huh, Maggie?" He could tell there was hardly any gold coming out of the mine. And Moses was shouting a lot lately because of all the accidents.

"No, I'm afraid we're not, Wilson."

His features turned solemn when he saw how sad she looked. "Do we have to go back to England?"

"I hope not, but it's possible. We hardly have any money left, and winter will be here soon." Snow clouds were already gathering on the distant horizon.

"I don't want to go back. Aunt Fionnula is mad at us."

"No, she isn't."

"How do you know? Has she answered your letter?"

"No," Maggie admitted. "She hasn't written, but that doesn't mean that she's mad at us. We're family, and if worse comes to worst, I'm sure she will let us come back if we need to."

"Oh, brother." Wilson had a more fitting comeback, but he'd just get his mouth washed out with soap again.

"What will happen to Gordie? We can't go back to England and leave him." Gordie was theirs now. He didn't have anybody but them, and they loved him. Aunt Fionnula might let him and Maggie come back, but she wouldn't even let Gordie through the front door. He'd have to go around to the back, just like all the other riffraff.

Sighing, Maggie took a bite of dumpling. "I don't know about Gordie." She wished she did. The crazy things they did together. Had she no shame? She grinned. Actually, she didn't, not when it came to him.

"Why is he acting so nutty?"

"Wilson, can I tell you something?" He suddenly seemed like the old, wise-beyond-his-years Wilson she'd always been able to share problems with, and right now she needed an old friend.

"Certainly. May I have more dumplings, please?"

"Yes, you may, and I'm very proud of you. Your language has improved considerably."

"I'm working on my English," he divulged. "And I'm trying to teach Butch the proper usage. He is a terrible speller. Just today, when Miss Perkins left the room, he went to the blackboard and wrote, I wish there was more piece on earth. I told him, no, it should be p-e-a-c-e, not p-i-e-c-e, but he said it was spelled right." He took a drink of milk. "I was embarrassed for him, but he just wouldn't listen."

"Where *are* that boy's parents?" Maggie asked rhetorically.

"I overheard Miss Perkins say she thinks he's being raised by wolves." He looked up. "Could that happen?"

"No, Miss Perkins was only teasing."

"Oh. What did you want to tell me?"

"You have to promise not to say anything to anyone about this."

"Who would I tell?" Hardly anybody ever talked to him anyway.

"T.G., for one."

Wilson quickly took another drink of milk, remembering how much trouble he got into for asking Gordie to marry them.

"Gordie says he's seen Butte Fesperman." She ladled more dumplings on his plate, watching his reaction.

He peered back at her, waiting.

"The ghost—T.G. says he's met the ghost," Maggie repeated, hoping he would think it as ridiculous as she.

"Did he like him?"

"Wilson! That's insane. There's no such thing as a ghost!"

"Who said?"

"Everybody *says*."

"Not everybody. I heard Moses and the other women talking and they believe there's a ghost. They said he was one mean son of a— Said he was real mean, and they were tired of fighting him."

"When did they say that?"

"Today." He looked away. "When I wasn't in the mine."

Her heart sank. If Moses walked out they were doomed. "I'm so confused. I don't know what to believe. The number of accidents and cave-ins is unusual." How much bad luck could one person have? "Maybe there truly is a ghost."

"Gordie said he saw him, didn't he?" Wilson spoke as if the matter were settled, if T.G. said it.

"Yes, he says he has, on more than one occasion."

"He doesn't carry his little flask in his left coat pocket anymore, does he?"

"No, I'm almost positive that he isn't drinking, Wilson. I think he was just confused and lonely when we first met him. Now he has a purpose in life."

Wilson nodded. "He just needed someone to love him, huh, Maggie?"

She smiled. "I guess so. It's true he isn't the same person he was a few weeks ago."

"And we love him, don't we?"

She looked away this time. "Eat before your dumplings get cold."

"But we do love him, huh? I won't tell him if you don't want me to. Honest."

"Yes, we love him," she conceded.

"A lot."

"A whole lot."

"Wilson thinks you're nuts."

Gordie looked up to see Maggie standing in his doorway later that night. It wouldn't do any good to deny that he was nuts, though he was reasonably sure he wasn't—except when she was around. He knew the incident she was referring to—Wilson overhearing his conversation with Butte in the mine today.

Shrugging, he lay back on his pallet. "Tell him to get in line."

"Honestly, Gordie." Maggie came into the tent, letting the flap drop into place behind her. "He overheard you today—you have to be more careful. Granted, everyone talks to himself occasionally, but when you start answering back, something's wrong." She moved to the fire to warm her hands.

Damn, she looked good tonight. Gordie had a hard time keeping his mind on the denunciation and off her. It wasn't the way she was dressed; she was wearing the same flowery thing she periodically alternated with a striped blue one. Faded, worn, neither garment was exactly designed to capture a man's eye.

It was the way she wore the dress, the pliant curves, the soft planes, the rounded hips. The mere sight of her brought on a heated rush.

He wanted her, not just wanted her, needed her, damn it. *Needed* her. He hated to admit it, but he did. And he didn't have to be reminded that she wasn't like Nell's women; he was smart enough to know the difference.

Trouble was *he* knew the difference, his body just didn't.

Common sense warned him to let the moment pass, as it surely would if he let it alone. Common sense told him he was obsessed with her and it had to stop.

His eyes slid over her supple curves, small breasts. It wasn't his imagination. She looked damn good tonight. The icy wind tinted her cheeks a rosy pink, and her lips were soft and shiny, fairly begging to be kissed. Last night's tent encounter returned in a hot rush, antagonizing his misery. Would he have made love to her if Wilson hadn't happened along? Had it been more than sultry eyes inviting him—no, beseeching him to make love to her, or was it merely foolish thinking?

Get a grip on yourself. Apologize for talking to Butte within Wilson's earshot, and promise to be more careful in the future. Now. Before you make a fool of yourself.

Send her back to the dugout, purity intact. And you settle down for one hell of a miserable night.

Getting to his feet, he faced her. "I'm sorry. I'll try to be more careful."

Her eyes softened. "I don't mean to be critical, but Wilson is fond of you, and I don't want him thinking you're nuts."

"I'll be more careful." She had a right to be concerned. Wilson was impressionable, and besides, he didn't want the kid thinking he was nuts, either.

The silence stretched between them.

"Was there something else?" *Just go back to the dugout while you can.*

"No," she said. "Just that."

And damn if it didn't happen again.

One minute they were talking—he keeping his distance, and the next, she was in his arms, he kissing her as if he didn't have good sense, both talking at the same time.

"This is crazy . . ."

"I know I shouldn't have come out here . . . I've thought of nothing but you since last night . . ."

"Me too . . . me too . . ." Their mouths devoured each other. Kissing down her neck, he held her tightly, powerless to regain control.

He would regret what he was about to do. So would she. She would be angry and accuse him of being a miserable human being for taking advantage of her in a vulnerable state. He'd swear it had been as much her fault as his; they'd both be right.

They would agree, civilly, that it had been a mistake, and mean it. They would vow to never let it happen again, but it would. Over and over, because their hunger ran too deep. As long as he was within a hundred miles of her, he was doomed, and he knew it. And he didn't give a damn.

Hands feverishly worked to dispose of clothing, urgency overriding common sense.

"I shouldn't tempt you like this," she apologized. "But I can't help it. Gordie . . . forgive me . . ."

"You've tempted me from the moment I saw you." He kissed her hard, demanding, unrelenting, punishing her, punishing him, hell, he didn't know.

"We shouldn't . . . I shouldn't ask this of you . . ."

"Ask me anything you want," he said gruffly. *Anything*. Hang the moon, walk on water, part the

sea, extinguish the sun, find the mother lode . . .
For her, he'd try.

"Oh, Gordie . . ." The neediness in her voice
matched his.

She was worrying about him thinking badly of
her, but she was worrying in vain. The recriminations would come, fast and furious, later. Women
like Maggie Fletcher didn't go to bed with men—
they married them, had their babies, rocked their
grandchildren. The sheer significance of her offering should have weighed heavily on him—would
have, if it wasn't for the more pressing weight in
his trousers.

Lips clinging together, they sank to the pallet,
their clothes tossed aside in a careless heap.

Smiling, her eyes issued an undeniable challenge. "I take this to mean you feel up to a rematch?"

"Wrestling you?"

She nodded.

His eyes devoured her. "Lady, you haven't got a
chance."

They gazed at each other in the firelight. They
didn't need words. Who needed words? Her eyes
told him all he needed to know.

"Is Wilson . . . ?"

"He's asleep by now."

That was good. He wanted her all to himself.

"You feel so damn good." His hands couldn't
get enough of her. His eyes couldn't adore her
enough.

Sliding his hold down her silky length, he familiarized himself with her, absorbing her beauty. Her body was all womanly softness, perfect. Her shivering acquiescence made him protective, wanting to shield her from the initial pain, but knowing after the pain came the pleasure. Incredible pleasure.

"Are you afraid?"

She shook her head, spellbound. "Not of you."

His voice dropped to a confidential whisper. "You should be."

"Make me be," she dared.

He kissed her, his mouth warm against hers. "Have I mentioned I think you're pretty?"

"No. Have I told you I love your red hair?"

"No," he grinned. "I hope you find more than my hair interesting."

"Oh, I do . . . by the way, is all the hair on you red?"

"This something you've given considerable thought to?"

"More than I should have," she conceded.

His lips moved along her cheek, softly along the jawline, up her brow, pausing briefly at her temple as his breathing quickened. "Why don't you see for yourself?"

She blushed. "You don't mind?"

"I don't mind."

Getting to her knees, her eyes traveled his full length. The flickering firelight allowed her her first real look at him. Her eyes mirrored, he hoped, if not admiration, then at least respect.

As their eyes found each other, her inhibitions fled. She grinned. "Am I lucky. You are truly gifted." Her hand became bold, confident, dangerous.

"Miss Fletcher," he teased, pretending shock.

"Mr. Manning." She lay back down beside him, kissing his ear, running her tongue along his lobe. "You are magnificent."

"You surprise me, though I don't know why," he murmured. Nothing about her should surprise him.

"Ah, just you wait, Gordie Manning. You're not going to know what's hit you."

Laughing, he fell back with her, kissing her, hugging her, holding onto her, afraid to hold on, afraid to let go.

Gradually, their laughter faded. Gazing at her, he said softly, "Is this what love is like?"

Her expression sobered. "I don't know—I think so."

His eyes clouded. "I can't promise forever, Maggie." He had no idea where tonight would lead. He was going to make love to her; after that . . . the answer wouldn't come.

Rolling to her side, she gazed up at him, brushing her fingers lovingly across his cheek. He had never wanted her more. "I don't recall asking for forever."

I can't promise more than tonight, he agonized as he elevated himself above her, consumed by desire now.

He had to hope it would be enough.

Chapter 21

"Quit? You can't quit, Moses!"

"Quit." Moses, sporting an angry bruise between her eyes, glared at T.G. This latest incident was the last straw. Butte had rigged the women's picks so when they swung them, the heads flew off and hit them squarely between the eyes. Sue Ann was knocked cold and hadn't come around for a full ten minutes.

"I know it's hard to fight a ghost—but if you'll be patient just a little longer," Gordie pleaded. Butte was out of hand, but given enough time, T.G. would find a way to thwart him.

The shady ladies picked up their shovels and walked off. There wasn't enough gold in Colorado to put up with this.

T.G. watched them go, realizing what it meant. There wasn't a man, woman, or child who was willing to work the Hellhole. All because of Butte Fesperman.

His anger began to build.

Pitching the shovel aside, he strode toward the

mine, with no thought of phobia. Rage blinded
him. He didn't care about the gold. Backus could
damn well do whatever he wanted to him, but
without the gold, Maggie was sunk. She wasn't
chasing luxury, she was fighting for survival, and
he was going to fight Butte to the death, if that's
what it took.

Snatching up the lantern, he entered the mine,
shouting, "Butte, damn it, show yourself!"

A startled bat darted up and away, vanishing into
the darkness.

"Butte!"

Butte, Butte, Butte, echoed back.

Moving deeper into the shaft, T.G.'s eyes
searched the darkness. "Butte, enough's enough.
You can't do this to Maggie!"

Overhead, a timber snapped and came crashing
down. Jumping aside, T.G. barely avoided the flying debris.

"You going to fight like a coward? Cut it out,
Butte! For once in your life, fight like a man!"

Water rushed the mine. Grasping the side of
the wall, T.G. struggled to keep his balance as a
whirlpool swirled around his legs. The lantern
fell from his hand, and the current swiftly carried
it away.

The shaft plunged into darkness. T.G. could
feel his lungs closing. Struggling for breath, he
held tight to the sides of the ledge. "If you want
to fight someone, fight me. Just let Maggie have
the gold. You can't use it. You'll never be able to

use it! You're *dead*, Butte. Dead men don't need gold."

T.G. ducked as an explosion rocked the mine, splintering rock and pitching timbers through the air.

He was going to die. He should have enough sense to be afraid, but he wasn't. He was just damn mad. The blackness closed around him, filling his senses, squeezing the life from his lungs.

The scent of wildflowers suddenly deluged him, the fragrance so strong it was staggering. Maggie. Good, sweet Maggie. The feel of her innocent body hungry for his flooded his memory. Sweat beaded on his forehead. Blast that Butte's lousy hide. The son of a gun was using everything in his arsenal against him.

Another thunderous boom rocked the mine, and T.G. heard the back shaft give way. Oh, Butte was playing dirty all right—real dirty. No one knew he was in here. He could be buried alive, and Maggie would never know what happened to him.

Walls collapsed and buckled in.

Racked by coughing spasms, T.G. clung to the side of the wall as dust fouled the air. A thick grit filled his mouth and stung his eyes. The air supply in the narrow chamber dwindled. "You're evil, Butte. Let go of the past," he choked out.

A sheet of fire burst overhead. Angry flames licked across the ceiling, searing the rotting timbers.

Strangling, T.G. fought for breath. And for life. Plowing through the rising water, he felt his way back through the shaft. He didn't want to die. The realization hit him harder than any of the rocks and debris. If he died, Maggie would have no one. Worthless as he might be, she needed him. And he needed her.

He didn't want to die; the revelation was exhilarating and sobering. The meaning of life, which he had forgotten, suddenly came back. Wallowing in self-pity was for cowards. It took guts to stand up and fight back when life got you down.

Damn. What had Maggie Fletcher done to him?

Bolts of lightning forked through the tunnel, bouncing off the walls, charging the air with electricity. The ground vibrated beneath his feet as T.G. felt his way along the shaft wall, inching his way toward the entrance.

Timbers shattered, dirt and shale hurled through the air as the tunnel became a living, roaring hell.

Stumbling out of the shaft, T.G. fell to the ground, gasping for breath as the mine entrance violently sealed shut behind him.

As the dust settled, Butte's voice shouted from somewhere deep in the shaft. "And *stay* out!"

A moment later T.G. passed out.

He awoke with the feel of a cool cloth on his face. Maggie was bending over him, softly cooing his name as she worked the wet cloth back and forth over his battered face.

"Gordie . . . please . . . wake up. Please . . . Gordie."

Cracking one eye open, he scowled. "What for?"

With a sob of relief, Maggie dropped her head to his chest, hugging him tightly around the waist. "I thought you were dead."

"With my luck?" He struggled to sit up, massaging the knot on the back of his head.

Wiping moisture from the corner of her eyes with the hem of her apron, she glared at him. "You scared the life out of me!"

Getting to his feet, he knocked the dust off his denims, grimly surveying the blocked entrance to the mine. "I apologize, but I can assure you, this wasn't my idea."

"Oh, Gordie!" She turned from him to survey the cave-in, the third this week. "Not again!"

"Afraid so." Reaching for his hat, he dusted it off before settling it back on his head. "This is getting a little old."

"It's really true, isn't it?" she whispered. "There really is a ghost, and he's deliberately doing these things to discourage us and keep us from finding the gold."

"I tried to tell you."

Whirling, she grasped the front of his shirt. "We can't let him beat us, T.G.!"

"The hell we can't." T.G. had had it. Butte Fesperman could have the mine *and* Colorado. "We're letting him have it, Maggie. The whole kit and caboodle."

She looked stricken. "But what will I do? I have no money, no home, no life!"

His eyes softened. "Maggie, it's over. Moses just

quit and took her crew with her. We've dug that shaft out too many times to think about. We haven't got a crew, we don't have enough money to buy one stick of dynamite, let alone the case we need. We couldn't hire another crew if our lives depended on it."

She gazed back at him, heartsick. "Wilson's and my lives do depend on it."

"No, they don't." Taking her by the shoulders, he made her look at him. "I'm not a quitter, but damn it, I know when I'm beat. You and I sure can't dig that shaft out again. We're beat. Butte Fesperman is never going to let anyone get that gold."

"But—"

"No." She wasn't going to talk him out of this. "I have enough gold to get you and Wilson back to England. Take it, Maggie, and go back to your aunt. You don't belong here. You deserve to sleep in a warm bed, take decent baths, and go to sleep with a full belly every night. You need pretty clothes and proper suitors." His eyes were incredibly gentle. "You need a good man, Maggie, one who can give you all you deserve."

"But that money's to pay off your gambling debts."

The muscle worked in his jaw. "How do you know about that?"

"I overheard you talking with those wretched men." She knew that he was endangering his life if he failed to repay the debt. "And I saw what those thugs could do the first day you came to work at the mine."

"I'm not worried about Backus. Take the money and leave."

Meeting his eyes, she bit back tears. "And what about us?"

He tried to look away but she wouldn't let him. "What about us?"

"There is no us, Maggie. I thought you understood that."

"No," she whispered, stung by his rejection. "I didn't understand that."

He looked away. "I worked your mine. That's all I promised."

"Yes," she said brokenly, "that's all you promised."

The hurt he saw cut him deeper than any knife. Tears welled in her eyes.

"Now, don't start that," he warned. "We gave it our best shot, and we lost."

Turning away, she walked off.

T.G. watched her climb the hill, wanting to stop her but knowing that he wouldn't. She felt wounded and betrayed right now, but someday she would understand what he'd just done. She would realize that he loved her enough to set her free.

A tear escaped from the corner of his eye and rolled down his cheek. Swiping at it self-consciously, he castigated his weakness. Now she had him crying, damn it.

But he couldn't deny the pain strangling his gut;

it hurt like hell. His hand automatically went in search of his left-hand pocket.

Hell, he needed a drink.

Chapter 22

Plunging the iron skillet into a pan of hot water, Maggie vigorously scrubbed it. She'd battled the blues all day, and this depression had to end. For one thing, she had to get a job. For another, she had only a few dollars left to her name.

Taking a job didn't bother her. She could cook; she was good at that, and she knew she could find work at one of the camp cafés. Madeline Baxter mentioned that Cleo's Fork and Spoon needed a waitress. The tips were good, and Cleo was reported to treat her employees fairly. The problem was Wilson. Although he spent his days in school, who would look after him in the evenings?

Tears surfaced anew. She was *sick* of these maudlin feelings. She wasn't the first woman to go to work in order to provide for her family. Jeanine Tabor had lost her husband in a mining accident last year and found herself with six hungry mouths to feed.

Grabbing the hem of her apron, she wiped her

eyes, reminding herself she'd better be thankful
that she was strong, healthy, and able to work.

Glancing at the pile of eggs she'd gathered for
breakfast, she sighed. Flour, baking powder, and
salt were in the bowl, carefully measured and put
aside for breakfast. All that was needed was lard
and liquid, and she'd have a pan of biscuits that
would melt in a man's mouth.

If only there were a man around to eat them.

T.G. hadn't eaten with them for two days now.
Maggie had barely caught a glimpse of him at all
lately. If he actually thought she was going to give
up and go back to England, he was sadly mistaken.

She was not going to be scared off. He might be
satisfied with his life, and clearly he didn't want
Maggie a part of it, but she wasn't leaving. Somehow, some way, she would get another crew and
reopen the mine.

Taking the last jar of blackberry jam out of the
packing crate, she set it beside T.G.'s plate just in
case a miracle happened and he showed up in the
morning. Like everything else, it was the last. The
last of the jam, last of the money, last of a dream,
last time she was giving T.G. a chance to redeem
himself.

"Wilson, feed the animals," she called.

And that was another thing. What was she going
to do with a turkey, a raccoon, a blackbird, six laying hens, and a hoot owl, once it got so cold they
couldn't stay outside any longer? The dugout was
barely big enough to house the two of them.

"Already did!"

"Thank you."

"Welcome!"

Maggie picked up the basket of wash and started sorting clothes. Outside, the wind howled through the mountain pass. Winter was setting in, and T.G. would return to camp any day. For the past two mornings, she had expected to see the tent gone, but it was still there.

"Hey, Maggie?" Wilson called.

"Yes?"

"Is tonight Halloween?"

Maggie had to think for a moment. Why, it was Halloween. The weeks had passed by so swiftly she had lost all track of time.

"Yes, I believe it is Halloween, Wilson."

He glanced at the front door apprehensively. "Does that mean there are witches and ghosts roaming around outside tonight?"

"No. Actually, Halloween is a holy night."

"A holy night?"

"In medieval England, October 31 was called All Hallow Even. The souls of the dead went to visit their former homes on that day."

"You mean ghosts would come to see people?"

"No, not ghosts. The people knew they wouldn't actually be visited by the dead; it was a festival celebrated by the Christian church. All Saint's Day celebrates the saints of the church on November first. The night before, what we call Halloween, but they called All Hallow Even, was celebrated with festivities and children playing pranks during the evening."

Wilson pushed his glasses up the bridge of his nose, scooting closer to the fire. "Butch said on Halloween witches and goblins eat little kids!"

Maggie folded a petticoat, wishing Butch wasn't so informative. "Well, once again, Butch is wrong—"

She looked up as a knock sounded at the door. Her pulse quickened with expectancy. *Gordie?*

Closing her eyes, she breathed a sigh of relief and sent a small thank you heavenward. He was back.

"Want me to let Gordie in?" Wilson asked.

Deliberately adopting a casual tone, Maggie said, "No, I will."

Wilson grinned. Boy, did she think he was stupid, or what?

Tucking aside a wisp of stray hair, Maggie hurried to the door, wishing she had put on her blue dress. It was much prettier than the drab gray she was wearing, but there wasn't time to do anything about it now.

Pulling the door open, her welcoming smile froze, and her face paled when she saw Fionnula Wellesford standing before her. Gwendolyn and Mildred huddled beside her, their generous dimensions quaking in the biting wind.

Slamming the door, Maggie leaned against it, stunned. *Aunt Fionnula, Gwendolyn, Mildred.* How had they found her? Her letter had vaguely implied that she and Wilson were living in a mining camp near Denver. How did Fionnula determine precisely which one?

Wilson looked up, frowning.

"Aunt Fionnula," Maggie whispered.

His eyes widened. "Where?"

"Here . . . outside the door!"

Wilson's heart started to pound. "Is Gwendolyn with her? She'd better not step on Selmore with her big old foot!"

A rap sounded sharply at the door again. "Margaret, open this door!" Fionnula demanded in a muffled voice.

Maggie's mind was awhirl. What could she do? Never in a hundred years had she expected Fionnula to come to Colorado!

The pounding grew more insistent. "Mary Margaret, open this door immediately. It's dark out here!"

"Don't do it, Maggie," Wilson begged. "Make her go away!"

"She won't go away," Maggie whispered. That much she did know.

Wilson got up and ran over to stand beside her. "Is she mad?" The persistent hammering was a strong indication that she wasn't exactly happy, but angry? Maggie hoped not.

"Open this door, Margaret! We're freezing out here!"

"Don't do it!" Wilson begged as Maggie moved him aside in order to open the door. "Let her freeze."

"Shush, Wilson. She knows we're in here. We can't let her stand out there in the cold."

"Yes, we can!" Wilson clutched onto her skirt.

But Maggie wasn't to be swayed. She calmly reached for the latch and opened the door. "Aunt Fionnula! What a surprise!"

Fionnula, eyes sharp as daggers, swept into the room. Gwendolyn and Mildred stormed toward the fire, their expressions as sinister as the Halloween night.

Maggie summoned her brightest smile. "How did you find us?"

Fionnula, teeth chattering, huddled close to the fire, thawing her frozen bones. Gwendolyn and Mildred sullenly elbowed one another for the warmest spot.

"*Motttthhherr!* Mildred is hogging the fire!"

"I am not, Mother. *She is!*" Mildred, shouldering her sister aside, centered both feet on the floor and held her ground.

"Girls, girls," Fionnula soothed in a catlike purr. "There's room for all." Her obsidian eyes swung to Maggie. "Margaret, make us a pot of tea to warm ourselves."

"Oh, yes, ma'am—right away." Maggie scurried to put the kettle on the fire. "How did you ever find us?"

Gwendolyn's eyes trapped Wilson as he shrank farther under the table.

Removing her gloves, Fionnula surveyed the small dugout with obvious disdain. "Your letter was deliberately misleading. Fortunately, Kingsley Dermot knew of your whereabouts."

Maggie ventured a hesitant glance her way. "Then you got my letter."

Fionnula's eyes fossilized. "I received it."

Wilson, crouched beneath the table, mouthed a silent *ahhhh* when Gwendolyn deliberately stepped on his fingers as she backed up to the fire to warm her ample backside.

Mildred shoved her, and Gwendolyn shoved her back.

"Mothherrr!"

"Motheeeerr!"

"Girls, girls, settle down."

"You're looking well, Aunt Fionnula," Maggie complimented as she set out cups. "I hope the long journey wasn't overly taxing." Now that the shock was wearing off, Maggie was happy to see her family. She couldn't believe they'd come all this way to visit.

"It was awful," Gwendolyn whined.

"Horrible," Mildred sniveled.

"It was hellish," Fionnula concurred.

Maggie judiciously slid the remaining jar of blackberry jam into the packing crate. "I'm so surprised to see you."

"Yes." Fionnula smiled at her coldly. "I'm sure you are."

The kettle began to boil. Maggie whisked it off the fire and poured hot water into the teapot.

"Wilson, come out from under that table," Fionnula ordered.

Wilson didn't immediately answer, but when he did, it was to ask lamely, "Do I have to?"

Sticking her toe under the table, Maggie nudged

him out. "Wilson, come out here and say hello to Aunt Fionnula."

Wilson eventually emerged, giving Maggie an uneasy look.

Fionnula viewed the boy's slight build captiously. "He's too thin. You haven't been feeding him properly."

"I have, Aunt Fionnula. We've eaten well," Maggie insisted.

Fionnula dismissed her with a sharp look. "Girls, you can take your coats off now. The tea is ready."

They all gathered around the small table, the girls and Wilson seated on pillows on the floor, Aunt Fionnula on the stool. Maggie poured steaming hot tea into cups. "Isn't Colorado lovely?"

"It's cold."

"No colder than England," Maggie commented.

"I can't breathe," Mildred complained.

"My lungs hurt," Gwendolyn muttered.

"It's the air. It's thinner up here," Maggie explained. "It takes awhile, but you'll get used to it."

The girls each stirred four heaping teaspoons of sugar into their tea as Maggie sliced bread and set out butter. Her mind was wondering where they would all sleep. The dugout was so tiny, and she only had two blankets.

Taking a sip of tea, Fionnula cut straight to the chase. "We are not here for a social visit, Margaret. As you might suspect, I am quite unhappy with Eldora's scandalous omission of Mildred and

Gwendolyn in her will. I have instructed my attorney to break the will."

Maggie looked up, stunned. "But Aunt Fionnula—"

"I know this comes as a shock, but I cannot sit idly by and watch my daughters hurt by an oversight."

"Oversight?"

Fionnula's eyes hardened. "Surely you're not suggesting my sister would intentionally leave my daughters out of her will?"

"No, of course not, I just—"

"Didn't think," Fionnula finished. "Rest assured you and your brother will be provided for while the matter is under advisement. Any gold that comes out of the mine will be set aside and evenly divided among the four of you once the legal matters have been resolved."

Wilson broke in. "We ain't got any gold, Aunt Fionnula."

"We 'ain't got any' gold?" Fionnula repeated.

"Wilson," Maggie corrected sharply. "We don't have any gold."

"Yeah, that's what I said. We don't have any."

Fionnula's censuring look silenced him.

"Naturally, any gold already mined will be taken into account and deducted from your portion at the conclusion of this unfortunate error. Meanwhile, you and Wilson will return to England with us. Once there, we'll speak no more of this matter."

"We don't want to go back to England," Maggie said softly.

Fionnula said coldly, "You have no choice."

"I'll be eighteen soon," Maggie reminded her.

"I am aware of that, Margaret. Under the circumstances you may remain under my guardianship until you have the funds to establish yourself elsewhere."

Stirring a teaspoon of sugar into her tea, Maggie quietly absorbed the ultimatum. Fionnula was going to squander money on legal fees to seize part-ownership in a mine that wasn't worth the paper it was written on? How very fitting.

"It was Aunt Sissy's wish that Wilson and I have the mine. I don't understand why, but don't you think we should honor her wishes?"

"Nonsense." Fionnula buttered a piece of bread. "Eldora was clearly out of her mind when she constituted the will. Her outlandish lifestyle addled her brain. My attorney assures me he'll have no trouble proving so in a court of law."

Mildred reached for the last slice of bread as Gwendolyn lunged for it. In the ensuing battle, cups and saucers were knocked off the table and the sugar bowl overturned. Wilson grabbed Jellybean, shielding him from the fracas.

"Girls, girls," Fionnula mollified. "Margaret will slice more bread."

Getting down on her hands and knees, Maggie picked up the broken pieces of pottery. That pretty well took care of that! They were down to strictly tinware now. She had brought so few nice dishes, only her mother's favorites, in her tiny bag when she left England. Oh well, it didn't matter, anyway.

How could losing a few dishes compare to the problem of her uninvited guests?

Fionnula peered over her nose domineeringly. "Mary Margaret, leave that for later. Slice more bread. Gwendolyn is ravenous."

Gathering pieces of broken cup into her apron, Maggie answered in a calm voice. "There is no more bread."

"No more bread?" Fionnula glanced around the small kitchen. "You baked no more than one loaf of bread?"

"I had enough flour for one loaf, no more." Dumping the broken pottery into the trash, she took her seat again.

"Are supplies scarce here?" Fionnula challenged.

"No, money is scarce here."

Fionnula's features registered thinly veiled triumph. "Girls, didn't I tell you she would regret leaving my protection in such a harridan fashion?"

"*Motheerrr!* Mildred's had three cups of tea and I've only had one!"

Mildred snatched the teapot and dumped the remains into her cup as Gwendolyn fought her for control.

"*Motheerrr!*"

"Hush, Gwendolyn, there's tea for all." Fionnula's eyes pinned Maggie. "Or is that in short supply, also?"

"I have more tea." Maggie got up to fix it.

Smothering a yawn, Fionnula dismissed her efforts. "The girls are exhausted. Just show us to our rooms, and we'll eat a large breakfast in the morning."

Maggie glanced at Wilson, who was giving Mildred and Gwendolyn plenty of elbow room. "I'm sorry ... we'll have to make pallets on the floor."

"Motheerr!" the girls wailed in unison.

"The floor?" Fionnula's brow lifted with repulsion. "There are no beds? You are living in such abject poverty that you have no beds?"

"Only a small one. You can take it, Aunt Fionnula. Wilson and I will sleep in the tent."

"In Gordie's tent?" Wilson exclaimed.

Fionnula's eyes swung to him. "Whose tent?"

Maggie hurriedly explained. "One of the miners' tents. It's all right, he isn't there anymore."

"Gordie's gone?" Wilson cried. When had he left? He'd seen him right after school!

"Get your coat on, Wilson. Aunt Fionnula, Mildred, and Gwendolyn are tired." Gathering whatever she could find to make pallets, Maggie prepared the beds.

When she finished, she put on her cloak and lit the extra lantern. "You'll be plenty warm," she promised. "The wood is just outside the door."

The women looked at each other as if someone had broken wind.

"Come along, Wilson." Smiling, Maggie shooed him toward the door. "We'll be back in the morning."

"What time is breakfast?" Gwendolyn called.

"Whatever time you say, Gwendolyn."

Closing the dugout door, Maggie pulled her cloak tighter around her. The wind was screeching now, swirling large flakes of snow in the air.

"Ha," Wilson said, the irony of it finally dawned on him. He pulled Jellybean closer, shielding him from the bitter elements. "Aunt Fionnula came all this way just to steal a haunted mine. Let's give her the whole thing, huh, Maggie. The ghost and all. That'll teach her."

"Yes," Maggie muttered. "We're gonna teach her, all right." Take their mine away from them? She didn't think so.

Doubled against the wind, they hurried across the frozen ground to Gordie's tent, where a dim light burned in the whirling snow.

Chapter 23

"T.G., let us in!"

Gordie stepped out of the way as Maggie and Wilson rushed into the tent on the heels of a blast of arctic air.

"I thought you said Gordie was gone!" Wilson cried, turning to Maggie in bewilderment.

"I only said that for Aunt Fionnula's sake." Maggie's eyes locked with T.G.'s, their gazes hungrily searching. The two days they had spent apart suddenly seemed like a lifetime.

"Aunt Fionnula?" Gordie asked.

"Oh, yeah," Wilson said, his eyes widening, awareness seeping into his voice. "She wouldn't have let us come out here if she knew Gordie was here, would she, Maggie."

Gordie listened to the exchange, puzzled. "Your Aunt Fionnula wouldn't let you come out here?"

"That's right, and she wants Gwendolyn and Mildred to have a share of the mine. She says her lawyer will have no problem breaking the will." Maggie began to pace the length of the small tent.

"Who?"

"Gwendolyn and Mildred. Aunt Fionnula. What am I going to do?"

T.G. tried to piece together the fractured conversation. "Do you mean she wrote you and said she wanted Mildred and Gwendolyn to have a share of the mine?"

"No, she's here."

"Here, in Colorado? You can't be serious."

"Right here—in the dugout. What am I going to do?" Maggie was rambling now, talking more to herself than to T.G. "I know what we'll do. We'll sign the mine over to you."

"*What?*"

"Yeah!" Wilson sang out. "Let's give Gordie the mine!"

"She's not going to take our mine away from us. I won't let her. We've worked too hard to let her take it away from us."

"Didn't I tell you she'd try to take it away?" Wilson blurted.

"You tried to tell me, Wilson, but I wouldn't listen. Aunt Fionnula has no right to our inheritance. If Aunt Sissy wanted Gwendolyn and Mildred to share in her estate, she would have included them in the will. She wasn't crazy—on the contrary, she knew Aunt Fionnula's miserly ways, and she wanted to protect us. We won't let her do it. We'll sign the mine over to T.G. Once she is gone, T.G. can sign it back over to us."

"Give T.G. our mine?"

"Not give it to him, only loan it to him for a

while." Maggie knew the ramifications if her trust were misplaced.

"Whoa," T.G. said. He wasn't sure what they were talking about, but he wanted no part of it. Not if it involved the Hellhole.

"Now, T.G." Maggie stopped pacing and faced him squarely. "You have to help us."

"No, I helped once, and look what happened." Not only had he lost the satisfaction of drifting aimlessly through life, he was actually now languishing over lost love.

"I'm desperate, Gordie. My aunt is here, threatening to break the will."

"Yeah, Gordie, it's Halloween and a witch showed up on our doorstep."

"Wilson," Maggie reprimanded. "No matter what Aunt Fionnula is trying to do, you are to show her respect."

"I was talking about Gwendolyn."

"Your Aunt Sissy's will?" T.G. asked, still trying to follow the fast-moving conversation.

"Yes, Aunt Fionnula is certain Aunt Sissy was out of her mind when she left the Hellhole to Wilson and me. She insists Gwendolyn and Mildred have been slighted. She's instructed her lawyer to break the will."

"Give it to her, Maggie."

"Give her *my* mine?"

"Our mine," Wilson reminded.

"Give it to her," T.G. repeated. "Think about it, Maggie. What could be more appropriate? Give her the mine *and* its headaches. Within a month, she'll abandon it, and some other sucker will come along to claim it. He will surrender it, in turn, and so it will go on and on until someone finally blows the thing up and seals Butte Fesperman and the whole damn mess for eternity."

Wilson agreed with Gordie. "Yeah, let Aunt Fionnula have the mine *and* the ghost, Maggie!"

"Never. We have worked too hard to let her take it away from us. I stood by silently when she stole Mother and Father's money, and I will not let her take away the one thing we have left."

"Maggie, be reasonable. The mine is worthless! It will take weeks, maybe even months to get it going again. Even if we can find anyone to work it, what will you have? Nothing. Butte Fesperman is never going to relinquish his hold on that gold!"

"Aha! Then you do believe there is gold in there!"

"I'd stake my life on it, but nobody's going to get it. I'll double stake my life on that."

Maggie thought of her father's fierce pride and tenacity. It strengthened her own resolve. Her chin shot upward. "I don't care. Good or bad, the Hellhole is mine, and no one is going to take it away from me."

"Us," Wilson put in, suddenly undecided again. Maybe Maggie was right after all.

"You and Butte," T.G. complained bitterly.

Maggie's brows lifted imperiously. "Butte and I what?"

"Sound exactly alike."

An idea suddenly hit her. "T.G., is Butte here?"

"I don't know."

"But he might be?"

"I don't know where he is. We've been out of touch lately." Since their last violent run-in, Butte had stayed away.

"Ask him to appear. Right here—right now." If the ghost did exist, this was the perfect time for him to prove it.

Wilson's eyes widened, and he clutched Jellybean tighter around the neck.

"Forget it, he refuses to let anyone but me see him."

"But if he is real he can help us. He can stop these useless acts of violence and let us work the mine."

"Butte isn't going to stop anything."

Maggie spied the metal flask lying beside the fire. Disappointment filled her eyes.

Recognizing the look, Gordie leaned over and picked up the flask. "Don't worry. I haven't drunk it yet. I've sat here staring at it for two days."

Maggie's spirits lifted, her faith restored. "What have you decided?"

His eyes met hers. "I haven't come to any firm conclusions."

She gazed back at him, all her pent-up love in her eyes. It had been two long, agonizing days since she'd been in his arms. "I'm sorry, I hoped by now you would know what you want."

"Maggie, what about Aunt Fionnula?" Wilson's voice brought them back to the present.

Maggie's eyes locked with T.G.'s. "I'm signing the deed over to Gordie."

"No, you're not. Not when I'm like this, Maggie."

"Like what?"

His eyes indicated the flask. "When I'm not thinking straight."

"When you're seeing ghosts?"

He didn't answer.

"I trust you."

"Don't be a fool." He didn't trust himself. If he took that first drink, he wouldn't be responsible for his actions. He could easily gamble the mine away, or worse, give it away in exchange for more liquor.

"I'm signing the mine over to you. When Aunt Fionnula learns that I've given it away, there will be nothing she can do. Once she leaves, you can sign it back to me."

"Go home with your aunt, Maggie. Give the Hellhole to her, and go back to England." He turned away. "There is nothing here for you and Wilson."

"I don't agree."

"Then you're a bigger fool than I thought."

Removing the deed from her cloak pocket, she moved closer to the light.

When T.G. realized that she was determined to go through with her plan, he said sharply, "No, don't do it, Maggie. I won't accept the responsibility."

"You don't have a choice." Scribbling a brief

note on the deed, she signed it. "Wilson, you need to sign this, too."

"Don't sign it, Wilson."

Handing Jellybean to T.G., Wilson stepped next to Maggie, looking up at her. Their eyes exchanged a private moment. Reaching for the pencil, he carefully printed WILSON FLETCHER JR. before handing the pencil back to her.

She smiled warmly at her brother. "Thank you."

"You're welcome." Reaching for Jellybean, he hugged the cat tightly to him.

Handing Gordie the deed, she said, "Our future is in your hands."

"Shit."

Wilson glanced expectantly at Maggie. "He's talking bad."

"Please disregard T.G.'s atrocious language, Wilson. He's just upset."

"Don't do this to me, Maggie."

"And another thing, we have to sleep here tonight. There isn't room for us in the dugout," she went on.

"Double shit." That's all he needed. A small tent, a cold night, Maggie in his bed.

And her little brother lying not ten feet away.

Triple shit.

It wasn't yet light when Maggie stirred. Barely awake, she glanced at Wilson, smiling when she saw his head burrowed beneath the blankets.

Sighing, she snuggled closer to T.G.'s warmth. It had been a tortuous night. Hands and lips had found each other. He kissed her for long periods, sweetly, not forward, but hungry kisses that let her know that he needed her as much as she needed him. Stolen whispers, urgent needs, and Wilson lying close by made for an unusually long night.

Her hands deftly unbuttoned the tops of his long johns, then slid inside to run along the furry edge of his belly, playfully giving little pinches here and there to awaken him.

Capturing her hand, he put it in a place that brought a hot rush to her cheeks.

Rolling over, his mouth took hers in a heady kiss. Their hunger was impossible to gratify.

"I have to go," she whispered, although she would have been content to stay in his arms forever. "Gwendolyn will be calling for breakfast."

She started to get up, but he caught her back to him, his fingers slipping down over her buttocks. "It was a long night."

"I know," she whispered.

"One day, Maggie Fletcher, we will be alone." His eyes delivered a reckless promise.

"I know." She brought his mouth back to hers. "I can hardly wait."

"What do I do now?" he asked when the kiss finally ended. He had a deed in his pocket he didn't want, granting him sole ownership to a mine he didn't want, involving him deeper in Wilson and Maggie's well-being, a component he sure didn't want. Or did he? Before Maggie came into his life, he had been so clear on what he wanted. Now, a vagueness plagued him.

"I want you to disappear for a few days. When I tell Aunt Fionnula what we've done, she'll be angry and want to return to England as soon as possible." After one night in the dugout, she would practically run back to England on foot.

"You honestly think you can convince her you've given the mine away?"

"I won't tell her I've given it away." Now that she'd had time to think, she knew her aunt was smarter than to believe that. "I've decided to tell her about Butte Fesperman and show her the havoc he's caused. I'll tell her I couldn't stand anymore, so I sold the mine to a passing miner for one dollar. I'll say Wilson and I were getting ready to return to England when she showed up."

"And in the meantime?"

"In the meantime, you'll vanish for a week—no longer, because I have exactly enough money to last a week—then we'll meet at Potter's Stream and you can sign the deed back over to me."

Cradling her face, he gazed at her. He knew he loved her and wanted only the best for her, even if it meant losing her. "Go back to England, Maggie. I sign the mine back over to you, and you're still facing the same problems. No workers, no money, barely adequate living conditions—you deserve more, Maggie. Go home. Marry a fine, upstanding man who can give you children, a comfortable home, pretty clothing, one of those new motorcars—"

She lay her fingers across his lips, preventing him from going on. "What about love?"

His eyes darkened to a cerulean hue. "You'll have no trouble finding love."

"I would rather have a horse."

He grimaced. "Than love?"

"Than one of those motorcars. I've heard they break down a lot, and they can't master a hill nearly like a horse."

He kissed her briefly. "Nevertheless, you should have one."

The teasing light faded from her eyes. "I know there are problems with the mine, but they're my problems, T.G. Please let me fight them as I see fit."

He gazed back at her, his instinct to protect her still the overriding consideration. "A woman's place is in the home, not fighting for survival in the gold mines."

"One week." She kissed him into submission. "I'll meet you at Potter's Stream in one week."

"And what are you going to do about Butte?"

"Fight him until there isn't a breath left in me."

"How do you fight a ghost?" She had no idea what she was up against.

"I don't know, Gordie, I just know I'm not giving up."

Wilson stirred, opening his eyes.

Exchanging one last kiss, Maggie and T.G. moved apart.

"Is it morning?" Wilson mumbled sleepily.

"It's morning," Maggie conveyed brightly. Crawling from beneath the blankets, she straightened her clothes.

Crawling out of his blanket, Wilson reached for Jellybean. "We'd better be getting back to the dugout. *Gwendolyn* will be wanting breakfast."

Draping her cloak around her shoulders, Maggie's eyes searched T.G.'s. "I'll see you soon?"

He lay on the pallet, staring up at her. His long johns were open at the neck, revealing a thatch of reddish hair. Desire flooded her. "Why would you trust me with so much riding on your future?"

"I don't know, T.G." She didn't claim to know all the answers. "I just do."

A moment later the tent flap closed, leaving T.G. alone with only the scent of wildflowers to remind him of his obligation.

Chapter 24

"You what!" Fionnula's eyes turned to shards of steel.

Cutting out biscuits, Maggie calmly laid them in the pan. "Honestly, Aunt Fionnula, it was such a relief to be rid of it. When I found out the mine was haunted, I had the same reaction as you. Why, that's ridiculous, I told Wilson, but after a while, when all the accidents, fires, floods, and cave-ins kept happening, I said to Wilson, 'Wilson, I think we should sell the mine and return to England, where we know we are always welcome in Aunt Fionnula's house.' " She glanced up, smiling serenely.

"You sold my daughters' inheritance?"

"Well, of course, when I sold the mine, I didn't consider Gwendolyn and Mildred a part of the will." Just as she didn't consider them to be part of it now. However questionable Aunt Sissy's decision had been, it had been hers to make.

"You silly twit! This is an outrage!" Fionnula shoved back from the table, furious.

Gwendolyn lunged for the last bite of biscuit dough, causing Mildred to bolt to her feet, fighting her for it. The girls scuffled, rattling tins and cups until Fionnula was forced to break up the tussle.

When the girls were seated again, they stared daggers at each other.

Fionnula asked sharply, "Who did you sell it to?"

Maggie shrugged. "A drifter."

Fionnula was fit to be tied. "You'll just have to return the money and get it back! I forbid you to sell it!"

"It's too late. I've already sold it."

"Get it back!"

Gwendolyn and Mildred got into a squabble over the sugar bowl. It looked closer to Mildred than to Gwendolyn, and Gwendolyn felt affronted.

Wedging the pan of biscuits into the fireplace oven, Maggie looked up thoughtfully. "That's not possible. He's a drifter—I haven't seen him since I sold him the mine."

She carefully avoided looking Wilson's way. She wasn't lying. She hadn't seen Gordie since she'd sold him the mine half an hour ago.

Fionnula looked faint. Sinking to her chair, she fanned herself with her fingers, suffering from the vapors. The tiny room, with too many occupants, was suffocatingly hot.

"Aunt Fionnula, the mine is haunted," Maggie consoled. "Believe me, it was nothing but a headache. I'm lucky to be rid of it."

Fanning more energetically, Fionnula glared at

her. "Young lady, if you have thoughtlessly sold that mine right out from underneath your cousins' noses, you will split whatever proceeds you have with Mildred and Gwendolyn. That's the only fair way to handle this matter."

"I have no money, Aunt Fionnula. Everything we've mined so far has gone to pay our workers."

"What workers? I see no sign of workers." The place looked deserted to her!

"They're gone now. They walked out after the last cave-in."

"Oh, my." She fanned harder. "This is all so distressing."

Maggie shrugged. "There's nothing left of my inheritance, honestly."

"Then you will *share* with your cousins half of what you received from the sale of the mine! Have you forgotten that I took you and your brother in when no one else would?"

"No, ma'am, I haven't forgotten." Moving to the packing crate, Maggie knelt, rummaging through the contents until she found the small tin where she kept her coins. Taking one, she replaced the lid and fit the tin back into the crate. Standing up, she handed the coin to Fionnula.

Viewing the coin imperiously, Fionnula inquired, "What is this?"

"Gwendolyn and Mildred's share of Aunt Sissy's mine."

"One dollar?"

"Exactly what I sold it for."

"*One* dollar. You sold the mine for a dollar?"

Maggie cracked eggs into the skillet. "Ask any-one around here. That's top price for the Hellhole."

Mildred dived for the empty shells as Gwen-dolyn tried to beat her to them. Picking up the skil-let, Maggie moved out of the way as the girls fought over who got to dispose of the shells. They wrestled, yanking each other's hair before Fionnula could separate them.

"In other words," Fionnula physically restrained the girls as she picked up the conversation, "you *gave* the mine away."

"I had to. I couldn't work it. In the past two months we've had eleven cave-ins, seven fires, been flooded more times than I can count, and lost our entire crew. If a mine isn't worked within a specified amount of time, the owner loses the claim."

There was no need to mention this rule was null and void if there was a reasonable excuse for not working the mine.

Cave-ins, fires, and floods were accepted as rea-sonable excuses, but with the Hellhole it didn't matter if anyone worked it or not. She couldn't give it away.

Wilson decided to add his wisdom. "You want to see the mine, Aunt Fionnula?"

Fionnula sniffed. "I most certainly do."

Smiling, Maggie scrambled eggs. "You don't be-lieve me when I say it's worthless?"

"I didn't say I didn't believe you, I've just never known you to be so selfish, Mary Margaret. Your poor cousins—just look at them. *How* could you do this to them? A gold mine would have insured their future." She was the proud matriarch as she gazed fondly upon her daughters. "There isn't an eligible bachelor in Wokingham who could have resisted both beauty and wealth."

Gwendolyn belched.

"Say excuse me, dear."

"Excuse me."

"Dear," Wilson added under his breath.

After breakfast they all trooped out to view the ruins. Nosing around in the dirt, Fionnula failed to come up with any sign of gold. A skiff of snow dusted the frozen ground, and the wind was blowing a stiff gale this morning.

Wiping mud off her hands, Fionnula viewed the sealed Hellhole entrance as the girls huddled beside her, quaking in the blustery wind. "Well, darlings, it seems it's true." She viewed the blocked shaft dishearteningly. "Apparently there's nothing we can do until Margaret comes to her senses and gets that deed back. We'll return to England immediately."

Gwendolyn stuck her tongue out at Wilson.

Wilson stuck his back, mouthing a silent yeaaaaaaah!

"Bah." Fionnula turned away with disgust. "Come along, girls. If we hurry, we can catch the afternoon train."

Later that afternoon, Wilson and Maggie stood at the train depot awaiting the Wellesfords' imminent departure. Fionnula had not asked what

Maggie and Wilson planned to do now that they no longer owned the mine. It was disturbingly clear to Maggie that she didn't care.

Directing an impersonal kiss in Maggie's direction, Fionnula ushered the girls aboard the train. Gwendolyn and Mildred darted to the benches, warring over the window seat.

"Mary Margaret, when you come to your senses, you may return to England. The Wellesfords and Fletchers will unite and take back the mine."

"And if I don't?" Maggie dared to ask.

Maggie had never seen Fionnula look so hateful. "You will. You have no way to support yourself. You'll come crawling back, and I wager it won't be too long."

"Are you saying you will let us come back, Aunt Fionnula?"

"If there's no other choice."

The words stung, but Maggie didn't want her to leave with bitter feelings. "I'm sorry you're angry, but the mine is haunted. It would have been of no value to Gwendolyn and Mildred."

"Bah, all this nonsense about ghosts. You get the deed to that mine back, young lady. If nothing else, we'll sell it for two dollars!" Climbing aboard, Fionnula held onto her hat to keep the blustery wind from snatching it away.

Maggie suddenly felt deserted. It was one thing to choose not to return to England, and another not to be invited. "Aren't you curious what Wilson and I will do now?"

Fionnula peered over the rim of her glasses at

her. "You're just like your father. You'll come up with something, but that, too, will fail. When you grow tired of struggling, you'll be back to England."

As the train pulled out of town, Maggie and Wilson crowded together in the bitter cold. Their breaths made frosty clouds in the air.

"We're not going back, are we, Maggie? I would rather starve than go back and put up with Gwendolyn again."

"I hope not, Wilson."

Wilson leaned forlornly against her side. Things just weren't working out the way they had planned. "Guess we really are on our own now, huh, Maggie?"

No mine. No money. No Gordie.

Wrapping her arms around his thin shoulders, Maggie held onto him tightly. At the moment he was *all* she had. "Don't worry, Gordie won't let us down."

One week from today, he would meet them at Potter's Stream.

Chapter 25

"What day is it?"

"You've asked twice already. It's Tuesday, both times." Chappy inspected the miniature hummingbird he was carving, silently chuckling. That boy had it bad for Maggie Fletcher. Real bad!

"And you saw Maggie's aunt actually getting on the train?"

"Her and her two homely daughters." Chappy held the carving up to the light. "That woman's got a problem on her hands with those two."

Gordie was killing time this morning. Perched on the hitching rail, he observed the wagons moving up and down the street. Tomorrow morning, he would meet Maggie at Potter's Stream. The deed she had entrusted to him had not left his hand for a moment.

His blood raced with expectancy when he thought of her. He missed her; the touch of her hand, her smile, the sound of her voice.

"You gonna marry her?"

Gordie swept the idea aside. "What would a woman like Maggie Fletcher want with a man like me?"

"Don't know—but 'peers she does." Wood chips from Chappy's knife flew to a scattered pile at his feet. "Well? You gonna take the plunge?"

"I don't have any plans to marry her."

Chappy didn't understand T.G.'s reluctance. A man would kill to have a woman like Maggie Fletcher in his bed. The union between him and the Fletcher woman was inevitable.

"You never talked much about yourself. Where'd you say you come from?"

"Phoenix."

"Phoenix, huh?" Chappy paused, brushing the cuttings off his lap. "Suppose you got family there."

"Some. Sister, father."

"Mother?"

"She died in '89."

"Sorry to hear it. Your father in good health?"

"I haven't talked to my father in awhile, but, yes, I'd say he's in good health for a man his age." Gordie thought about the long hours Gordon Sr. worked, delivering babies, treating dyspepsia with doses of bismuth, rheumatism with bicarbonate of soda laced with lemon juice. T.G. had apprenticed four years by his father's side before going on to Boston for another four years to get a medical degree. His life had turned out so differently from what anyone expected.

"Suppose you'll be going back someday?"

"I'm not sure of what I'll do." He wasn't sure of anything anymore.

Smiling, Chappy turned the carving over in his hands, critically examining his work. "What d'you think the Fletcher woman will do now? Heard the Hellhole was sealed tighter than a tick."

"We'll open it again." T.G. had been doing a lot of thinking the past week. Odds were against them, but if Maggie wanted to reopen the mine, he was going to do his damnedest to get her another crew.

"You ran into Butte yet?"

"Yeah, I've run into him."

Chappy glanced up.

T.G. nodded. "The stories are true. Fesperman's spirit lives in the mine."

Chappy eyed him skeptically. "You're pulling my leg, boy."

"No, he's there. I've seen him."

"Butte Fesperman?"

"Butte Fesperman. Ornery as hell. If it weren't for him, Maggie would own the mother lode right now."

Chappy cocked his head, trying to see T.G.'s left coat pocket.

Ignoring his misgivings, T.G. went on. "I'm more certain than ever, it's in there."

"The mother lode? In the Hellhole?"

"In the Hellhole."

That was every man's hope. Hit that one big

payload that would make them rich beyond their wildest expectations. "Anything in particular make you think that way?"

"Butte said it was there. If you think about it, it makes sense. He wouldn't be caught where he is, refusing to give up his hold on the mine, if it were worthless."

Chappy looked up again. "Caught where he is . . . where is he?"

T.G. turned cagey. "He's not certain."

"I thought you said he was in the Hellhole."

"He is . . . at least in spirit." T.G. hoped Chappy wouldn't press the subject.

"Uh huh." Word had it Manning had stopped drinking. Chappy had to wonder about that.

"I have to figure a way to make him give up the mine and move on." Even if the mother lode were not there, if T.G. could just mine enough gold to keep Maggie and Wilson here with him, he'd be happy.

"Uh huh."

The two men sat in silence, mulling over the conversation.

"This is Tuesday, isn't it?"

"Yeah, it's Tuesday, still."

Eventually, T.G. got up and absently wandered off.

Rubbing the carving between his hands, Chappy watched him go.

That boy was a tad weird lately.

* * *

As a cold sun surfaced above the mountain-tops, T.G. was already on his way to Potter's Stream.

He had tossed and turned most of the night, unable to get Maggie out of his mind. The brief separation had been a revelation for him. For someone who thought he didn't need anyone, he'd discovered he needed her.

Contented for the first time in a long time, he whistled as he walked along the road. The brisk, pine-scented air filled his nostrils. The sky, overcast and dreary, failed to make a dent in his mood. Pewter-colored clouds promised snow by nightfall, but T.G. knew by that time he, Maggie, and Wilson would be sitting before the fire, eating popcorn, catching up on the past week's events. He was anxious to hear how Fionnula had taken Maggie's news, and eager to tell her about his plans to reopen the mine. If he were lucky, Wilson would drop off to sleep early, then T.G. would have Maggie to himself. He smiled, admitting that she was a fire in his flesh, in his soul, in his heart.

Near the outskirts of camp the sun came out, touching the frozen earth with pale, icy fingers. Potter's Stream was a mile or so down the road, not a long walk, so the cold didn't bother T.G.

Up ahead, T.G. spotted Edgar Miller's outhouse. The small building with a half-moon notched in the door was active this morning. Edgar himself emerged, fastening his suspenders on his way back to the homestead.

As T.G. drew nearer, he frowned, spotting Abe Norris, one of Backus's thugs who'd been hounding him for payment, walking up ahead of him.

Slackening his pace, T.G. let Abe get well ahead of him. Abe hadn't been paid recently, so he'd just as soon not inflame an already volatile situation.

Veering off the road, Abe made a beeline for the outhouse as the sausage and fried apples he'd had for breakfast suddenly kicked in. Abe, who wouldn't miss three hundred pounds by much, would be a tight fit for the small quarters, but when nature called Abe, she shouted.

The door closed behind him, and the little privy rocked back and forth as Abe worked to get his pants down and his tail end over the hole.

Ordinarily, T.G. would have left well enough alone. But this wasn't an ordinary day, or an ordinary opportunity. Abe Norris had given him one hell of a shiner that day, and T.G. wanted retribution. Glancing around, he noted he was the only one on the road.

Even better.

Sounds coming from inside the privy assured T.G. his approaching footsteps would never be noticed. Pausing in front of the door, T.G. grinned. Revenge was sweet, even if the air surrounding the outhouse wasn't.

Bracing his shoulder against the door, he mustered all his strength and shoved.

The outhouse toppled backward amid a flurry of Abe's startled oaths.

Whirling, T.G. ran. When Abe crawled out, T.G. wasn't going to be within a country mile.

He was half of that country mile down the road before his pace started to moderate.

Trotting along, he threw his head back, laughing out loud as he pictured the look on Abe's face when he went down. Confident Abe would never know who or what hit him, T.G. relished the brief victory.

Three hundred pounds, give or take a few ounces, suddenly slammed into him from the back, felling him like a shotgun blast.

Grunting, two figures rolled around on the ground, each trying to gain the upper hand. Abe outweighed T.G. by a good hundred pounds, so Gordie was outmatched.

Dazed, T.G.'s eyes stung from the rotten smell. Abe's clothes were pungent with urine and excrement.

Anger flushed Abe's fleshy cheeks. His nostrils engaged, retracted, fury boiling over in his eyes as he pinned Gordie to the ground.

"I'm gonna break your damned neck, Manning!"

"Come on, Abe." T.G. tried to break his headlock but wasn't having much luck. "Can't you take a joke!"

"Joke my arse!"

T.G. saw it coming. Planting his knee in the

middle of Gordie's chest, Abe drew back, murder in his eyes. A belated thought crossed Gordie's mind: You should have toppled the outhouse on its *door*, stupid!

That was his last coherent thought before Abe coldcocked him.

Chapter 26

Snow began falling around ten o'clock. Pacing the banks of Potter's Stream, Maggie tried to blow feeling back into her hands. Her eyes anxiously searched the road for T.G. Though no certain time had been agreed upon, he should have been here by now.

Her mind tried to justify his delay. Since she hadn't known his whereabouts the past week, she didn't know how far he had to come. Potter's Stream was halfway between Hoodee Doo and the Hellhole.

While she assumed he had stayed in the vicinity of Hoodee Doo, that didn't necessarily mean he had. He could have decided to visit friends at a neighboring camp. After all, he had been told to disappear. Wincing, she prayed that he hadn't taken her literally.

Wilson, huddled on a fallen log, was losing heart. They had been waiting for Gordie since early this morning. Now, his hands and feet were numb with cold. Teeth chattering, he voiced

Maggie's worse misgiving. "Maybe he isn't coming."

Her tone came out more caustic than she intended. "Don't say that. He's coming."

Her eyes stubbornly returned to the road. He would come. He wouldn't walk away with her mine like a common thief. He might have shortcomings, but who didn't? He certainly was not deceitful and cunning; nothing would make her believe that about him. There was a reason he hadn't come—and he would be there. If only she waited long enough, he would.

Another hour passed. Snow blanketed the bare tree branches. The pines were taking on their winter finery.

Periodically, Maggie's eyes returned to the road. Wilson's always followed. Yet no matter how long and hard they looked, Gordie's comfortable, familiar figure didn't appear.

"Are we gonna stay here forever?" Wilson finally asked.

Maggie continued to pace. She hadn't been able to feel her feet for an hour now. Where could he be? In her heart she believed he would never betray her trust, yet what could possibly delay him this long?

A new thought assailed her. Was he ill? Had something happened that physically prevented him from coming?

No, he would have sent word. He wouldn't just let her wait without knowing.

Another hour passed, then another. Wilson's lips were beginning to turn blue.

Sinking down next to him on the log, Maggie stared blindly at the falling snow. It was getting late. They couldn't stay much longer.

"We better go now, huh, Maggie?" Wilson realized Maggie didn't want to give up, but they couldn't stay here all night. It would be dark soon, and it was still a long walk back to the dugout.

Maggie's eyes yielded to the road again, desperately praying T.G. would appear. Perhaps he had forgotten. Hope flared, then died away. There was nothing wrong with T.G.'s memory. If he could remember anything, he could remember to meet her at Potter's Stream this morning.

But morning had come and gone. Now afternoon. She had to conclude he wasn't coming.

Getting up, she winced from the pain in her icy limbs.

"Are we going now?"

Maggie stared at the road, but it was as it had been all day, empty. "Yes, we can go."

Wilson's eyes darted to the deserted road, his voice strained with emotion. He couldn't believe Gordie hadn't come. He said he would. "He isn't coming, is he?"

"No." Maggie stiffened her resolve. She wanted to be strong for Wilson, but she was crying inconsolably on the inside. "He isn't coming." Her heart ached.

"Well, maybe a bear got him or something."

Wilson searched for any shred of hope. "There're a lot of them around, you know." They started walking.

"Maybe he got mixed up and went to the dug-out instead. That's it, Maggie, I bet he's at the dug-out right now, waiting for us. I bet he's waited all day long, just wondering where we are."

When Maggie didn't immediately answer, Wilson tried to look up at her, but his glasses were frosted over. He sensed her despair because his own heart was filled with the same sadness. "Don't you think?"

"Perhaps, Wilson . . . perhaps."

Their footsteps left deep tracks in the snow as they labored to walk. It was bitterly cold, the snow blinding them now.

Wilson suddenly started crying. Softly at first, then deep sobs. He'd tried to be brave for Maggie's sake, but his love for Gordie overpow-ered him. He'd prayed all day that Gordie loved them enough to return—at least enough to give Maggie back the mine, so they'd have enough money to live on.

But he didn't love them at all. He didn't care that they had sat in the cold, waiting all day for him. Knowledge that he cared so little about them was unbearable.

"Shush," Maggie said quietly, blinded by her own tears.

Salty, warm rivers rolled down Wilson's cheeks as he tried to keep up. The snow was deep, he hadn't eaten since early morning, and Gordie was never coming back.

He was suddenly so tired, so awfully tired.

As T.G. slowly came around, he was aware of sounds. Logs sizzling in the fireplace, a ticking clock, the metallic chink of a spoon scraping across the bottom of a kettle, a cat lapping cream from a saucer, the faint brush of slippered feet against a wooden floor.

Smells permeated his thick fog. Wood smoke, a subtle detection of lye soap coming from the woolen blanket, meat sizzling in a skillet.

Ensnared in a murky haze, T.G. struggled to orient his thoughts, but his mind refused to serve him. A raging fire wrenched his gut. Even a small motion brought excruciating pain.

Maggie!

Breaking into a cold sweat, he started shaking, his feverish body burning up beneath the heavy blanket. Throwing it aside, he tried to sit up. His head swam and blackness momentarily encased him.

Hands penetrated the darkness, bearing a cool cloth. T.G. moaned as he was lowered back to bed. Even the small act of kindness brought a cry of anguish from his swollen lips.

He stilled the faceless hands, trying to speak. "Deed . . ." he murmured.

A dipper of water found his mouth and he drank thirstily. The water spilled over, splashing onto his

bare chest. Each place the droplets touched re-
sulted in more suffering.

"Deed," he whispered hoarsely. "Maggie . . .
Potter's Stream . . ."

When he'd drunk his fill, his head was gently
lowered back to the pillow. A pungent smell filled
his nostrils, and he cried out again as hands that
had once been benevolent became instruments of
torture. Each place they touched produced hellish
agony.

T.G. prayed for death, but the torture continued.

"Maggie . . . Maggie . . ." The hands restrained
him as he struggled to sit up again. He had to get
to her, she would be waiting for him. "Let me
go . . . Maggie . . ."

As he succumbed to pain, the hands adminis-
tered to his body. The pain was unspeakable.

When the ordeal finally ended, T.G. was lying in
a pool of sweat. Once again, he was gently turned,
the cool cloth cleaning his heated body. The sheet
beneath him was whisked away and replaced with
a soft, dry one.

"Deed," he mumbled, praying the angel of
mercy would understand. Maggie was waiting for
him at Potter's Stream.

But the angel didn't understand. Deed was mistaken to be dead.

A gravelly voice penetrated his fog. "Not dead.
Very sick."

Groaning, T.G. lapsed back into unconsciousness.

* * *

The return trip up the mountain was harrowing. Since she'd planned to be home long before dark, Maggie hadn't taken a lantern. When darkness fell, she and Wilson were still a mile away from the dugout.

As darkness closed around them, Wilson stumbled often, his short legs having to work hard to keep from falling behind. He knew he had to keep up. They had to get to shelter before the storm vented its full fury.

"Don't look down!" The screeching wind caught Maggie's words and flung them away. The mountain pass was steep; one slip of the foot could prove fatal.

Latching onto Maggie's skirt, Wilson clung tightly as they battled the howling wind and blowing snow. By following the outcrop of shale that lined the trail, Maggie slowly gauged her way.

Responsibility for Wilson weighed heavily on her mind. She had risked his welfare, and now perhaps his life, for a man who apparently cared so little, he had left them in dangerous peril.

Yet, it wasn't anger that broke her heart, it was love. Love for a man who she had been so certain loved her back. She didn't realize that she was crying again until she tasted tears.

It didn't matter that he was gone, she told herself. They had lost others they loved and survived. They would survive this, too. After all, they'd only had T.G. a few weeks—how much could you love someone in a few weeks?

Yet her duplicitous heart told her sometimes with love a moment is enough.

But nothing mattered now except their safety. She had to get Wilson to the dugout. Tomorrow she would make the necessary arrangements to return to England.

The decision to stay or go had been taken away. Without the mine, there was no reason to stay. She couldn't go on jeopardizing Wilson's future with her foolish dreams.

By not returning with the deed, T.G. had left her no choice. She would be forced to wire Aunt Fionnula and ask for money to get them back to England. Had he purposely done this so she would have to go back? Didn't he know that she loved him enough to endure whatever the future held, as long as they were together?

Only one thing was certain. Winter was full upon them, and her last hope to remain in Colorado had vanished.

Chapter 27

"Eat."

T.G. pushed the bowl aside as he'd done for days.

"Eat!" The bowl was back at his mouth, and he was forced to swallow the tepid broth or choke to death.

After he managed a few swallows, the bowl was taken away.

Stirring, T.G. slowly opened his eyes. Moses stood over him holding a bowl of the strong-smelling concoction she had been using to coat his wounds. The aroma was obnoxious.

Shoving her hand away, T.G. murmured. *"Don't* put that on me."

"No talk. You sick." Dipping her large fingers into the bowl, she gobbed more on, but again his hand reached out to block her.

"Stubborn man!"

"Sadist!"

"You sick! Moses fix!"

"What is that stuff?" The smell was so vile it made his eyes water.

"Bear grease, skunk oil, herbs. Good for you." She scooped up another handful, determined to nurse him. Once more, his hand shot out to stop her.

Bringing her hand to her ample hip, she glared at him. "You *very* sick. 'Bout got *brains* knocked out. Must have medicine."

"Not that kind of medicine I mustn't."

"Mulehead!"

"Torturer!"

Dropping his head back to the pillow, T.G. groaned. How long had he been like this? The brief periods of awareness had left him with no idea of where he was or how he had gotten here.

"What day is it?"

"Wednesday."

"Wednesday." *Thank God the day wasn't over yet. He still had time to meet Maggie.*

T.G.'s voice was weak. "You have to do something for me, Moses. It's important."

Moses stared back at him dispassionately.

"Go to Potter's Stream and get Maggie. Bring her here."

"Fletcher woman?"

"Yes, Maggie Fletcher. She's been waiting all day for me to meet her. Bring her here, so I can explain what's happened." He paused. "What did happen?"

She answered in monotone. "Someone beat you."

He frowned. "Who?"

"Not know. Just someone."

"Apparently they did a pretty thorough job of it."

"You bad sick."

His strength was ebbing. "Go get Maggie."

"She not at Potter's Stream."

Opening his eyes, T.G. tried to focus. "Have you been there already?" He vaguely recalled mentioning the deed and Maggie in his feverish ramblings. Could Moses have made the connection and gone after Maggie?

"She leave—gone back to foreign country."

"Gone back—?" T.G. tried to sit up. His head whirled.

"No sit up!" Moses had just got him to where it looked like he might live. He didn't need a setback!

"Why would she have gone back? I'm supposed to meet her, today, at Potter's Stream."

"You loco in head."

His ears were ringing. "What?"

Moses circled her ear with her finger. "Beating make you big loco. You not think right."

A cold fear gripped him. "Moses, how long have I been like this?"

"Two weeks. I try to tell you. Very sick man. Almost dead man."

Visions of Abe Norris suddenly came back to him. Abe had beat him senseless!

"Dear God," he murmured. "Two weeks?"

Maggie. She must think he had betrayed her.

Without the mine or money, she had been forced to go back to England.

Picking up the bowl of salve, Moses made another attempt to treat his wounds, but again he stopped her. "Put that away."

"You sick!"

"I know I'm sick, but I need medicine, real medicine."

"No have real medicine. Have nice bear grease, skunk oil, herbs. Make you well."

"Makes me sick," he snapped. "Do you have a pencil and paper?"

"Pencil and paper no good medicine! Bear grease, skunk oil, herbs!"

"Do you have a *pencil* and *paper*?" He wanted to scream obscenities at the woman, but he knew he had better keep a rein on his emotions. "Please."

Moses went to search. Men. They plain idiots.

When she returned, she looked at him. "Have pencil and paper."

"Write this down." T.G. rattled off a list of things he needed from the general store. "They'll have to order some of the items, but I'll give you a slip granting my permission."

Moses looked up. "What you? Doctor?" she taunted.

"Yes, I'm a doctor, damn it."

"No." Her eyes narrowed. "You miner."

"No, I'm a doctor who became a miner."

"No, *you* miner," she insisted. She'd seen doctor. She not loco. Doctors don't look like miners.

T.G. was too sickly to haggle. "Just go get the medicine."

Though she thought him double loco, she left shortly, list in hand.

Another week passed before T.G. began to show improvement. Moses watched as he applied medicinal salve to his wounds and changed the dressings on his broken ribs. His work was slow and laborious, but his obvious knowledge convinced Moses that he was indeed a doctor. He shared some of his magic ointment, and within days, her corns were hardly noticeable.

"How did you find me?" A blizzard roared outside the tiny cabin as T.G. and Moses weathered the storms that were coming regularly now.

Moses shrugged. "Feeling."

"Feeling?" T.G. asked.

"Feeling. Walk to town that morning. No need to, but go anyway. Find you by the wayside."

"How did you get me here?"

She looked at him. "Carry you."

T.G. stared into the fire. "When I'm well, I'm going to kill Abe Norris." He had taken the one thing in life that meant anything to him. If it weren't for Abe, T.G. would have met Maggie, and they would be together now. Instead, she was thousands of miles away, believing that he had deceived her. He should write to her, explain what had delayed him, but he was too ashamed. How could he call himself a man?

The rawboned Eskimo listened, knowing that

grief, not Gordie, was talking. Gordie Manning was not violent. "Abe Norris bad man, but you should not kill. Two wrongs not make right."

He looked up with pain-filled eyes. "Maggie is the only woman I have ever loved. I waited too long, Moses. I was a pigheaded fool, and I've lost her."

Moses nodded, the sound of her knitting needles replenishing the silence.

The days grew shorter. Darkness came early to the mountain. Heavy snow nearly buried the small cabin with its curl of smoke coming from the chimney.

Moses looked over T.G., coaxing him to eat, and quietly tending his needs. Yet there was one thing she could not do. She could not ease the pain he carried in his heart for Maggie Fletcher.

Gwendolyn picked up the small bell and rang it. "My pot of chocolate, Margaret!"

Maggie's harried voice came back from the kitchen. "I'm on my way, Gwendolyn!"

"Gwendolyn can't have her chocolate until my dress is ready!" Mildred screeched from the top of the stairs. "Mothheerr, I can't be late for Della Gadfly's sleighing party! It's the talk of the season!"

"Margaret," Fionnula called from the parlor, "see to Mildred's needs first. Gwendolyn can wait a few minutes for her chocolate."

Snatching up the bell, Gwendolyn rang it harder. "My chocolate, Margaret!"

Maggie tried to keep the peace. "Your dress will be pressed in plenty of time, Mildred."

"*Mothheerr*, Margaret is fixing chocolate for Gwendolyn when she should be ironing my dress . . ." Mildred's voice faded off down the hallway.

Pouring chocolate into the silver pot, Maggie slapped Wilson's hands away from the plate of scones.

"Gwendolyn's going to eat all of them!" he exclaimed. "Every last crumb!"

"I'll make more, Wilson."

"When! You're busy all the time. Since we've come back, Aunt Fionnula treats you like a slave. I don't like it." Maggie could tell he was getting worked up again. "I *hate* it here! I hate not having Jellybean and Selmore. I hate Gordie. I hate Gwendolyn and Mildred. I want to go back to Colorado."

"I'll make more scones after dinner," Maggie said calmly, accustomed to Wilson's frequent outbursts. He was not adjusting well to being back under Fionnula's roof.

Nor was she. Her nights were agony as she lay in bed and recalled the feel of T.G.'s lips on hers, his hands touching her, exploring her, inciting her hunger for more. Tossing for hours, she found sleep impossible as her body yearned for his. By morning, she was drained of emotion.

Fionnula called her a thousand fools for signing the mine away, but her love for T.G. was resolute. Deep down, she knew he would come for her. Her biggest concern was for him. Was he ill? Did he need her? Were his nights as unbearable as hers?

Picking up the serving tray, Maggie pushed through the swinging door, Wilson's voice following her.

"I hate school! I hate England! I hate my teacher! I hate this kitchen, I hate this house, I hate this table, I hate these dishes, I hate this butter dish, I hate . . ."

Chapter 28

"Outside!" Moses pointed toward the door as she cleared away the breakfast dishes. He was getting on her nerves. The sun was out, a welcome relief from the recent storms. Good day for a walk. Not a day to sit in cabin moping.

"Not today, Moses." T.G. got up from the table and scooted his chair in front of the fireplace. With the exception of the outhouse, the fireplace was as far as he'd ventured for weeks. Moses knew he would never regain his strength if he didn't put his heart into his recovery.

"Go for walk. Need fresh air." Moses physically made him get up, shooing him toward the door. She'd been after him for days to move around more, but he had no interest in anything. Today, she wasn't taking no for an answer.

Before Gordie knew what was happening to him, his coat was around his shoulders and he was being pushed, bodily, out the front door.

The sun glinting off the newfallen snow blinded him. Shielding his eyes, he gazed across the frozen countryside, taking his first breath of fresh air in weeks.

Colorado's beauty stretched for miles around him. Snow lay in enormous, deep drifts. The sky was a brilliant hue, glistening above the undefiled wilderness.

A whitetail deer and his doe stood at the base of a tall ponderosa pine, chewing bark off the tree. A large hawk circled overhead, stalking fresh prey. Fresh rabbit tracks led to the grove of firs behind the cabin.

Glancing over his shoulder, T.G. noticed Moses standing in the doorway watching him.

"Go! Move!" Her voice did not invite argument, or even polite discussion of choice in the matter.

"I'm going!" It was fine with him. He was tired of her bossy company anyway.

Reluctantly, his feet began to move. His footsteps were hesitant at first, then more confident when he discovered his legs would support him. He kept moving, uncertain of his destination.

His lungs ached with every breath as he laboriously waded through the deep snowdrifts, making his way up the hillside. He felt as weak as a newborn kitten. When he reached the top of the hill, he paused, catching his breath.

In the distance, he could see the Hellhole. The deserted shaft brought back a flood of memories. Memories of Maggie.

Beads of sweat popped out on his forehead, and he quickly turned and started back down the hill.

He felt sick to his stomach, unable to cope with the sudden rush of emptiness.

He hated Moses for making him come out here where he was so exposed to bittersweet memories of what almost was.

Yet oddly enough, two days later, T.G. found himself walking up the same hill again. It was a gray, overcast day. Flakes of blowing snow peppered the air.

Standing at the top of the hill, he stared down on the mine. Snow drifted deep around the dugout, obstructing the doorway. The irrational thought that he should clear it away crossed his mind.

Squinting, the scene began to change, and he suddenly imagined it was fall again. Aspens, a resplendent gold, shimmered in the distance.

Smoke curled from the dugout's old smokestack. Selmore was staked outside the door, and Jellybean pawed the air at a passing butterfly.

As he watched, Maggie stepped out the door, her laughter coming to him on the icy air.

Pausing at the clothesline, she waved up at him, her eyes bright with mischief. The gentle breeze caught her hair and tossed it about her face. For a moment he smelled wildflowers.

She waved again, calling his name.

Hesitantly lifting his hand, he smiled, waving back.

Blowing him a kiss, she started to hang wash, humming under her breath. The musical strains of "Jeanie with the Light Brown Hair" floated through the frozen countryside. He could even hear the soft refrain she had whispered as they danced, how long ago was it? It could have been a million years, or maybe only a day.

He stood on the hilltop for over an hour, oblivious to the wind and the cold. Moses peeked out occasionally to make certain he hadn't fallen. Each time she found him standing in the same place, staring toward the mine.

On his third outing, Gordie took along a shovel.

Moses stood in the doorway, hands on hips. Now why crazy man need shovel?

This time, when T.G. reached the top of the hill, he disappeared over it and continued down the steep incline, the shovel slung over his shoulder.

It was over a mile to the mine. Today he wore snowshoes, so walking came easier. But by the time he reached the dugout, his strength was sapped.

Resting for a spell, he sat on the log, trying to invoke Maggie's image again. This time his imagination refused to cooperate.

As his strength returned, he got up and began to shovel snow away from the dugout door.

"Better save yore strength, Buddy Boy."

Closing his eyes, T.G. remembered, too late, that Butte would be around.

"Yeah, ya should have thought of that. It's not like I have places to go, things to do."

Butte was up to his same old rhetoric, but with a different tone. He didn't sound as ornery. Materializing, he appeared on the log. "Missed you, Buddy Boy."

T.G. ignored him.

"Pert near got yoreself killed. Gonna have to be more careful."

"We'll concede that I'm just plain stupid. Since you didn't finish me off that day in the mine, I thought I'd let Abe have a shot at it."

"Now, Buddy Boy, I didn't *hurt* you, did I? I was jest making a point."

Gordie shoveled a spade full of snow aside, ignoring him.

"Mad at me, ain't ya?"

"Actually, I don't give a damn about you, Butte."

"Yeah, yore mad all right." Butte scratched his beard sheepishly. "Guess I was a might hard on Maggie."

T.G. didn't need to answer. Butte knew his thoughts, and they weren't friendly.

"Got my own woman troubles, you know." Butte sat on the log, hands crossed, watching Gordie work.

"Come on, son . . . so I am a heartless, angry, old man . . . I did save yore life."

Gordie glanced up.

"Since I'm still . . . well, limited, I couldn't do nothin' to help you when Abe lit into you, but I made sure Moses found you that morning."

T.G. recalled Moses mentioning that she had a feeling she should go into town.

"That was you?"

Butte nodded. "That was me. Fool thing you done, shoving that shithouse over with Abe in it."

"Well." Gordie lifted another spade of snow. "Face it, I do a lot of foolish things."

"There you go, being hard on yoreself again. You was on yore way to Potter's Stream to meet Maggie, wasn't you?"

"Before I was detained."

"Then what's the problem? You didn't steal the mine. You did what you said you'd do—or least you would have if you hadn't let your orneriness get the better of your common sense. Son, you don't fool around with a man Abe's size. Ain't anyone ever told you that?"

Pausing for a moment, Gordie's eyes traveled to the mine. "She thinks I've stolen the mine from her."

"No, she don't."

"How could she not? I didn't meet her that day at Potter's Stream. She must have waited, but I never came."

"She doesn't think you stole the mine. Just the opposite, she's worried about you. She thinks something bad happened to you."

Gordon looked up, the skin beneath his eyes still a bruised, greenish yellow. Deep lacerations across his cheeks, his jaw, the evidence of his wounds were still clearly visible. "Does getting your brains beat out count as something bad?"

Butte hung his head. "Yeah, that ought ta do it."

"Wonderful. Too bad Maggie doesn't know."

"Yeah, that is too bad." Butte had no way of letting her know. Sissy could tell her, but Sissy was getting ready to move on, to reach for the light.

She'd been after him to do the same, but the gold
... the gold was holding him back.

T.G. shoveled a few more minutes. It was a
while before he spoke. "Is Maggie okay?" he
asked softly.

"She's all right. That witch of an aunt is taking
advantage of her. She misses you, but she's all
right."

"Wilson?"

"Wilson? He hates everything, but guess it's his
age."

T.G.'s voice dropped. "I love her, Butte."

"Yeah, I know, Buddy Boy." Love could be hard
at times.

T.G. rammed the shovel into another drift, angry
now. "I fell in love with her. I told myself a thousand times I wouldn't, but I did."

"Yeah." He wasn't telling Butte anything he
didn't already know. "Well, now, there's still time
to do something about it. Not all's lost. She might
be back in England, but they got boats that go over
there, boy. You can go after her."

When T.G. kept on shoveling, Butte looked at
him. "Why are you shoveling that snow?"

"I don't know ... it makes me feel closer to her,
like she was still here, and I'm doing something to
help her."

"Shoveling all that snow's only gonna sap yore
strength. Better save it, son. Once you're back on
your feet, you can go over thar to England and get
her back."

"I haven't got enough money to get me to Hoodee Doo, let alone England."

"Well, we can figure out a way to get money." That was the least of their problems. "Word's going around up here that they're jest about to repeal the Sherman Act law. You know anything about that?"

"I haven't seen a newspaper in weeks."

"Hmmm," Butte mused. "If they was to do that, it would make the bottom fall out of silver and gold shoot sky-high."

"I wouldn't know about that, since I don't have silver or gold."

"Yes," Butte mused. "But you are gonna go after her, aren't ya?"

"Forget it, Butte. She's better off without me."

"Feeling sorry for yoreself again?"

Maybe he was. He'd faced the grim reaper, and lost the only woman he ever loved. If anyone had a right to feel sorry for himself, it was he.

"Oh, you have a right," Butte agreed. "But you shouldn't. Here you are, a doctor, and yore still feeling sorry for yoreself."

"You know I haven't practiced in years."

"Don't mean you couldn't, if you took a notion. You forgot what you learned?"

Before T.G. could answer, Butte answered for him. "No. You know jest as much as you ever did. Wire your pop in Phoenix, and tell him you're coming home. Then, go get that little gal and her brother and start livin' again. You can do it."

It wasn't that the thought hadn't crossed T.G.'s

mind. It had. But he wanted a different kind of life for Maggie. "Being a doctor's wife isn't easy, Butte."

T.G. recalled the days of his youth when his family lived on Pop's fees: fresh eggs, vegetables from a grateful patient's garden, a butchered hog come fall, fryers and stewing hens throughout the summer.

There were times when an outbreak of cholera gripped the community and Doc Manning wouldn't see his family for days. When he did come home, he'd be so tired he could do little more than eat leftovers and fall into bed for a few hours sleep. People came and went at all hours of the night. He could never be counted on to be around at important times: Christmas, birthdays.

Delivering babies, tending the terminally ill, hovering over the desperately sick, never enough time for his own loved ones. It was no life for a family man.

That was the reason Gordie sought his fortune in the gold mines. He wanted more for himself than hard times and charity. He wanted wholesome meals on his table, new shoes for his children every winter, a big house, and a fine motorcar to take the family for a Sunday afternoon ride.

"You could always become one of them doctors," Butte offered.

"No thanks. I've had my fill of doctoring."

"Want Maggie, don't you?"

"I want a lot of things."

Slinging his shovel over his shoulder, T.G. walked away from the mine.

"Hey . . ." Butte sat up on the log. "You coming back?" He shore hated to see him go. It got real lonely around here nowadays.

Gordie never looked back. Butte watched as he slowly made his way through the deep snow and eventually disappeared over the hilltop.

Glancing at the barren, winter landscape, Butte sighed. It shore did get lonely around here.

Cocking an ear, he looked up. "What? . . . Yeah, I can see he's hurtin'." A fool could see Manning loved the Fletcher woman.

"Why me? I didn't take him to raise."

A cagey look entered his eyes. "Yeah, I know about love. . . . Yes, dadburn it, I want my due reward." He'd been studying the light, just like everyone else. The vitreous light beckoned, drawing him. Yet if he accepted it, he would have to give up all earthly desires.

"Your niece and nephew's safe—they got a roof over their heads, and food on their table. . . . Yeah, I know *that*. But Manning loves her. Those two are bound to get together, and he'll take care of her. . . . Well, now, you can't blame me for that! He's a doctor; he could make 'em a good livin'. . . . No, not as good as the gold, 'course not. They'd be rich beyond their wildest dreams if they had my gold."

He frowned. "Don't nag me, woman!" If there was one thing he couldn't stand it was a carpy woman.

"Well, sure . . . I don't want to stay around here forever, I told you that." Where he was wasn't bad, just not real permanent-like. Every day he saw people reaching for the light, being drawn upward, their faces filled with glory. . . .

His eyes traveled indecisively back to the mine. It shore 'nough was getting to be more trouble than it was worth. Sissy nagging him to go with her, that beautiful light drawing him . . . If he stayed, he would always have another miner to fight, another battle to win. Truth was, he was jest plain gettin' tired of the bother.

Dadburn, 'peered like death was as complicated as life!

Chapter 29

It was over a week before T.G. ventured back to the mine. He had vowed he was never going back. Maggie was gone, and he sure didn't want Butte's company.

Yet, early Sunday morning, he set off in search of Maggie's memory. Climbing the steep hill, he made his way slowly down the other side of the incline.

A cold sun glinted off the deep snow. T.G.'s heavy boots broke through the crusty surface as he plodded toward the mine.

The little dugout looked bleak in the early morning light. What a difference Maggie's presence had made.

Taking a seat on the log, he gazed at it, wondering what Maggie and Wilson were doing on this Sunday morning in England.

They were probably eating blackberry scones, he surmised, breaking into a grin as he recalled the tasty bread. His eyes sobered. It wasn't the scones he missed, it was Maggie. If he had a cent to his name, he would go to England—not to bring her back to a life of misery, but rather to see her, to hold her, to absorb her scent. The smell of wildflowers he could conjure easily, but during the long nights, it was difficult to call forth her sweetness.

Cold saturated his bones, aggravating his injuries. Oblivious to the pain, he sat lost in thought.

"Hey! You! Buddy Boy!"

T.G. glanced up as he heard Butte's voice. His eyes searched the area for the apparition.

"In here!"

T.G. looked, but Butte, for once, didn't materialize. "What do you want, Butte."

"I'm trapped."

"You're what?"

"Trapped. Over here."

Now what was he trying to prove? "Where?"

"In the mine."

"Good Lord." Getting up, T.G. walked in the direction of the mine. Butte was more trouble than a kid. And more aggravating, he might add. "Where are you?"

"Over here."

"Where?"

"Toward the front of the shaft."

"What are you doing in there?"

"I live here, remember?"

Turning away, T.G. went back to the log. He was in no mood to play games.

"Hold on a minute, Buddy Boy. I got myself a problem, this morning. A bad one."

T.G. sat back down. "Join the crowd."

"I'm serious. Git back over here."

"No."

"Just git over here!"

Getting up again, T.G. walked to the entrance of the sealed shaft. "You are getting on my nerves."

"I hate to tell you this, but I'm stuck."

"Stuck?"

"Stuck."

"How could you be stuck? You're a ghost. You come and go as you want."

"I don't know how it happened. One minute I was moseying through the mine, and the next I was trapped. Cain't move a muscle, Buddy Boy. You're gonna have to help me."

"What can I do about it?" T.G. wasn't a miracle worker.

"Help me figure out a way to get unstuck."

"Fade out," T.G. advised simply.

"Done tried that. When I faded back, I was still here."

"Well, I don't know what you're going to do about it. The shaft's sealed. I can't get in there."

"You cain't just leave me here."

T.G. laughed. "Why? You could die?"

"I'm serious, Buddy Boy. You gotta do something. I'm a mite uncomfortable."

"Ask someone up there what to do."

"Cain't, they're all busy."

"You can feel pain?"

"Yeah, I feel pain. Now get to thinking. What are we gonna do about this?"

Kneeling, T.G. ran his hands around the sealed entrance. "Butte, the dirt's packed tight. I can't get to you."

"Yes, you can. Think."

T.G. thought. "Where are you?"

" 'Bout fifty or so feet just inside the shaft. You know that outcrop of shale just to the left as you come into the mine?"

"Yes." T.G. knew it well. Went by it every time he entered the mine.

"That's where I am. Wedged in between two big rocks."

T.G. looked around for something to dig with, but there was nothing.

"You can't *dig* me out, boy." Butte read his mind, exasperated. Was he gonna have to draw him a map? "You're gonna have to *blast* me out."

"Blast you out? Why that would—"

"Kill me?" Butte mocked. "Now listen, there's a couple of sticks of dynamite in the dugout. Go get 'em."

T.G. glanced toward the dugout, puzzled. "Maggie didn't keep explosives in the dugout."

"Just go look," Butte said crossly. *Land o'mighty*. "This ain't no picnic in here."

When T.G. returned he was carrying the two sticks of dynamite he'd found in the dugout. They had been lying in the middle of the kitchen table, a situation he found bizarre.

"You find 'em?"

"I found them."

"Good, tell me when you're gonna light the fuses. I'll plug my ears."

"Butte—I don't know about this—" Ghost or no ghost, when he lit that dynamite, things were going sky-high.

"Jest do what I say! You ain't gonna hurt me!"

"You just said you could feel pain!"

"Don't worry 'bout me! Just light the blasted fuses!"

T.G. searched his pockets. "I don't have any matches."

"Good Lord, boy!" Butte had picked an idiot to befriend. "There was matches laying right next to the dynamite. Didn't you see them?"

"No."

"Well, go look."

"Hold on."

"Yeah, like I'm going somewhere," Butte muttered.

T.G. was back in a minute.

"Got 'em?"

"I have them."

"Get to blasting."

"Hold on a minute." T.G. began to set the charge, still not sold on the idea.

"Now, you are going to marry Maggie Fletcher, ain't you, Buddy Boy?"

T.G. looked up. "What?"

"I said you *are* gonna marry the little Fletcher gal, aren't you?"

"Why would you be asking that now?"

"Just curious. What's your answer?"

"Were we talking about Maggie?"

"No, but you *are* gonna marry her, ain't ya? You ain't gonna let that pride of yours stand in the way of love, are you?"

"To be honest Butte, I don't know what I'm going to do about Maggie. But I do love her," T.G. admitted softly.

"What?"

"I said, I love her!"

He had given up thinking he could live without her. He couldn't. While he had thought he was in bad shape before, his misery was nothing compared to life without her. Somehow he would scrape up enough money to get him to England. From there, he would have to see what the possibilities were for setting up a family practice. If Maggie were willing to marry a dirt-poor doctor, then by damn, he was going to marry her.

"Gonna take good care of the boy—see that he gits a good education?"

"What's the sudden interest in Maggie's and Wilson's future? You never cared before."

"Well, like I told you. Me and Sissy's been talking lately. She's kinda worried about Wilson and Maggie. She knows her sister's ugly ways, and she don't want Wilson and Maggie livin' under Fionnula's roof any longer than necessary."

T.G. finished rigging the fuses. "Stand back. I'm going to light the fuses."

"Hot dingy. Light 'em, Buddy Boy!"

Touching a match to the fuses, T.G. ignited them. Running for cover, he shouted over his shoulder, "They're going to blow in a couple of minutes, Butte!"

"I'm ready, Buddy Boy! Let her blow!"

Smiling, Butte reached over and took Sissy's hand. "That thar weren't so hard."

Sissy smiled, patting his hand. "It never is, and the Lord will forgive you for the tiny infraction."

"Ready?"

Sissy nodded. "Ready."

Holding hands, they started walking toward the light. A sucking sound ensued as they were gently lifted up . . . up into the swirling vortex.

A thunderous explosion rocked the Hellhole, showering dirt and catapulting debris skyward.

As the dust settled, T.G. stood up, waiting for Butte to appear. When a few minutes had past, he stepped closer, peering into the mine. "Butte?"

"Butte?" he called louder when Butte didn't answer.

A ray of sun suddenly caught a shining speck on the ground. A moment later, a second ray caught another, then another.

The brilliancy that suddenly surrounded T.G. was blinding.

Dropping to his knees, he picked up a handful of gold nuggets, stunned. Lifting his head, he looked around, realizing that he was sitting in a pile of more gold than he'd ever seen in his life.

Huge, unbelievable stones covered the ground for as far as the eye could see.

Laughing now, he scooped up handfuls of the enormous nuggets, tossing them into the air deliriously. The mother lode! He had hit the mother lode!

His laughter died away as he looked for Butte. Had he done this? Had he finally relinquished his claim to the gold?

"Butte!" he said hesitantly. "You still there?"

When the silence lengthened, T.G. grinned. Why, that old fool!

Clutching handfuls of gold, T.G. realized what had just happened. Butte Fesperman had just given Maggie and him a future. Gratitude swelled his heart.

"Thank you, you old coot," he murmured affectionately.

From high above, he heard Butte say: "I heard that."

Chapter 30

"Gordie's here."

Maggie looked up from the open oven door, wiping a stray hair out of her eyes.

"Who?"

"Gordie."

Lugging the heavy roaster to the cooling board, Maggie set it down with a thump. "That isn't funny, Wilson."

"I'm not being funny. He's really here."

Maggie turned, her heart hammering, halfway believing him. "Where?"

"At the front door. Aunt Fionnula was gonna send him around back where the other riffraff has to go, but she can't. He doesn't look like riffraff, Maggie. He looks *rich*."

"Rich?"

Wilson nodded. "Really rich." He'd never seen Gordie looking so good.

Dropping the hot pads, Maggie bolted out of the kitchen door. Dear God, *please* let it truly be him, she whispered. It had been two months since she'd left Colorado, and she hadn't heard a word from him.

Shrugging, Wilson sneaked over to steal a bite of the roasted hen. "Filthy rich, actually," he murmured.

Racing down the hallway, Maggie wondered what she looked like and immediately decided that it didn't matter! She could be wearing sackcloth and ashes for all T.G. would care—if it were really him!

Fionnula was standing in the doorway, her eyes surveying the handsome stranger dictatorially.

Rounding the corner, Maggie came to a sudden halt. Standing in the doorway was the most handsome man she had ever seen in her life.

T.G.'s eyes met hers over Fionnula's head. Gazing at one another, there was no need for words. His eyes said everything she needed to know.

With a squeal of joy, Maggie flew into his arms, nearly bowling Aunt Fionnula over in her exuberance.

Clasping her to him, T.G.'s mouth hungrily found hers. Rockets exploded, colored lights flared, whistles sounded as their mouths consumed one another's.

"Mary Margaret!" Fionnula gasped.

The taste of him, the feel of him—Maggie couldn't get enough! The shameless passionate embrace was embarrassingly prolonged.

When they finally parted, Maggie took both his hands, smiling up at him. "You're a little late."

"I have a good excuse." Leaning forward, he

kissed the tip of her nose. "By the way, I love you."

"Mmm," she whispered, kissing him back. "I love you, too."

"I insist this appalling display cease, immediately!" Fionnula demanded. What had gotten into Mary Margaret?

Realizing her lack of propriety, Maggie quickly apologized. "I'm sorry, Aunt Fionnula."

Still holding tightly to T.G., Maggie pulled him inside the door. He looked utterly smashing today. Decked out in a striking royal blue cloak, vest, and matching pants, he looked quite the young entrepreneur.

"Aunt Fionnula, I would like for you to meet T.G. Manning."

"Manning?" Fionnula peered over her aristocratic nose. "And who might T.G. Manning be?"

"T.G. befriended Wilson and me in Colorado." Squeezing his hand, Maggie grinned at Gordie. "I don't know what I would have done without him."

Removing his coat, hat, and gloves, T.G. handed them to Fionnula. She looked down, uncertain of what to do with them.

Taking them from her, Maggie quickly deposited the items in a chair. Totally confused, Fionnula allowed herself to be led into the parlor.

After Fionnula was seated comfortably on the settee, Maggie reached for T.G.'s hand again, unable to keep her hands off him. "Aunt Fionnula, this is the man I'm going to marry."

"Marry?" Fionnula's mouth dropped open.

Maggie lifted her eyes to T.G. "I certainly hope so."

T.G.'s eyes held all the assurance she ever needed.

"Madam Wellesford, I have come to ask for your niece's hand in marriage," T.G. announced. "It would be well and good if you were to grant that permission, but I must warn you: I love your niece with all my heart and soul, and I shall marry her no matter what your verdict."

"Oh, Gordie." Maggie was so proud of him she could burst. "You said that so well!"

He nodded, courtly indeed. "Thank you, Miss Fletcher. I thought I did a rather smashing job myself."

"Marry her? Why, I know nothing about you!" Fionnula protested.

Seating himself, T.G. crossed his hands. "What would you like to know? I shall begin by noting that I am an extremely wealthy man, Madam Wellesford. Your niece and nephew, as well as all of Maggie's family, will want for nothing." His eyes met hers, frankly. "Absolutely nothing."

Fionnula's nose lifted. "Wealth is quite subjective, Mr. Manning."

"Two billion isn't, Madam Wellesford."

He heard Maggie's soft intake of disbelief.

"Two . . . billion," Fionnula repeated lamely. "Dollars?"

"Give or take a few hundred thousand."

"Well, goodness," Fionnula fanned herself. "Mary Margaret, get Mr. Manning a pot of tea!

And he would certainly enjoy some of those delicious scones you make! Oh, shoot. Never mind, I'll get them." Springing to her feet, she trilled, "Oh, girls! Come meet Margaret's new fiancé! He's such a joy!"

Two very homely looking heads popped over the banister rails to see what all the excitement was about.

"Come dears, hurry now!" Fionnula gazed at T.G. fondly. "Tell me, Mr. Manning, do you have younger brothers?"

Later, Maggie drew T.G. into the kitchen where they could be alone. As the door closed behind them, she went back into his arms.

"Oh, I've missed you so," she whispered as his mouth ravished hers. Between long, voracious kisses, he managed to tell her why he failed to meet her that day at Potter's Stream. He explained how he would have died if Moses hadn't found him and nursed him back to health.

"But the money," she whispered. "Were you just making that up?"

Chuckling, he held her to him, thanking God he had found her again. "No, the money is real. Butte gave us the mother lode, darling."

Frowning, Maggie looked up at him. "Butte?"

"The ghost."

"Oh," she said lamely. "The ghost."

Resting his lips on hers, he whispered, "It doesn't matter if you ever believe there was a Butte Fesperman. He believes in us. And so does your Aunt Sissy."

"Aunt *Sissy?*"

Laughing, he kissed her bewilderment away. "There is so much we have to catch up on and to learn about each other." Briefly, he told her about the incident with Abe.

"I realize we know little about each other," she whispered.

"We know we love one another. That's the only thing we need to know for the moment." They had the rest of their lives to share their past experiences.

"Then, we are rich?" she finally asked.

"Honey, we can burn money for fuel."

"Oh, T.G., I would love you if you didn't have a single pound," she reminded.

"I know, my darling." She had proved that a hundred times over. "The deed to the Hellhole is in my pocket, but I warn you, I'm not going to sign it back to you."

Her eyes clouded. "You're not?"

"No, fortunately you sold your worthless inheritance." He kissed her lightly. "Most fortunately, you're marrying a man who owns an extremely profitable mine. Have you heard they have repealed the Sherman Act?"

"No ... you mean gold is now the rage again?"

"Quite the rage, my lovely."

"But about Gwendolyn and Mildred. If the mine is now that lucrative—"

He lay his finger over her lips to stop her. "What about Gwendolyn and Mildred? They were not included in the will, that was Fionnula's idea."

"But if Fionnula ever learns that it was you I sold the mine to—"

"Darling, your family will never want for anything, but that mine is yours and Wilson's, and no one, including me, is going to take it from you."

"Oh," she whispered. "I truly, truly love you."

Lowering his mouth, he murmured softly, "I want you, Maggie Fletcher." The proof of his desire was blatantly evident against her middle. "I need you so damned bad I hurt—"

"This is all well and good, but what about me?"

Springing guiltily apart, they saw Wilson sitting at the table, calmly eating cookies.

"What about you?" T.G. reached over and rumpled his hair. "You can have your own zoo now, kid, complete with elephants, if you want."

"I'd like an elephant—perhaps two, but that isn't the point." Wilson wasn't to be deterred. Maggie might forgive Gordie, but Wilson wasn't going to let him off the hook that easily. "I *know* you'll take care of me because Maggie will make you."

"I would take care of you regardless, but knowing you, you're about to make a point. What is it?"

"The point is, you hurt my feelings."

T.G. glanced at Maggie, and she shook her head warningly. Wilson had been angry at Gordie from the time they left Colorado.

"I'm sorry I hurt your feelings. Do you want to tell me what I did, so I can try and correct it?"

Wilson's countenance was grave. "Maggie and I waited all day for you to meet us, Gordie, but you didn't come. It was cold, and we waited, Gordie, all day. You didn't come."

"Wilson." T.G. knelt beside his chair, feeling Wilson's pain. "I didn't come because I couldn't."

"Because that man beat you up?"

"Because Abe beat me up. I did a stupid thing, and I paid for it by temporarily losing the two people I love most."

Tears brimmed in Wilson's eyes, his anger starting to thaw. "You love me, Gordie? Honest?"

"Honest." Leaning closer, they shared a private moment. "Next to your sister, I love you more than anything in the whole world," Gordie whispered.

Throwing his arms around Gordie's neck, Wilson hugged him. "That's how you hurt my feelings," he whispered back. "That day, when you didn't come, I thought it was because you didn't love me."

"Never," Gordie assured him. "And from now on I won't be pushing over any more outhouses. But that's another story entirely. If you need me, I'll be there for you."

"Always?"

"Always."

Epilogue

Years later in Phoenix, Arizona

"There he is! I see him!" Maggie stood on her tiptoes waving at the long cap-and-gown procession coming down the aisle.

A tall, handsome, red-headed boy in the ninth row broke into a grin, lifting his college diploma in the air triumphantly.

"Doesn't he look handsome, darling!"

T.G. took the baby from her, freeing his wife to hop excitedly up and down on one foot.

"Mommy, I want to see Uncle Wilson!" Three-year-old Gordie tugged at Maggie's skirt, demanding to be held.

"Lionel, help your brother," T.G. gently instructed his oldest son.

"Here you go, squirt." Swinging the child up onto his shoulder, fourteen-year-old Lionel waved at Wilson. "Guess he's well on his way to becoming a doctor, Dad."

T.G. smiled, proud as punch of Wilson. "Looks

like it, son." Glancing over at Maggie, they both grinned, sharing the happy moment. Just because T.G. hadn't liked the medical profession didn't mean they weren't thrilled that Wilson was following in Grandfather Manning's footsteps.

As the band played on, the noisy crowd waved and cheered the graduates' accomplishments.

"Kinda makes you want to cry, don't it, Buddy Boy?"

Yes, Butte and T.G. still visited on a regular basis. Heaven had more than one reward for Butte.

"It does, and none of it would have been possible without you."

"I know, Buddy Boy, I know." Butte blew his nose noisily. These family occasions always got to him.

"In a way, I guess it's your graduation day, too," T.G. noted.

For the past four years, Butte had spent every day in the classroom with Wilson. Wilson wasn't aware of his unusual classmate, but Butte worked every lesson right alongside of him.

Why, Butte could hardly wait for the day when he'd know how to take out a gallbladder.

Maggie glanced at T.G., barely able to hear over all the confusion. "Did you say something, darling?"

"Yeah." He leaned over and kissed her long and hard. "I love you, Mary Margaret Manning."

"Oh, Daddy!" Rebecca groaned, embarrassed when Daddy talked to Mommy like that in public. He did it *all* the time!

"What?"

"I said, *I love you*, Mrs. Manning!"

"*I love you too*, Mr. Manning! Lots!"

Eight-year-old Rebecca just rolled her eyes, humiliated.

T.G.'s eyes lovingly took in his family: wife, four children, Wilson, and one incredibly sentimental curmudgeon of an old ghost.

Pulling Maggie closer so he could whisper in her ear, he confided softly, "It just doesn't get any better than this, darling."

Smiling, Maggie turned and whispered back. "No my love, it doesn't get any better than this."